ARMIST...

'There's a raw, urgent power to Stafford's depiction
of the grief and desperation of the postwar world'
Guardian

'This is the story of a heroic quest, a painstaking
sifting through the rubble of war by a heroine back
at home unafraid to fight her own battles. Stafford's
fans won't be disappointed'
Observer

'It is a powerful and absorbing first novel. Stafford
brings all his characters vividly to life, from his
damaged hero and heroine to the egotistical and
amoral Anthony, and Philomena's determined
crusade to honour the memory of her lost lover has
a poignancy that will linger long in readers' minds'
Waterstone's Books Quarterly

'It is a good, light read'
Daily Mail

'Opening with a series of vivid, sharply rendered
scenes, Nick Stafford's debut novel is an unusual and
powerful story'
Good Book Guide

Also by Nick Stafford

PLAYS

Battle Royal
Luminosity
Love Me Tonight
Katherine Desouza
War Horse

ARMISTICE

Nick Stafford

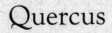

First published in Great Britain in 2009 by Quercus
This paperback edition published in 2010 by

Quercus
21 Bloomsbury Square
London
WC1A 2NS

A CIP catalogue record for this book is available
from the British Library

ISBN 978 1 84916 023 0

10 9 8 7 6 5 4 3 2 1

Printed and bound in Great Britain by Clays Ltd, St Ives plc

ARMISTICE

PROLOGUE

This particular November morning we would much prefer to remain hunkered in our captured trench than go over the top again, but orders are still orders even now at this late stage, so once more we plunge side by side across No-Man's Land in that habitual hunched running position – with Death's hot breath on our necks we urge ourselves and the others on, praying that it really is going to be all over in minutes at eleven a.m.

Are the enemies' watches set to exactly the same time as ours? Has that been sorted out?

Run harder this time. Run harder than ever before. Not harder, better. Crouch more expertly. Be invisible, or bullet permeable – hope, believe that you can survive. The end is close enough to see, to smell, to touch. What will peace, what will no-war be like? Not like before, that's for sure.

Jonathan yelps and lurches sideways into a shallow crater and I dive after him. The toe of his boot has been shot off but his toes are intact, pink under the dirt. He wriggles them and they look – illogically - more vulnerable than the rest of him. Hundreds of rounds *phutt* from a heavy machine gun splicing the air above our heads and then, aimed lower, they rip spurts from the rim of our friable haven, spitting soil in our eyes. We press ourselves down and curse. There's a pause.

I can hear Jonathan's rasping breaths. We twist our necks to look at each other.

'Reloading?' I say.

'Or jammed?' he says.

The pause continues. Mouths agape to drag in maximum air we nod to each other and stumble to our feet and will our bodies on over the clinging, uneven terrain—

When *kerrump!* A six-pounder. Dive flat. Merge with earth. Peer up. Enemy tank, one of ours, captured British Mark IV grinding towards our left flank, desperate Krauts sheltering in its wake. That'll be our undoing. We have nothing to touch it.

But then *owoooeeeee . . . pang!* One of ours – a twelve-pounder shell – only a glancing blow but tearing tank's armour, stopping it! And bonus! Metal on metal at that velocity gives birth to shrapnel; savage, spitting, indiscriminate bastard offspring; death multiplied, it scythes the enemy infantry at waist height and lower, some falling like skittles in fast-motion, and some flying up feet-first backwards as if a rug has been snatched from under them. All when they land are untouched above the waist but shredded scarlet mush and shocking white bone below. Untouched above the waist but lifeless. Some with eyes open. Like obsolete mannequins dumped round the back of a shop. I blink, still surprised, after all, at the sudden transformation from living to dead, movement to stillness.

But the tank is only wounded, stunned. It appears to shudder, and like a great beast regaining consciousness it groans and lurches into motion again. The six-pounder *kerrump*s and machine guns clatter. The beast must die.

Me and Jonathan run at it from the flank and poke grenades into the jagged rip in its side, whereupon there are shouts of alarm and when we are a few yards clear, terse explosions, short cries of distress; men inside the tank – I can't help imagining them – must be sundered and smashed, or slumped and deafened, the latter uselessly pressing their hands to their ears.

Main weapon eliminated, the battle's shape immediately becomes more irregular. We combatants intermingle, khaki versus grey. Now separated from Jonathan I can see Major Chiltern caught in a pincer movement by two of them. I shout to him but my voice is swallowed up in the cacophony of war. I fire from the hip at one of Chiltern's predators but my pistol's pin clicks impotently on a dud round – simultaneous to this I see Major Chiltern judder, penetrated from two different angles and he falls and lies still.

I am surprised at how upset I feel: both those shooters must die.

The dud jams my pistol. I have to clear it. I checked all these bullets personally when I loaded them; what more can you do, clean your weapon, check all the ammo? One of Chiltern's attackers twists and falls. The second clutches his chest and drops onto his face. I turn and from the angle of Jonathan's body I can see it is he who has shot them and that he is now hurrying to snap a new magazine into his pistol because for these few moments he is like I am, without a loaded gun – naked, defenceless, blinking in the light. I shout to him and gesticulate wildly because a big man has appeared out of nowhere and is almost upon Jonathan wielding a home-made club bristling with vicious spikes.

I hold my breath whilst Jonathan by a fraction avoids the first blow aimed at his skull, then twists, eluding the second to his neck, and sways, in control now, in the opposite direction, so that the third blow, destined for his shoulder, swishes past. Jonathan hoiks his pistol up, rams it into the German's chin – it should be a knock-out blow but the man takes it without going down and when Jonathan wields his knife the blade only nicks his opponent's cheek instead of slashing his eye or his nose or his cheek or his lips over bared teeth right open, and now Jonathan and the German close and try to kill each other face to face.

I want to go to help Jonathan but my way is barred by a child so pale and thin that he might be an apparition, who appears to be no more than twelve years old, in a uniform far too large for him, who tremblingly points a rifle, far too heavy for him, directly into my face. The fleeing Kaiser has sent his children against us.

The shouts begin to go up: 'It's over! *Der Krieg ist vorbei!*'

The child is soiling himself – the tell-tale wet patch spreads down the legs of his grimy uniform and I fear that he is trembling so much he might discharge his rifle by accident. Out of the corner of my eye I can glimpse white being waved and for a moment I think it is men waving their own exposed bones and offal hoping that someone will know what to do with it. I close my eyes and shake my head to dislodge that picture and see cloth, whiteish cloth – how absurd it would be to die at a terrified child's involuntarily twitched hand just as the war is ending!

I try to smile reassuringly and to hold the child's gaze as the sounds of war subside. The boy begins to tentatively lower his rifle – it's probably too much for him to hold up any longer – and to me this seems good, the first good thing to happen, the first after-the-war good moment, but then I hear a crack from behind me and the boy collapses and is still. I half turn, just glimpse – ah, there you are, coming at me like a coward, and there's another crack and I fall backwards and sideways, down on my front, looking at an ant going about its business, scaling peaks in the muddy earth.

I can smell blood and metal and decay.

Mud presses into my nostrils, seeming to want to invade me, to begin burying me already.

I can feel my blood pumping warmly out of the exit hole in my chest.

I have an image from school – geography – a cross-sectional diagram of the water table, the surface of a saturated subter-ranean sea – but now it is the blood table – all the blood from all the men and women who've leaked their lives into this contested earth, and mine is adding to it, fast-rhythmic-ally gushing – I must get up! I try to place my palms on the ground and push but only succeed in inhaling fragments of the land we've been fighting over. I automatically cough as my vital organs stutter and hiccough, gasping for fuel. Through my ear to the ground I can sense running feet pounding the ground.

I have a vision of myself and Philomena, and Jonathan, and the fiancée that he will acquire some day; all going about together, by the sea, living it up, dressed all in white, possibly back here in France, but definitely by the seaside, and no expense spared. I try to grasp this vision, to anchor myself to it, but it is slipping, agonisingly, away from me, out of reach.

Someone picks me up – it is Jonathan – and I feel myself begin to shake, and I can feel Jonathan holding me, and I think that I can see Captain Dore to the side of Jonathan, looking on anxiously.

More images of Philomena flash before me at machine-gun speed, as if my memory is rapidly discharging its final rounds. One day: her in a white blouse and long skirt on her bicycle, giggling as she struggles up a hill; her letting out a small cry as she slips naked into the freezing waters of that hill pond, her back arched away from the cold; later her warm breath in my ear as she moves slowly on top of me – was that the best day of my life?

Past tense?!

No! No! I think I cry.

Jonathan is holding me and I can see him calling but his voice is as if from afar. 'Dan. Dan. No. No. Daniel Case: can you hear me? Dan!'

If I am about to die I know that I have to tell Jonathan . . . It is imperative . . . If there is just one more sentence, or phrase, or single word left to me to utter then I know what it— I must tell Jona— If I can just spea— Or if I can just make a— indica— slide my eyes towards— move any part of my bod—

CHAPTER ONE

Some men had started a war, other men went off to fight it; the living were left with the mess.

She'd left a note at work. 'Back the day after tomorrow. Nothing to worry about. Sorry. Philomena.' Her train slowed down and the smoke from the funnels fell and swirled about the carriages rather than streamed above them, thus her first views of central London, of Euston, were wreathed in vapour. Philomena's hands, which had lain together in her lap, lifted slightly and parted, and began to describe small, slow shapes in the air. They seemed to move independently of the rest of her, they had recently begun to do this, as if responding to a quiet, sad orchestra playing inside her, or if moving more swiftly, betraying her anxieties. Jo should be seeing her scribbled note about now. Should she have told her where she was headed? She didn't know where, exactly. London, yes, but she had nowhere yet to stay tonight, and the note was written in a rush, on an impulse; she'd had to come. Philomena knew no one in the capital. All she had was three names and two addresses of men she'd never met. Who weren't expecting her.

She could hear the elderly guard along the corridor calling: 'All change! This train terminates at Euston. London and North Western apologise for the late arrival of this train. All change!' When he passed her compartment he met her eye for a fleeting moment, then she resumed her watch through the glass. The platform appeared below. The train's brakes screeched intermittently as it slowed more. The couplings clanked as they contracted and stretched, jolted and bumped. She directed her hands to take out, from her worn leather everyday bag, a sheaf of envelopes held together by elastic bands. Locating one, an official letter, she nervously checked the sender's peacetime address for the umpteenth time and returned it to its envelope. She touched several of the other well-thumbed envelopes in succession, divining which, if any, she should next revisit. As the roof of the station slid over-head obscuring the faint stars in the end-of-the-night sky her eyes welled with tears. 'This won't do.' But another voice butted in, 'This might be the way things will be for some time to come.' Voices in her head; was she mad? On the spur of the moment she had decided yesterday evening to travel alone to London, then had been unable to wait for the first train of today, the eight thirty, for that would not have delivered her until lunch time – half a day wasted. So she had caught the last yesterday, the midnight – had banked on sleeping on it, if it felt safe enough. It had, but oblivion proved only fitful, despite the mesmeric rocking of the carriage. Now she felt ragged, but so what? Her life since mid-November had been chaos: breathless lungs racing heart scrambled thoughts, interrupted by periods of torpor; slow, leaden hours with a black dog in a long dark lane.

She wiped her cheeks with the backs of her hands then stood. There was no one to help her down with her overnight luggage from the rack so she stood on the seat and hauled herself up. On boarding at Manchester last night an officious guard had quite unnecessarily shoved the bag up there, wordlessly, scowling, she felt, because of something about her. After he'd gone she'd put on the wedding band, precautionary lump on her finger, sad reminder of what was not going to happen.

As the train glided in, the glass window in the compartment door took a heft to get down before she could reach out for the handle on the outside. She looked along the smoky platform to the ticket barrier, and waited for the train to come to a complete rest. Whilst it still moved some doors in other carriages opened and the air was filled with the sound of shod feet hitting stone platform – crack! Men in suits and ties carrying briefcases forged ahead, as if using the train's final velocity to launch themselves, stealing precious seconds in what appeared to be a race to urgent business in the heart of the metropolis. Philomena felt herself infected by the rush, tensed as if ready to spring. Trying to relax her body was hopeless – the surge of human energy was irresistible, pointless to buck. She tried to join in but in stepping down onto the platform she stumbled and had to take another three or four steps to balance herself, by which time other disembarkers were nudging into her from behind. Some veered then converged ahead of her as if she were an obstacle that they must flow around, but the mass swept her up and along, crammed through the narrow gate – breathlessly squeezed – then spewed out into the Great Hall of the station, where it spread and dispersed and she was deposited, sediment, a particle, forgotten.

Everyone but her seemed to know exactly where they were going, but she'd been in a crowd before, just not a London crowd – she wasn't completely naive as to the ways of crowds. Used to at least the principles of urban navigation, she sped up, dropped her left shoulder, slowed down, paused on her toes to let a man cross, dropped to her heels, dipped her right shoulder, thrust her bag ahead of her to part a way and slipped through the gap. Now she was in an eddy. Here, because she wasn't having to concentrate on avoiding collisions she became aware of all the voices – hundreds, perhaps thousands of voices reverberating back off walls and floor, amplified by the towering ceiling. Cutting through this hubbub were the specific cries aimed to catch the attention: the newspaper vendors, shoe shiners, coffee and sandwich sellers – just like Manchester only bigger, louder, taller, fuller!

As she had planned en route she purchased a cheap map of central London. Unbuffeted at the side of the stall she unfolded this but immediately felt dismayed by its complexity. Famous names: Buckingham Palace, Westminster Abbey, Pall Mall led her bewildered eye this way and that but for the most part it was a maze, a blur of routes and names, too much to take in. She folded it and headed out through the station entrance in search of a bus. That was the sensible thing to do. Look at the first address again; find the correct bus. Out came the envelopes. That one was on the top.

Feeling the massive portico as she passed underneath she turned to look up at it. She craned her neck to see to its tip, pale against the lightening sky. The slightly darker shapes of scudding clouds made it appear that the station was swaying – she felt dizzy, reached out a hand to steady herself, unwittingly touched a passer-by, a man in a three-quarter double-breasted in blue chalkstripe, who muttered 'sorry' without even glancing at her. More sights and sounds assaulted her senses: the hooves of hundreds of horses on Drummond Street, the engines of motor cars, motor bikes, motor lorries, motor buses – the latter, from competing companies, swooping at queues of passengers as soon as they formed, the drivers in their exposed cabs impatiently sounding their horns, waving each other out of the way. Familiar names on the buses' sides: Iron Jelloids, Heinz Pickle, Veno's Cough Cure, like the faces of friends in a crowd of strangers. She consulted her map again and this time was able to locate Euston Station. But where on the map was she going? Her finger shakily traced the names of roads in the index. She found a grid reference. There! But which bus was headed that way?

Feeling very much like the country mouse, she searched the impassive faces of those around her for the least unapproachable, to ask for help.

A soldier in uniform ushered Philomena into Major James' office.

'He won't keep you waiting long. Sit there, miss.'

The room was plain and formal: a desk, a portrait of the king. It didn't feel like anyone's room in particular. He might not have been back here very long. The leather seat creaked as her weight shifted upon it.

She looked down at her hands and found that they were moving slowly, like fronds in water; little ripples. She made no attempt to influence them, instead trying to remember all the potential questions she had for Major James. She told herself off for not having written them down and decided to try to do that now. Rifling through her everyday bag she found a stub of pencil and the sheaf of envelopes. On the back of one she began to scribble a question. She drew a line from it and scribbled a sub or supplementary question. Then more lines to additional queries. What began as an orderly list quickly became a diagram, as if a structure was being exposed, or she was inadvertently mapping the truth that there never was, nor could be, a single consequence of an action.

She was hunched over engaged in this when Major James swiftly entered the room so she sat up straight a little too swiftly to be dignified. She noticed that he looked anxious in his body if not in his face, losing his stride a little – it wasn't a trip, nor was it enough to be called a stumble, but there was a definite malfunction and correction. Caused by the abrupt way she had sat up?

'Miss Bligh?' His smiling eyes looked practised.

'Yes,' replied Philomena, suddenly worried about military etiquette, gathering herself to stand.

'Please, stay seated,' said the neatly uniformed major as he made his way to the other side of the desk and put down his cap. Then he looked as if he changed his mind, and came to the front of the desk, nearer his visitor, where he perched, working off his tight gloves, which he afterwards held in one hand. He was stiff-backed. He sported a bushy moustache. In his early forties? His ears stuck out a little.

'Thank you for seeing me without an appointment,' Philomena said, 'and so early in the morning.'

'It's a pleasure to meet you,' he said, taking in the overnight bag on the floor by her feet. 'Travelled far?'

It was a new bag; paisley. When Philomena had bought it she'd worried it might have a bit too much pattern. Now, in that austere room it looked positively brash. If in the shop it had quietly burbled, in Major James' office it screamed.

'From Manchester.' She examined the word 'pleasure', turning it over in her mind's eye. It jarred but she decided that the major wasn't being haphazard or insensitive; it was just a word. As if he knew what she was thinking the major went on:

'I'd rather not have to meet you in these circumstances, of course. It was especially poignant, your fiancé's death.'

He spoke with clipped consonants, long vowels; very Standard English.

'Poignant because it was the last day?' she asked.

'Yes,' replied the major.

He'd entered the room possibly anxious and now Philomena could sense – from how he looked away, eyes flickering, that he was embarrassed or awkward in some way.

'Yes,' she said, 'the day of the Armistice, first post I had a letter from him, then last post next day the notification and letter from you.'

She searched a while for the next thing to say. Major James frowned and she realised her hands were doing their moving thing. She asked them to stop and they dropped to her lap. It was as if her hands slipped her consciousness from time to time and had to be reminded that she was supposed to be in charge.

'Daniel Case was a very good man,' said Major James.

Philomena felt her pulse quicken. There was something about the major – it *wasn't* that he was embarrassed or awkward; she felt that he was engaged in some sort of evasion, and decided to test him a little.

'Dan was always a little wild,' she said.

'Not incompatible with being good,' replied Major James without hesitation, and she could see that he meant it. Notwithstanding, her doubts about the major hardened into a suspicion that he was concealing something. Was she reading the major wrongly?

Feeling a little flustered by her possibly misguided reaction she said: 'It's a shame that they had to fight on the last day,' then immediately thought that shame was altogether too mild a word. 'It's appalling that they couldn't have all got together and agreed that as it was the last day they'd stop there and then, and make the day before the last day.'

As she said this she feared she was being stupidly naive

about how things happen on a battlefield, but the major gave no sign of passing judgement. He explained, as if she were his equal: 'We had to keep going; to take ground if possible. Some thought that we shouldn't stop until we were in Germany; give them a taste of their own medicine.'

Philomena suddenly felt like crying again and didn't want to in front of the officer, so to distract herself she stood up and made moves to go. Out of the corner of her eye she could see the major's brow had furrowed and his mouth had dropped open.

'Thank you for seeing me,' she said, making herself look him in the eye.

Major James' mouth closed, and Philomena thought that he looked a little relieved that the meeting was ending; she didn't blame him. He certainly reached the door quickly enough.

'I just wanted to see some of the men who knew him,' said Philomena.

'Who else have you met?' asked Major James, lightly.

'No one yet. You're the first.' She took a few steps then remembered she hadn't got one of the things she'd come for.

'Actually, I wonder if you might be able to help me. I have one address but I need another. I have the names of two of Dan's friends, but only the peacetime address for one of them. I have Captain, or, rather Mr Jonathan Priest's name and address.'

Major James nodded stiffly. The way he was holding himself, she wondered if he was feeling quite well. Perhaps that was what she had been sensing. Or, she wondered if he had met many women since the end of the war, and if mostly, like her, they didn't really want to know very much apart from that it had been quick, but they had a tendency to break down and cry, and that was awkward for him, and he'd feared she would be the same.

'Would you be able to help me with an address for the other man?' she asked.

'I shall do what I can,' replied Major James, returning to his desk, reaching for the card index. 'What name is it?'

'Captain, or Mr Anthony Dore,' she said, noticing a slight twitch in Major James' fingers just before they flicked through the index. Having found an entry he sat behind the desk to write.

'Here,' he said, beginning to copy a few lines onto a piece of crisp white letter paper. His hand made a strange movement, a sort of spasm, and he changed his grip on his pen and wrote the next words awkwardly, almost illegibly, muttered to himself, shook his head and resumed his former grip on his pen.

Everyone was a bit funny since the war started, weren't they? Philomena knew that you couldn't blame everything on it but neither could you ask: do you do that because of something in the war?

In her room in the Holborn hotel, 'The Daphne', the wall-mounted gas lamp cast a shadow of itself on the heavy purple paper behind. In the muffled light she could see that the ceiling was once possibly painted off-white but now was off-yellow on the way to light brown, and that the counterpane on the bed was shiny with age. The room was cramped; she could reach from the end of the bed to touch the cold glass of the window. The faded rug curled at the edges. There was no sink. The wardrobe rocked when she opened the doors. The predominant odour was of mothballs and what could be old feet – old some part of the body – feet hopefully, feet rather than other noxious zones of unwashed bodies. And still the room wasn't cheap. London was very, very expensive. Only one night, though.

She put her paisley bag on the bed then from her everyday bag extracted the bundle of envelopes. She fanned through until she found the photograph of Dan pretending to smoke a stick as if it were a cigar and propped this upright against the paraffin lamp she hoped she wouldn't have to use that stood on the bedside table.

In her mind she could hear Dan declare that one day he would smoke a real cigar that size.

She placed particular envelopes at the photograph's foot, as if constructing a shrine. From another envelope she took a letter and read it again. It was from the man called Jonathan Priest. There was an address, his office address; legal chambers. In this letter he explained that he didn't yet have a permanent home address – after being demobbed he couldn't decide where to settle. It was a friendly letter, almost chatty, as if from someone she knew. A few minutes ago the hotel receptionist – Philomena didn't know what else to call the slovenly man who provided the key to this room – had squinted at Jonathan Priest's address and peered at her map, stabbed the location with his forefinger, leaving a grubby mark. 'Fifteen to twenty minutes' walk,' he'd barked, 'if you don't get lost, for it's a proper labyrinth. If you do get lost, we'll sell your belongings in a month to pay your bill.' He'd winked to show that, despite appearances, he wasn't being unpleasant. 'On your own?' he'd said. 'Yes,' she'd replied. 'Hmm,' he'd said.

A rare shaft of sunlight slanted in through Philomena's grubby window creating a narrow beam over the top of the bed. On an impulse she raised her hand and brought it down flat on the counterpane with a *whump!* She watched the dust motes thrown upwards dance and twinkle in the sunlight, the glinting detritus of the room's previous occupants. She recalled home, about how the light beams could be caught in the glass of the magnifiers and redirected to all corners of the workshop. It was the tip of the tail of the winter, still in the months when daylight was in short supply. When the days grew longer and the sun rose higher they worked all the hours they could in the bright natural light. Work. Home. Loneliness.

The thought of work made her consciously straighten her spine. She was determined to avoid becoming hunched like the others. An occupational hazard, they all said. It could be avoided, she had decided; didn't want Dan going off her because she was all bent over. There; she caught her thoughts. Dan wouldn't be going off her, would he? How long would this forgetting take? She didn't mean forgetting – *I'll never forget you* – she meant how long would these ambushes continue? These aftershocks? It was the middle of March, and Dan had died on 11 November. She'd begun to understand those photographs she'd seen of women in black; foreign-looking women, who stayed in mourning for the rest of their lives. How long would that be – the rest of her life? Future. Don't think. Just live now. Or black dog in long dark lane. She felt sick, and unbalanced by lack of sleep.

She lay down. She stared at the ceiling. She began to see patterns in the cracks in the thick paint and its patina when she didn't want to see anything. She shut her eyes but still she could see; at first mostly blackness, with flashes of red and yellow, then, unbidden and unwelcome, images of war: men, bits of men, their insides on the outside, obscenely glistening, hands trying to push portions back inside mushy holes. She imagined groups of men, faceless. She was trying not to hear the sounds of war, the explosions, screams, whimpers. The smells: blood, faeces, rottenness, stale breath, damp— no, wet— no, *sodden* wool, that's overpowering – suffocating, in a confined space, like a dugout, or a grave. She opened her eyes and deliberately widened them and looked to the limit of her periphery, stretching and blinking, sucked in daylight in the hope of dislodging the war images. She sat up and poked her fingers into her ears and waggled them to create a rushing noise to drown out the war sounds, and she cupped her hands over her nose and mouth and inhaled the smell of her palms. There was the counterpane – the last thing she had touched.

Having reset herself, she lay down again, picked a quiet spot on the ceiling and tried to concentrate on it, to block everything else out. She lay on her back and sent her gaze like a beam to the spot on the ceiling.

CHAPTER TWO

It was still not yet mid morning when, nearing the receptionist's smudge on her map, Philomena crossed a busy commercial street and continued into a low brick passage, which opened out at the other end in to a surprising garden square. On her left ran an ancient, bulging brick wall. Past this there was an entrance, through which she could see another square of manicured lawns surrounded by grand buildings. Over the tops of them, turrets and spires. There were men passing swiftly, singly and in pairs, dressed in closely woven black cloaks and white wigs, carrying thick bundles of papers tied with wide ribbon. Expensive motor cars purred past, their black paintwork shiny as lacquer. *Keep Off the Grass!* a sign commanded. An elegant terraced row to the right showed a date, 1787, built into its brickwork. A mature purple wisteria ran several yards along it and a vast magnolia threatened to bloom, its buds standing ripe, upright, swollen, parted, revealing furled pink-tinged petals.

A man in a black three-piece suit and bowler carrying a large bunch of keys crossed Philomena's path. She expected him to challenge her, but he did not. She moved on, passing an ancient-looking cracked wooden door studded with black bolts. Beyond that there was what looked like a miniature barn. It had a roof, and columns, but no walls. The ceiling was decorated with stone carvings of foliage and fruit. A sign: 'This chapel was reopened after being enlarged. 8 April 1883'. Another sign, by a door in a wall: Flat 1, Lord and Lady —. Flat 2, Lord and Lady —. Titled people lived here!

Retracing her steps Philomena located a list of names in gilt transfer on a painted black background, but Jonathan Priest's wasn't among them. Another man, in a grey three-piece, left one door and entered another a few yards ahead (in a way that reminded her of the White Rabbit in *Alice*) and she pursued him. Entering the low door she called:'Excuse me, please,' as he was about to disappear around a corner.

'Yes, miss,' he replied over his shoulder.

'I am looking for this gentleman, please,' she said, showing her letter from Jonathan Priest.

'Follow me, miss,' said the man, as he ducked back out of the low door they had just entered.

He guided her to a full-sized door where *Mr Jonathan PRIEST* appeared on another gilt list. Behind this door a sharp-nosed clerk looked at her letter and informed her that 'sir' wouldn't be back until late afternoon. He encouraged her to leave a note. She became anxious. What should she write? In her mind she tried 'I am Philomena Bligh, Dan's fiancée. I've come down to London on the off-chance of meeting Dan's surviving friends.' She examined whether she really did want to meet them. If she had really wanted to

meet them she would have made contact in advance and
secured proper appointments, wouldn't she? The clerk's gentle
cough brought her back and she quickly wrote her name
and the name and address and telephone number of her
hotel on a card the clerk provided. On her way out she
learned, from an announcement on the wall, the court that
Jonathan Priest was 'performing in' – as the clerk put it –
that morning.

'Could I meet him there?' she asked. 'Is he returning here
at lunch?'

'Do you know him at all?' asked the clerk, whose name
was Jones.

'No,' Philomena admitted.

'You can watch him if you like,' suggested Jones.

'Watch him?'

'He's due to be on his feet this morning, summing up. If
you hurry you'll catch him. I shall furnish you with a description, so's you don't get the wrong man by accident. He's tall,
he's dark in colour – his eyes and hair that is, which is wavy
if you were able to see it under his wig – he's medium build,
his type is restless. And that should be enough to distinguish
him from the other barristers who I happen to know are
there in that court: one fat and grey, one bow-legged, and
one short in the arms.' All this said flat, rapidly, but with a
slight twinkle in his eye.

Thus it was that Philomena found herself – after a short
walk down to Fleet Street, and a turn east – seated in a

25

public gallery at the Old Bailey, watching Jonathan Priest conducting a defence. He was tall as Jones had said, but also graceful, and not restless; animated to an abnormal degree. Not that he was waving his arms about – it was his energy that was extraordinary: the amount of it, its intensity, and the way he marshalled and channelled it. The whole focus of the wood-panelled courtroom was on him, the jurors', particularly.

Jonathan Priest stopped moving and pinched the bridge of his nose for a few moments and Philomena swore that he had all twelve of them holding their breath. He dropped his hand, sent his weight upwards, balanced on his heels and turned his face upwards, towards her. She slid back in her seat, leaning away from him, peeking down, but he was oblivious to her. His eyes didn't take her in; they flickered from side to side, their movement and lack of focus revealing that he sought inspiration not from the surface of the material world but from somewhere inside himself.

He turned back, his weight dropped down again and he was in full flow, voicing his thoughts. He could be an actor, a proper actor, who appeared in plays, and was paid for it. The people in Philomena's hometown, Saddleworth, who got together and put on productions – none of them had his presence. He was compelling, but he had a tentativeness about him too, a hesitancy, a delicacy, even.

Jonathan Priest passed in front of the judge, who looked down on the court from his wooden throne – was that the right name for his big seat? The judge appeared to be the opposite of Jonathan Priest in nature, just as compelling but giving off no sense of struggle, no uncertainty. And he looked much bigger, heavier, thicker. The only lighter thing about him was his hair colour, which was grey in his eyebrows. Regardless of their dissimilarity, he seemed to be listening favourably as Jonathan Priest continued his summing up to the jury.

'So, if you believe in justice then you must acquit my client of this petty crime committed out of desperation.'

The young accused, dressed in army uniform, frowned, as did several others present, including Philomena. Had the defending barrister just admitted that his client had actually done what he was accused of?

Jonathan Priest continued: 'If you do not acquit this war veteran and he goes to gaol – I say veteran because he is one, but let us remind ourselves of his actual age; eighteen . . . he is an eighteen-year-old war veteran – and you must acquit him! You must acquit this boy! Put yourselves in his shoes – some of you can, I sense. No doubt some of you served; he is a boy called by his country – one of millions who has literally given his body for his country.'

Indeed, noted Philomena, the young man in the dock had an empty sleeve to his khaki tunic. It was pinned to his breast by the cuff.

'If you were he, and you were found guilty of taking just enough food and drink to feed yourself and quench your thirst and were sent to gaol for it, would you feel that justice had been done? Would you feel that?'

There followed a silence during which it appeared that Jonathan Priest might go on. Philomena could see that most of the jury were sat forward slightly, if not actually on the edge of their seats, inclined towards him. He was now looking floorwards, apparently at the toe of his own shiny shoe. He shook his head.

The judge raised a quizzical eyebrow. Jonathan Priest tapped his top lip with his fingers and looked up. He turned towards the jury and gave an almost imperceptible shrug, and then he sat down, not looking at anyone. The judge pursed his lips and looked doubtful, but most of the jury were visibly impressed. Their eyes were on Jonathan Priest, then, as if he directed them, on the accused, who was looking pitiful. In the silence that continued in the court Philomena imagined that she could hear the jury asking themselves, 'Yes, what is justice for this young fellow?'

Philomena's eyes settled on Jonathan Priest, searching for any signs that he was conscious of his performance. Any little smile, or flicker of the eyes. If Dan were in his place he would have been unable to prevent a smile to himself now – his habit, infuriating to some, after he'd done something well. Was Jonathan Priest acting? Only someone who knew him in another context would be able to tell if his current disposition: head down, angled slightly, nodding occasionally, as if running the whole thing over in his head in case he'd missed something, indicated he was acting. Acting or not, he was definitely leading, setting an example as to how the jury should conduct themselves when contemplating the very serious question: what is the right thing to do?

In the marble-floored public areas at the entrance to the courts where members of the legal profession and others can mingle Jonathan Priest was standing alone. Philomena wondered if she should exploit this proximity and make herself known to him. She observed him reach a finger under his wig to scratch his head, screwing up his face as he did so. Something about this unguarded gesture made her decide that she should introduce herself, but after she'd moved a few steps in his direction he suddenly became agitated, for no reason she could see, and he made off, entering – she discovered on closer inspection - the men's lavatories.

Now in the public area there began a bit of a flap. Hurried footsteps clacked on the shiny floor as various officials moved swiftly hither and thither, passing between them, in hushed tones, some urgent news. Philomena edged nearer to where two such men were about to converge and successfully eavesdropped on one telling the other that the jury had already sent a message to the judge asking what the lightest sentence would be should they return a guilty verdict. All the officials seemed to know exactly the significance of this, and it seemed to please them, but later, when the court reassembled to hear the jury's verdict, Jonathan Priest didn't appear to share this pleasure.

As the stiff-collared foreman declared the accused 'not guilty' the winning barrister remained in a reverie, tapping his top lip with his index finger, ignoring the grateful young veteran's attempts to gain his attention. Philomena puzzled at Jonathan Priest's behaviour towards the boy he had just so successfully defended. Able to see both without turning her head she watched the acquitted's celebration sour. His brow furrowed and the grimy-looking heel of his remaining hand beat nervously on the wood of the dock. Philomena sensed that more than anything he needed Jonathan Priest to look at him, but the barrister remained oblivious for a few more moments before he looked up and smiled at his client, who appeared more relieved now than when the jury's verdict had been delivered. Jonathan Priest got to his feet, courteously shook his youthful client's surviving hand, politely accepted his heartfelt gratitude.

Philomena accidentally caught the judge's eye and realised with a start that he was studying her. She looked away and felt immediately, automatically guilty, of course, as though if the judge pointed at her she would find whatever his accusations were, were true: 'It wasn't this young man who stole those items, it was her, her up there in the gallery!' And she would admit, 'Yes it was me!' and be arrested, tried, gaoled.

When she glanced back at him the judge had already looked away. She saw him nod imperceptibly towards Jonathan, as if to agree, 'Yes, fascinating.' Jonathan Priest looked around. Philomena could tell that the judge and he made eye contact. The judge made a tiny gesture, three swift little claps of his hands – not mocking or ironic.

Once out of the court Jonathan entered another lavatory. God, this case, he thought. How he'd had to bend it. Empty cubicle. Anyone about? That melodramatic speech he'd made earlier was more than was required of him – what had he been thinking of when he'd admitted the guilt of his client? He'd entered a plea of not guilty, so it was up to the Crown to prove his guilt beyond reasonable doubt – which they had done in terms of objects unpaid for found in his client's possession. But he'd sensed that whilst the court knew a guilty verdict was evidentially correct, it wasn't necessarily right, so he'd made his extremely unorthodox intervention, winging it on behalf of a young man he didn't even particularly like. It wasn't because he was a fellow veteran, that much Jonathan was sure of. He didn't like veterans for their own sake. Damn right he didn't.

Jonathan shut the cubicle door, wiped the varnished wooden toilet lid with his sleeve to ensure its dryness, lowered himself to his knees, took out a phial from his waistcoat pocket, removed the stopper, laid out a fine line of cocaine and inhaled . . . He rubbed the residue on his gums, stayed kneeling for a few moments, forearms resting on the toilet lid, as if in prayer. He took out a pocket mirror, checked no powder was visible on his face or in his nostrils.

In one of the corridors behind the courts where the public may not go he happened across the judge travelling in the opposite direction. Oh no, the judge wanted to talk. Their cloaks settled about them as they slowed to a halt. Standing too close the judge bantered: 'Guilty, wasn't he? The empty sleeve won it, of course.'

Jonathan had to make some reply; to do otherwise would

be unutterably rude, but instead of joining in with the judge's light-hearted teasing he surprised him by replying evenly: 'It really is empty.'

'What?' barked the judge. In the dimly lit, windowless thoroughfare he cocked his head and after a moment's pause added: 'I was complimenting you. You're in the ascendancy, Priest. People are talking about you,' expecting, as in the normal way, for a young lawyer to bow his head in humility, or to gush some thanks. But again the judge didn't get the response he expected. He received only a blank stare.

'Have I caught you at a bad time?' the judge growled, his rebuffed overture making him aggressive. 'You see, it might be worth your while to appear even slightly enthusiastic that I'm at all interested in you. I'm not saying you should kiss my arse or plead to rejoin my chambers, but—'

'I'm sorry, sir,' offered Jonathan, keen to placate his very powerful superior. 'I didn't mean to appear rude.' After all, the poor man didn't know what he'd done.

CHAPTER THREE

She had been here, to his chambers. Dan's girl. Might she return?

Jonathan desperately concentrated on the notes for his next case. '. . . I went in and heard the cry of a child from another room and I searched and searched but there was no child in any of the rooms that I could see or so I thought at the time, and when questioned he said that he hadn't been there all day or even ever at all before, he didn't know the victim—'

Who was this? Flick back through notes . . . ah yes, the police officer. He writes as he speaks:

'—and the other one she said she didn't know the accused but there was blood on the broken window pane and a neighbour said that the man had been there before, they were always at it—'

A knock at his door – not Jones' knock. Jonathan sat still, waiting. It was going to be her, wasn't it? He remained silent. The knock came again. He glanced towards the window, contemplating a dramatic escape – had a vision of himself as a silent movie comedy hero taking ridiculous, completely-out-of-proportion risks to evade minor threats. No; no need to flee. All he had to do was talk to her. It was bound to be emotional; he was just feeling the emotion. The physical symptoms of fear and excitement are the same.

He placed his elbows on his desk, made a cathedral of his fingers, and called, 'Come!'

There followed a few moments while he waited for the green baize door to open, but it did not. He dropped his hands and pretended to be reading so that he could appear unconcerned when she entered.

Having heard 'Come!' Philomena wavered. Open the door, or walk away? Why was this simple act so difficult? Knock on a door, receive an instruction to enter, open the door . . . She knew he wasn't going to have two heads, that he was a professional man, not too much older than her; what was this ominous feeling? It was as if she had one toe on the end of a bridge; she wanted to get to the other side but she couldn't quite put her foot down and step forward. Likewise in the real world, she could feel the round brass doorknob cold in her hand but couldn't bring herself to grip it tightly enough to turn it.

She jerked a little away from the door then immediately jerked back towards it. Both movements felt as if commanded by some remote part of her – she wasn't conscious of instigating either. 'Philomena,' she said her own name under her breath, and waited a few moments until she felt more whole. She deliberately let go of the doorknob, wiped her hand on her skirt – though her hand wasn't sweaty, shifted her stance slightly, and the brass knob turned easily. Still irrationally afraid of what might happen next but making herself go on, she entered the room, took a further three steps onto the heavy, dark green carpet, so that she stood just inside the threshold, the door ajar behind her. Jonathan Priest put down some papers and rose from his seat. He felt a force, a charge enter the room. Philomena. Striking, as he'd expected. More striking than in her photograph.

Unsettled, he thought to close the door and set off from behind his desk to do so. As he moved, so did she. She stepped more fully into the room and revolved, keeping her front towards him. An image of opposing magnets flashed through his mind; like poles repel. When he reached the door they were angled slightly away from each other like two animals meeting for the first time, watching each other with their sideways eye. He shut the door and turned to her. She took half a step backwards, which prompted him to think that they *had* been too close and that he should acknowledge this by also taking a step backwards.

For a few moments the muffling effects of the carpet, the heavy purple velvet curtains, the baize, the shelves full of books, combined to render the room silent apart from, it seemed to Philomena, her own and Jonathan Priest's life-sounds: the beatings of their hearts, the passage of blood in their veins, the sighs of slightly quickened respiration.

Jonathan was taken by her eyes, which were green, and bright when they caught the light so you felt that they were backlit. They reminded him of the luminous eyes of men in the war, who were intent on surviving some intense period of activity, and of people he encountered through the law, ordinary citizens caught in some great upheaval.

'I'm Jonathan Priest,' he said, trying to sound cheery about it.

'I know,' she replied. 'It says so on your door. But another man might have been using your room. But he isn't. You're Jonathan Priest. I know.' She faltered and glanced down at the carpet. Why was she babbling and why hadn't she admitted that she recognised him because she'd watched him in court – and why had she just thought the word 'admitted' as though she were embarrassed, had done something underhand? She knew that he was who he said he was because she'd watched him in court, but the moment she could tell him that had passed. Nerves: tell them what to do, not the other way around. She looked up at him and took a deliberate step forward. 'I'm Philomena Bligh; Daniel Case's fiancée.' And she proffered a photo of Dan pretending to smoke a stick, as if it were her calling card. Jonathan looked at it but didn't reach for it, so it remained in the air between them until Philomena took it back and tucked it in her bag without looking at it. Jonathan had recognised Dan's pose in the photograph. He'd seen him adopt it numerous times, not always with a stick, with whatever was to hand at the time: a cutlery fork, a Mills bomb, and several times nothing, just a mimed shape.

Feeling under pressure, he moved further away, saying: 'Please, sit down,' moving a chair for Philomena, trying to make a fresh start, begin a new exchange that wouldn't be as disquieting.

But 'No thank you,' said Philomena, staying where she was, on her feet.

'Oh,' he said.

Why wouldn't she accept the offer of a seat? He feared he knew why; she remained on her feet the better to confront him – she knew his secret. But how could she know that about him? Get a grip. Nobody knew that about him.

You don't know that about me, or, if you do, are unable to communicate, which is not quite the same; it leaves me with my fear, the knowledge that it's possible that you know.

He let go of the chair and there was a catch in his throat that he had to cough out before he could say: 'How are you?'

Having done the wrong thing in offering a seat – or rather having done the right thing but having had it treated as if it were the wrong thing, it seemed now that using one of the basic everyday introductory phrases in the English tongue – how are you? – was the wrong thing to say, because her only visible response to it was to shift her weight.

Philomena wasn't reacting to Jonathan's question; she wasn't thinking to herself that it was obvious how she was: 'I'm grieving of course, you fool.' She didn't understand her own behaviour but knew it was stimulated by the strange premonition she was having – a furthering of the ominous feeling outside the door – that everything she had known, or held, was falling away.

'I'm sorry, that sounds silly – how are you?' ran on Jonathan, 'I mean, are you visiting London— I'm sorry, that's a stupid thing to ask, too; what does it matter whether you are visiting?'

As he spoke more she could hear his – to her – reassuring Yorkshire accent emerge from underneath his 'working' voice. She hadn't meant to make him uncomfortable, but found it endearing that he clearly was.

'I am visiting,' she said surprisingly brightly, making it sound as if he was quite clever to have worked this out.

And that seemed to settle him a little. They were now looking directly square on at each other for the first time. His eyes were brown, and Philomena thought that a strange thing about them was that their edges didn't seem fixed. Under her gaze he reddened, and fidgeted, and seemed almost about to take a step towards her, which he checked.

He said: 'I have to say . . . I was so . . . sorry—'

'I know, I can see that you are,' she interrupted, experiencing an urge to save him, almost reaching out a hand to steady him, for he suddenly seemed as if he needed help, a lifeline, even.

'I have to say—' he went on, stopped, shrugged, leaned back as he inhaled, forward as he exhaled, reached for an expensive-looking black and silver fountain pen on his desk, began fiddling with it. 'I have to say—'

'I know, yes, I know,' she said.

'I mean . . . You got my letter?'

'I did, yes,' she confirmed, raising her bag to indicate that she was carrying said.

'Well then. You know. He didn't . . . he didn't suffer or anything. It was quick. If that's any comfort to you. Shall I just shut up?'

'No, please, don't,' she said, and moved to where he had left the chair, positioned it to face him and sat down. Perhaps now he'd be able to get through a sentence. He was much more upset than she'd ever imagined he would be, almost as if he was having to *break* the terrible news to her.

'Well. That's it really,' Jonathan continued, almost sitting in his own chair, bending his knees in preparation, but apparently changing his mind, standing tall again. 'As I said, it was quick. And, er, he was my friend. Really. I mean, I didn't know him very long, but—'

There was a knock at the door and it opened and Jones showed his face, smiling apologetically.

What was that 'but' leading on to? thought Philomena.

'I've a case, a client, you know,' Jonathan apologised to her. 'An appointment. Sorry . . .' Jones withdrew discreetly.

'Can I make an appointment with you?' she interrupted. 'I mean is there another time today or tomorrow before I go—'

'There's not much more I can tell you,' said Jonathan, more sharply than you'd expect. She narrowed her eyes. Yes, there was more he could tell. And there were things she could tell him. They could play 'Did Dan ever tell you about the time that . . . ?' They could exchange anecdotes: 'One day, Dan did/said/laughed about such and such' and they could confide; 'What is your favourite/least favourite thing about Dan?'

She said: 'I'd like to, just, talk. I haven't . . . There isn't . . . It's not—' Now it was her turn to be unable to complete a sentence.

'Well, you know,' came in Jonathan, putting down his worry pen, heading for the door, 'it's there in my letter and whatever you received from the army—'

'Please,' she asked firmly, arresting Jonathan's movement towards the door by her voice alone. He stopped mid stride, watched her stand up, appeal: 'I'd just like to—' Those eyes were looking right into him – say something to make them stop.

'Yes, yes, yes. Of course. I'm being stupid, and impolite. I'll write an address for you.' He returned to his desk. 'It's a good cafe. Small – less busy than a Corner House – we'll be able to find each other. Ask my clerk, Jones, how to get there. Six thirty do you? And bring anyone you are travelling with.'

'I came alone,' she said, raising her chin.

'Oh,' he said, narrowing his eyes. 'Well, why on earth not?' speaking almost to himself, giving her an image of him arguing aloud when alone.

'Yes,' she said, suddenly full of anxiety about going for a meal in an unknown place with this bewildering man. Her hands, one gripping her bag, must have started their telling movements in the air again because she realised Jonathan was watching them. His demeanour had changed once more. He'd resumed a persona she recognised from the courtroom: slightly distracted and thinking deeply, considering. She became very self-conscious, felt herself blush, abruptly moved towards the door to cover it, saying: 'Six thirty, then.'

And before Jonathan Priest could move Philomena Bligh

opened the door out of his padded room and entered the corridor beyond. On her way she sensed him moving to be in the doorway behind her, felt his eyes on her back.

CHAPTER FOUR

A few yards along the corridor Philomena turned a corner, thought she heard the soft click of his door shutting. No longer under Jonathan's scrutiny, as she proceeded she tilted her neck both sides to release tension. She had a strong sense of events unfolding, forces stirring into action. Lengthening her stride, she felt acutely aware that the war, and now the aftermath, were driving large-scale changes, and she felt part of this. But she also intuited developments that were personal to her, to do with the wider world but in some way about her in particular; her stride faltered and she came to a halt. It was as if, she thought, she had been set an as yet unarticulated quest, and that if she followed her instincts she would learn what it was. Or were any thoughts of a quest just wishful thinking, a way of tricking herself into optimism?

Just take the next step. Do the next thing.

She asked Jones for the location of the cafe and whilst he drew it in on her map she took the opportunity to ask the way to Anthony Dore's address, which Major James had given her. Jones lined her up along his sharp nose, said: 'That must be quite a place,' and held her eye for a few seconds, as if hoping she would elaborate. Philomena took his reaction to the address to mean that it was one she was too humble to be likely to frequent.

She walked down to Fleet Street again and turned right this time, west. Walking efficiently in London was still a challenge to her, but passage through the crowds was becoming easier as her peripheral vision rapidly evolved to the standard required. At the northern end of a bridge over the brown-green Thames, looking down its span, it slipped into her mind that nobody from home knew where she was. In fact, nobody in the world knew. Loneliness suddenly lumped in her throat and she took a few moments in the lee of a police box to steady herself. Around her, humanity poured in every direction — even upwards in the case of the tribe of urchins who ran alongside, leaped on, and cheekily ascended the curved stairs of a speeding motor bus. Their glinting eyes and smiling faces pleased her, and she allowed their glee to warm her heart. Her mood swung. Her anxiety at being alone, anonymous and unreachable by home began to be replaced by almost relish that she was, in some sense, free amongst the multitudes, none of whom seemed at all bothered by her.

As she continued to thread her way west, every few yards or so a narrow gap between buildings appeared, some, even in daytime, artificially lit, but others — the perversely enticing ones — fading to pitch dark, dangerous-looking corridors. Should she try to contact Captain Anthony Dore before meeting Jonathan? Dan had never mentioned him. She paused at a bright shop window. In it were all manner of scissors.

Some were mounted on a revolving display. They took it in turns to glint in the steady electric light. Very good for work – one day she and Jo would have electric light – but not so good as gas for heating, she'd heard. And how much was it costing? Dread to think. No wonder their scissors were so pricey.

According to the map the cafe was around the next right turn, but it took some searching for because the row in which it was situated was in such a state of disrepair. Scaffolding along both sides, hammerings and bangings and indistinct shouts. The street was narrow, which made the terraced build-ings climb higher, and the shallow pavements were barely wide enough for two people to pass. The feeling was that the sun's rays never hit the ground except, perhaps, at its zenith in summer. The large mirrors fixed to the walls, angled to catch whatever light there was and redirect it in through the windows, bore this out. Philomena listened to the sounds of work being carried on around and above her. Inside, the cafe – or dining room – looked welcoming. Yes, she thought she could meet Jonathan Priest there.

She set off to return to her hotel for a wash and brush up, then stopped. She should go to Anthony Dore's address now, perhaps even see if he was at home. Studying the map again in the light of the scissor shop she began to piece together what she knew so far of London geography. Her hotel was over there. Jonathan's chambers were there, Major James' offices were there, The Conduit cafe was there. Already she was getting a picture of London and her place in it. She began to walk, and the nearer she got to Anthony Dore's address the grander the buildings became, until each house seemed more like several homes amalgamated. She felt very conspicuous because she was obviously not a servant – her clothes were too beautifully tailored, but, if challenged, what was her business thereabouts? In a square with private gardens at its centre, Philomena kept near to the railings and their overhanging foliage. She couldn't imagine ever entering one of these grand houses by the front door. What was she doing there? She saw herself as a diminutive girl in a children's picture book. She'd wandered into a land of giants. These were giant's houses. Behind the windows, giants were looking down on her, a speck of a creature who should not lift her eyes above the horizon of her own world.

Jonathan met his new client, destroyed his defence, created a new one, then took himself off to an obscure Picture House where he felt it was his extreme good fortune to have the place entirely to himself. Up on screen the heroes in a series of short films escaped death or serious injury over and over again in various comedic episodes, none of which made him laugh. But to laugh wasn't the reason he was here. It was dark, and warm, and better than being home alone. As a falling house narrowly missed one hero because he'd bent down to pat a dog a second man entered the cinema auditorium and almost immediately began to laugh uproariously. Jonathan felt irked by this noise, this too-loud laughing. His pleasure was being ruined by the newcomer's ostentatious expressions of appreciation. Whilst he had to admit that his own behaviour in this public cinema showing comedies was perverse, he also thought the man was being ridiculous. Why laugh like that when there's only one other present and they're not laughing at all? For God's sake! He feared that at any moment the man might turn to him to demand, 'Did you see that? Did you see that?' when all he wanted was to watch the screen alone, or as if alone, and brood. This desire thwarted, Jonathan experienced a flash of anger, but rather than remonstrate with the other fellow, who was after all behaving more appropriately than he was, Jonathan vacated his seat, leaving the other man to laugh too loudly alone.

He headed for the cafe, The Conduit. Once there he took a seat at a table and began to drink inexpensive red wine, French, and he waited.

Arriving opposite Philomena could look from the darkness into the brightly lit cafe without being detected. It was busy inside – most of the twenty or so tables were occupied, some by couples, not speaking, one by a group of men in office suits, talking over each other, and to her relief, two by single female diners, also office workers by the look of them; and there was the one at which Jonathan sat.

As she crossed the street, he drained his glass and refilled it from the bottle. He seemed to be drinking without much pleasure. What was his life like? Nobody ever asks anyone that, do they? What's your life like? Up at home nobody asked such a question because everyone thought they knew what your life was like. It was like their life. Dan hates that – Philomena caught herself – Dan *had* hated that. Dan would never have returned and remained there.

Stepping forward to put her hand on the cafe door handle, a terrible feeling overwhelmed her. She found herself absolutely stricken, unable to move. Without warning, inertia had invaded and made her rigid. She would have toppled but fortunately there were only inches to go before her shoulder met the glass of the cafe window, where she leaned, wide-eyed.

From inside the cafe Jonathan stared out at Philomena. He had been about to take another swig of wine – the glass was still inches from his lips, held there because he was gripped, watching her in some sort of distress. Her eyes were open but her focus was elsewhere. The top of her chest rose and fell rapidly. Jonathan put down his glass and, continuing to watch her, he stood. But instead of going to help Philomena he looked over his shoulder towards the back of the cafe, to the door marked exit. He imagined Philomena as being on the edge of a great hole of sorrow, a terrifying void that he knew, only too well, existed, and that he believed could receive and accommodate all the many souls that fell into it without any prospect of it ever being filled. Glancing again at her, seeing that she was coming to, Jonathan threw some money down on the table, seized his hat, and skedaddled.

When Philomena entered the cafe Jonathan was nowhere to be seen. She looked around for him, blinking to clear her vision. The waitress approached and Philomena explained that she was due to meet someone. Indeed, he was here a few moments earlier. At that table.

'Ah, yes,' the waitress replied. 'He's gone, I think.'

'Gone?'

'He's left money for his bill.'

'Gone where?'

The waitress showed she was sensitive to the implications of what was unfolding by smiling apologetically and discreetly indicating the rear exit. Philomena looked suitably baffled.

'Would you like a seat?' asked the waitress. 'Would you like to eat? Are you sure he was the man you were expecting?'

Mumbling that perhaps it wasn't him, Philomena accepted a seat at a table, and a menu to hold. The Specials: Leg of Beef Soup, Sausage and Mash, Steak and Onion Pie. What was that smell behind the food? Fresh paint. The place was immaculate. Chairs, tables, all new. And what had been that smell she'd inhaled when she leaned on the glass? Fresh putty, yes.

Outside, in the darkness opposite the cafe, watching her, Jonathan mused on opposing magnets again; she approached, he was forced away. Another man headed for The Conduit. When he entered it Philomena glanced up, then her eyes went back to the menu she was holding. The normality of her reaction reassured Jonathan. Perhaps she wasn't as needy as he had felt. Perhaps it was his own feelings, his needs that he was projecting onto her. He made himself cross to the cafe and go in, all set to pretend to Philomena that it was his first entrance. He winked at the waitress to gain her compliance.

'Sorry I'm late,' he said, as he sat.

'You're not really,' Philomena replied.

The waitress came to their table. They ordered some food and Philomena accepted the offer of a glass of red wine. As the waitress took the menus she shot her a look as if to say she thought Philomena was handling the situation impeccably.

Still shaken, and preoccupied by the strange episode outside, she murmured: 'So, you're a barrister.'

'Yes,' said Jonathan, nodding, and he added unnecessarily, 'I was before the war. Well, I could hardly have qualified since the war. And you sew.'

'I'm a seamstress, yes. High class.'

Jonathan looked slightly sideways at her to see if she was being ironic. But no, she gave no indication that she was being anything other than straight with him.

'I'm a high-class seamstress. I work on expensive garments and fabrics. Alterations for the wealthy, mostly.'

Jonathan located her hands, resting on the table. Was he wondering at her wedding band? She let him look, determining that the strange movements of her hands that had begun after she heard of Dan's death must cease at some point. Philomena had an image of Dan's mother, her stifled cry on seeing her son's fiancée stumble into the shop to tell bad news – was Dan ever intending to end his estrangement with his parents? A few hours later, lying on her bed looking out at the bright, night November sky Philomena had noticed her hands moving independently of her. First thought was that they were ghost-sewing, doing the work she had planned to do over the previous two days but forgotten about. But her hands weren't doing anything so prosaic. They had taken on a life of their own. This strange innovation, because she felt dislocated anyway, hadn't alarmed her. It was another novelty in the terrible new world.

As if in the distance she heard Jonathan say: 'And Dan's family have a shop?'

'*The* shop, in their village,' she replied. 'They have *the* shop.'

She watched Jonathan absorb this piece of information then drift. Was he remembering when Dan told him his parents were shopkeepers? Or something else about Dan? Or was he thinking about something else entirely? Was she boring him? Was he very rude? She felt a surge. 'Where did you go?' she asked, belligerently.

'What?'

'I said, where did you go? You went out of the back door.'

Jonathan appeared to be about to protest that he hadn't done any such thing but at that moment the waitress returned with their drinks and it was clear from her expression that she had heard what Philomena had just asked and wasn't going to stand any nonsense, that is, corroborate any lies Jonathan might be trying to tell, no matter how many times he'd been there and how many times he'd winked at her.

'I had second thoughts about meeting you. But here I am.'

'Why did you have second thoughts?'

'Because the war's over.'

'I won't restart the war; I'm not meaning to make life at all difficult for you in any way. And I'll be gone tomorrow,' stated Philomena.

'I know,' said Jonathan, replying to all statements.

Thinking of going home the next day, Philomena felt a pain in her heart. She could see into his eyes. The strangeness of them wasn't because the edges of the iris weren't fixed. Due to streaks of grey in the brown, they looked as if they had movement, like thick smoke trapped in glass. She thought; those are fall-into eyes. What would you see if the smoke cleared? Trouble.

Needing to take in the whole of Philomena, Jonathan leaned back slightly, to widen his focus.

'You know,' she said, deliberately taking any sadness out of her voice, 'I was up there at home and I, I just couldn't . . . anymore. So I came down here. I'm not tragic. I'm a war widow – not even a widow! I'm one of the "surplus women" you hear about.'

One of the single female diners glanced ruefully across. Philomena made what Jonathan took to be a clan gesture, a little nod of greeting. She lowered her voice.

'Two a penny. So I thought I'd come down here and try to talk to his friends, the men, and the women – if there were any. Were there any women?'

Jonathan shook his head. How brusque she was. But perhaps less brusque, more blunt, not unlike the girls he grew up amongst.

'I've seen Dan flirt, you know. I've seen him in action,' said Philomena. 'It was all right women wanting him as long as I was there to beat them off.'

'He only ever talked about you,' reassured Jonathan.

'Yes, but I wasn't there, was I? When he was feeling frisky. We all feel frisky from time to time.'

Jonathan tried not to laugh but 'frisky' was such a perfect word to describe Mr Case.

'Not that I was unfaithful,' continued Philomena, 'but . . . you know.'

'If that's what you're worried about,' offered Jonathan, 'I can put your mind at rest.'

'I mean,' continued Philomena, 'I wouldn't have minded, given the circumstances. Not minded too much, anyway. So there. Thank you.'

Why had she asked that about other women? She hadn't planned to. Was she worried that another woman had figured? Was that what Major James and Jonathan were anxious about? She had a definite sense of something pulsing in Jonathan, some incident or detail about Dan that he wasn't offering up to her. She felt a little bit of the overwhelming feeling that immobilised her against the cafe window return and she raised herself slightly off the seat of her plain wooden chair as if in preparation to leave. Jonathan grabbed her arm and just as quickly let go of it.

'I'm sorry,' he said.

'Sorry for what?'

'Grabbing you,' said Jonathan, 'but I thought . . .'

'It's all right,' she said.

'Are you okay? I thought for a moment that—'

'How could I be un-okay?' she said, using that new American word clumsily. 'You only grabbed my arm.'

'I grabbed your arm because I thought you were feeling—'

'Feeling what?' she demanded. Relenting, she remarked, 'We're all feeling all the time, aren't we?'

'I thought you were about to go—'

'If I did you wouldn't be able to stop me,' she said. 'And I'd go out of the front, not the back like some.'

Then she regretted saying all that, because it sounded too harsh and spiky, not like her, and he looked wounded. Rather than waiting to allow the ill feeling to pass in its own time she dived straight in to change the mood: 'Are you in court tomorrow?'

'Yes,' replied Jonathan.

'On what charge?' she said, as deadpan as she could.

He looked at her, puzzled. Her eyes crinkled and the corners of her mouth curled up and she laughed, which made him smile. He'd not imagined her laughing. It was a sudden enlightenment.

She has a beautiful, beautiful mouth, and an enviably unselfconscious throw of the head. She's full of surprises. But you wouldn't have saddled yourself with a dimwit, would you? And of course, she is striking. Not pretty-pretty, or beautiful, but very attractive.

The atmosphere between them completely changed. As the waitress put Philomena's plate down Jonathan saw that she gave her a 'going well, then?' look, which Philomena either didn't notice or ignored. But the waitress, as she went about her business, kept looking over, perhaps drawn, like Jonathan, by the sparks now glinting in Philomena's bright green eyes.

They tucked into their food in companionable silence. Between mouthfuls Philomena rummaged in her bag with one hand and slid out a clutch of envelopes.

'There's a couple of letters here that mention you.'

'Really?' Jonathan exclaimed, delighted.

Philomena continued to rummage one-handed. 'You know; Jonathan did this, Jonathan did that.' Her hand found the envelope she sought. 'He had another friend,' she said. 'Anthony Dore.'

Even though she wasn't looking directly at Jonathan she couldn't fail to register the impact that this name made.

'What's the matter?' she asked, wondering if some awful tragedy had befallen Anthony Dore.

'The matter about what?' snapped Jonathan. Mistake. Relax jaw. Unclench teeth. 'Anthony Dore. Yes.'

'He was another friend of Dan's,' said Philomena.

'Dan said that?' asked Jonathan, too casually.

From this moment Philomena knew that her quest, her fate, had led her here. She knew that she was meant to travel to London, to meet Major James, then Jonathan, and now the challenge was to discover exactly what was being concealed from her. There was a purpose; there was a future to which she was attached.

'You had quite a strong reaction to Anthony Dore's name,' she said.

'Just eat your food.'

'I beg your pardon?' she retorted.

'I meant eat it before it gets cold,' said Jonathan, unconvincingly. 'Who else?'

'What do you mean, who else?' asked Philomena, being deliberately obtuse.

'Which other friends did Dan mention?'

'All the other friends were killed,' she replied. 'He'd write to me mentioning a friend he'd made. Later he'd mention that they'd been killed.'

She could tell that Jonathan's mind was working furiously, turning something over and over. He set to eating, chewing fast. He filled his mouth and chewed and swallowed, filled his mouth again whilst also trying to speak.

'Look, it's best if I tell you—'

'Tell me what?'

Infuriatingly, Jonathan loaded his fork again and almost added another mouthful, but when he saw her scowl he paused.

'I don't know what to tell you. What did the army say?'

'About what?'

'About Dan?'

'I don't know what you mean,' she said.

Jonathan looked at her, mouth open, panting slightly. He appeared hounded – shrunken one second, full of something the next; clearly struggling.

'You want to tell me something,' she said, gently.

Was he going to tell her? What was he going to tell her?

And how? And when? Where to begin? It was too much: 'I thought you said you were a seamstress, not the fucking Inquisition,' snapped Jonathan, in his most native accent yet.

Refusing to be put off, Philomena allowed a pause before asking in deliberately level tones, 'Tell me about Anthony Dore's friendship with Dan.'

And when Jonathan didn't reply: 'Treat me with respect, please. Respect me.'

'In what way am I not respecting you?' asked Jonathan.

She looked deep into his eyes, trying to increase the pressure on him. Her brilliant green boring into his smoky brown.

'What sort of thing do you want to know?' he asked.

'That's a trick question,' she replied, 'because I don't know what I don't know. I don't know what I need to ask about.'

Jonathan was gazing back at her. She was someone he'd never imagined existing before. Although terrified of Philomena and what he might tell her, he also felt lifted, exhilarated even. He tried to relieve the pressure with a joke.

'Are you sure you're not a barrister?' which was pretty weak, because being a woman she couldn't be one, of course.

But she wasn't having it anyway. 'I'm not sure about anything,' she replied, tartly, which with her stern look made sure he understood that she wasn't going to let him off. Jonathan chewed the food in his mouth. He swigged some wine, and became thoughtful. He grew unable or unwilling to look Philomena directly in the eye and she guessed he was preparing himself. Choosing his words with minute care, he said: 'Anthony Dore is a captain. He was there when Dan died.' He stopped.

'They knew each other,' said Philomena, prompting him.

Again Jonathan meticulously weighed his words before saying: 'Dan died after I'd got to him. It wasn't instantaneous, but it was pretty quick.'

He looked at Philomena as if that were all he had to say.

Go on, she thought, more than interested as to why Jonathan had strayed off the subject of Anthony Dore. You can't begin to say something, and in that way, then just stop. For pity's sake!

'Go on,' she invited calmly, and watched his face crumple and line and he looked away.

'There was a feeling . . .'

'What did you say?'

'There was a feeling,' repeated Jonathan, turning back so she could hear his lowered voice.

'What feeling?' she asked, her hand going to her breast-bone as she scented he was about to divulge something momentous.

'A sense,' said Jonathan, clearly wavering on some brink.

'A sense of what?' she almost cried, tears filling her eyes.

'You're going to try and speak to Anthony Dore?' whispered Jonathan, glancing around furtively.

'No. I don't know. Maybe. Yes.'

'I have to be very careful what I say,' said Jonathan, infuriating her. 'There was a fuss . . .' He appeared to lose his nerve. His hands flapped: 'Look, I can't—'

He rose from the table and reached in his pocket.

'Please!' she implored.

'I can't. I'm sorry. Please leave me alone.'

'Leave you alone? What do you mean, leave you—'

But Jonathan exited by the front door and was swiftly enveloped in the darkness. What on *earth*?!

Philomena realised that she was half out of her seat as if to go after Jonathan, and that the whole cafe was silent – everyone was watching her. She shuddered, or shook herself, sat down fully on her seat, deliberately picked up her cutlery and resumed eating, trying not to look upset. The waitress appeared at her shoulder.

'Are you all right, luv?' she asked, quietly.

Philomena nodded several times, but was unable to look her in the eye.

CHAPTER FIVE

Once her solitary meal was over, in an attempt to work off her disquiet Philomena decided to try to walk back to her hotel. She kept to the main, well-lit thoroughfares, aloof to any looks she was getting. At the Aldwych she changed her mind. Instead of turning towards her hotel, she headed in pursuit of a particular landmark. After a while she knew from her map that she should be nearing St Paul's Cathedral but its foot – massive as it was – actually took some finding, it was so hemmed in by inferior buildings. Even though she hadn't been to church in ages she felt awe as the dome rose higher and higher, until it was as a mountain peaking above her, darker than the sky around it. None of the other people she saw about were behaving like her, like a tourist – they were all en route in that incredibly busy way everyone seemed to have in London. How much time had to pass before a person new to London EC4 became complacent about the fact that they were passing St Paul's Cathedral? People can get used to anything: beauty, grandeur, grief.

She climbed the deep stone steps leading up to the front doors. They were too big, too thick, too heavy, to be called doors, surely? They must have a special name. The wood was cold when she touched it. How could both these and the little thing on the front of her cottage be called by the same name? She looked guiltily about herself before trying a tentative knock. The wood was so dense it swallowed it up. Her knuckles were puny against it. What was Jonathan so . . . scared wasn't the word, was it? What was he so agitated about?

She took out her envelopes, locating the official letter from Major James. In the flare of a succession of matches she read it again, searching for any hints, finding none. The wording was completely unambiguous. So to what had Jonathan been referring when he said there was a 'sense', a 'feeling' and a 'fuss'? She was going to have to talk to him again. And to Major James. And what about this other man, Anthony Dore? Philomena could think of numerous possible explanations for Jonathan's strong reaction to Anthony Dore's name but it was all speculation. She found the envelope that contained all she knew of Anthony Dore – the one she'd had her hand on, that she was about to show Jonathan when he'd gone funny. Reading its contents with new intent she was unable to detect anything untoward. She put the letter away, pressed her hands flat against the doors to St Paul's, pressed her cheek to them, and felt vibrations; far-off, deep, like when, out in the hills above the village, she couldn't decide for certain if she'd heard thunder from behind a high ridge or felt a tremor underground. Was the wood of these vast doors, being so very dense, still alive somewhere near its middle? Feelings rose up from inside her and again threatened to overwhelm. She leaned against the wood, focusing inside her chest. It was as if a terrible battle had broken out inside her, and all she could do was hang on and await the outcome.

Jonathan nodded to the man on the door and made his way up the familiar stairs of the dimly lit nightclub, swaying slightly from the effects of all the alcohol he'd consumed. He'd handled the situation with Philomena about as badly as it was possible to have done, and was cursing himself for it. He had hoped he'd managed to put some daylight between himself and his emotions but tonight they'd come rushing back, and in fact what he'd revealed to Philomena was only a tiny fraction of what he felt. What was he going to do about 'it'? He went over some of the old arguments in his head. His feelings swiftly came into play and the arguments disintegrated; fragments shot off in all directions and he was left with one predominant emotion, anger, and a burning sense of injustice. There were traces of other emotions, too: sorrow, love, and guilt – that bastard guilt nagged away. Should he be acting? Well, he had, as far as he was able, as far as he reasonably could. Was this excusing himself? Was his 'as far as he was able' actually an excuse? Was he really a coward? No one had ever told him so, and he'd never believed that something he'd done or not done was cowardly. He'd felt fear, of course, and had, on occasions, acknowledged that fear prevented him from acting as he might. But also, fear had sometimes saved him. No, fear wasn't the problem here. Nor cowardliness. Not his, anyway.

Had he done absolutely everything he could have? Yes and no. But the sense of injustice was always burning within him; it never died down except for the brief periods when he was totally intoxicated. It burned mostly on a low flame, but the times it flared up were maddening to an intolerable degree because they were a reminder that he knew in his heart of hearts that someone was still getting away with about the worst thing that they could get away with. And he didn't know how to rest because of it.

He turned left at the top of the stairs in the nightclub and entered a medium-sized room suggestively lit by chandeliers of red bulbs. In the nearly colourless, airless room cigarette smoke curled down from the ceiling, deepening the sense of being slightly underground rather than three floors up. He'd been oblivious on the stairs to the normal goings-on but now he saw what he expected to see: men and women in various states of intoxication having a damned good time even if it killed them. More women than men, of course. More young women than young men, anyway. And a few of the young men had visible disfigurements. The post-war euphoria had worn off to be replaced by quiet desperation as it became progressively more unclear exactly what it had all been for.

He nodded to a middle-aged woman, dressed for the night in a slick gown and gauze veil, sitting on a bar stool smoking a cigarette in a long black holder. Didn't know her name. Didn't want to. She nodded back and, with an incline of her head activated a grizzled hulk of a man, unlikely in evening-wear, to come to Jonathan's side. He barely paused as Jonathan slipped money into his paw. While waiting for the return part of the transaction Jonathan's hand went to his scalp, to his scar. He absent-mindedly ran his fingers along it, whilst trying to imagine how and when Philomena would discover what the 'fuss' was about. Could he trust her, if he told her, to not let on it was him she had learned it from? Obviously he took the threat of libel seriously. But if she heard it first from someone else what version would she be given? No, not what version; whose version? And what would she think of him? He watched the woman at the bar accept his money and give her simian emissary a tiny packet in return. Was this subterfuge really necessary? Now the stuff had been deemed illegal, then yes, he supposed it was. The grizzled man neared. Jonathan got his prickly feeling at the back of his neck. This sensation had saved his life on more than one occasion so he paid it due attention. Stepping sideways, he gave a discreet hand signal to the deliveryman, who changed course, looking slightly puzzled. Jonathan manoeuvred himself so that he was able to see what was behind him. His heart skipped a beat and the blood roared in his ears. What had triggered his sixth sense was Anthony Dore, around the corner of the bar, taking a seat. The human being he loathed above all others was calmly sitting down alone, oblivious to being glared at.

Shocked to find his enemy in one of his own haunts Jonathan slipped directly behind Anthony Dore as he settled. Jonathan studied the crown of his foe's head as he sipped his drink, and not for the first time, but never before in such proximity, contemplated smashing it in some way. The various times he had followed Dore about the streets he had fantasised about hurting him, and now as Dore held his glass to his lips Jonathan imagined reaching over to ram it hard into his face, breaking glass against skull, changing grip, screwing glass into tissue, gouging, tearing and severing.

Why couldn't anyone else know what Jonathan knew? Or did they know but didn't care, had no stomach for the fight? What fight? The fighting had stopped, hadn't it? The arguments in his mind spiralled and spun. He had to get away. And he wasn't just running away from what he wanted to do to Anthony Dore, he was running towards Philomena. He had to tell her before someone else did. She had to hear his version first. He had to go to his chambers, find the address of her hotel, and go there. But first, to make the world seem a much better place than he knew it to be, he must snort some dope. He smiled at the grizzled man, who now advanced and slipped his purchase into his hand.

A while later the night porter at The Daphne was being distinctly uncooperative. He was able to confirm that the young northern lady was in her room, or at least the key wasn't on its hook, but he couldn't contact the room because they didn't have that sort of thing – an internal communications system – not even strings and bells, and he couldn't go up and knock on the door for Jonathan or deliver a note because he couldn't leave his post, such as it was. He was able to put a note in the pigeonhole for the room but he couldn't guarantee that the young northern lady would get it first thing. Much exasperated, Jonathan tried to appear as if he agreed that the night porter's concerns were legitimate and paramount, whilst figuring a way to be allowed to pass. But what logic could sway a pedant as rigid as the scrawny wretch who stood in his way? No logic. He'd have to use the authority of his personality. He banged his fist down on the counter, making the droning porter jump.

'Look. If she doesn't get it, I might never see her again, so you are just going to have to let me up there,' Jonathan declared. 'Turn your back if you want, pretend you never saw me. But don't dare try to stop me.'

The Daphne's night porter, finding the gentleman quite tall and fierce, did turn his back, pretended to busy himself, humming under his breath.

Philomena was in her nightclothes when the gentle tap came on her door. She had just been sweeping the bed. Her earlier appraisal that the room was the cleanest she'd seen at the price she could pay had had to be abandoned once she'd slipped between the sheets and the fleas had awoken. At the door she called, 'Who is it?'

'It's Jonathan,' came the reply. 'I'm sorry to come up here unannounced and I'm sorry about earlier, but it's desperately important that I speak with you.'

He'd had a change of heart, of mind? She mustn't let him go off again, but nor could he see her this undressed. She grabbed her coat from the rickety wardrobe and threw it around her shoulders, calling, 'I'll come out. You can't come in.'

'Of course not,' replied Jonathan. 'I'll wait out here, shall I?'

Philomena opened the door a crack so she could see his face.

'Is it about the sense and the feelings and the fuss?'

Jonathan looked blank for a moment, before: 'Yes! Yes, that's exactly what I'm here about.'

'Wait there,' she said, and shut the door. Immediately she opened it again: 'Where are we going?'

'To another cafe,' said Jonathan. 'Where we can talk. I can tell you a story.'

'Okay,' she said, and shut the door. She snatched it open again. 'You won't run off whilst I dress, will you?' she demanded.

Jonathan shook his head.

With her door closed she hurried into clean underwear, followed by the previous day's outfit, topped by her hat, rammed down to cover the unkempt state of her hair.

While Jonathan queued for mugs of tea Philomena looked around the cafe, thinking that that day had been the second strangest of her life, after the day following the Armistice when, as Dan's declared next of kin, hungover from the celebrations, she had learned of his death. There were all sorts of men seated at the tables. Some wealthy by the look of them, some drunk, one asleep. The majority were manual workers, filling up before work or on their way home. No other women, bar those behind the counter, until the arrival of a mixed party of night owls, slightly the worse for wear. The

women didn't wear wedding bands, and they smoked cigarettes.

Jonathan seemed much calmer now. He hadn't wanted to
start his story on the way here so Philomena knew no more
than before. She had had, then put aside, an idea that whatever Jonathan was about to tell her might involve something
Dan may have done – something wrong; bad, even. She
momentarily feared that everyone had been concealing from
her a misdeed of his, protecting her. Perhaps it would be
better not to know. Jonathan arrived with the teas. Thick,
brown stuff in tin mugs. He sat opposite her.

'Okay,' he said.

She noticed that despite the appearance of equilibrium, his
hands shook.

'Okay. I'll start with when I met him. When I met Dan.
It's material, in a way. It helps to explain why I think what
I think happened, happened.'

'Okay. I understand,' said Philomena, nodding, not understanding, but humouring him. She just wished he would stop
procrastinating.

'I met Dan six weeks before the end of the war, during a
skirmish. A bit more than a skirmish, really. We'd been out on
a recce when they started lobbing stuff at us, quite big stuff. I
got separated and a bunch of them decided to do for me. So
I jumped into this crater, well, I fell in, if truth be told. Running
along, tripped over, found myself at the bottom of this pit.'

Philomena noticed that Jonathan's working voice was almost
gone. He was speaking in his native accent.

'So they see what's happened and start fanning out around the rim and I'm firing up at them – got one or two – but I didn't see another one of them taking a bead on me because the first thing I know is that something's hit me on the head and I'm down and I can't move. I think what Jerry did was to stand still and aim at me. He just stood still and I didn't see him. Anyway, I opened my eyes to see if I was dead. I could hear movement but I couldn't move myself. Jerry who'd stood stock still and shot me had come down to the bottom of the pit – I don't know why, it was his mistake, don't know what he was thinking of; he shouldn't have been thinking at all. I could feel a bit of movement returning to my limbs and I could feel that my pistol was still in my hand so I thought if Jerry hangs about a bit more I might be able to finish him before he finishes me. He guessed what was up and raised his rifle and I was looking right down the barrel and I heard a shot and thought that I really must be dead now but no, Jerry had himself been shot by one of our blokes who had run down the pit, across it, and was now running up the other side. He hadn't seen me at all so when I yelled 'Hey!' he swung around and was ready to shoot me but he saw my uniform and I hoisted my hands up to surrender just in case and screamed 'I'm alive!' and he said 'just'. And already we knew certain things about each other. Neither of us was posh, we had northern accents, we were both offi-cers. Later we learned that both having been promoted 'in't field', the only difference between us was that I'd elected to enlist as a private whereas he'd had no choice. But, you know, we recognised kindred spirits, I suppose. He was Dan, of course.'

Philomena nodded eagerly, unexpectedly filled with a strange rapture.

'I had quite a lot of blood coming down from where Jerry's bullet had creased me. It was going in my eyes and I was having to wipe it away but I managed to see another Jerry taking a bead on Dan's back. He was almost lined up behind Dan but I could just see him at the edge, if you get the picture. I thought to shout but it wouldn't have been quick enough – Dan would have had to turn – so I just took a chance and shot. Dan went down, and the other bloke, and I thought hell, I've shot them both, but Dan was all right, just a bit disgruntled because my bullet had passed through his trousers and just missed his, you know—'

Philomena felt herself redden.

'I told him that I hadn't meant to do that – I was aiming for the edge of him, not there, between his . . . He swore a lot, didn't he?'

She smiled and nodded, afraid to speak in case she distracted Jonathan.

'Anyway, they started lobbing more stuff our way so Dan joined me at the bottom of the crater and we got to know each other a bit better.'

Philomena's eyes started to fill up. She could see Dan and Jonathan together in the hole – could see it as if she were there – imagined exactly how Dan and Jonathan would have been together.

Jonathan paused a second. 'I can see that you're crying, Philomena, but I'm just going to plough on,' he said.

'This isn't really crying,' she muttered, taking out one of the cotton handkerchiefs she'd recently taken to carrying in duplicate at all times.

'Dan claimed that I'd ruined his best trousers and my reply was that there was a Chinese laundry around the corner – he could drop them in and pick them up before work; I'd pay. Then he wanted to know, because I was a captain whereas he was a second lieutenant, where we were or where we were supposed to be. I admitted that for some time I hadn't had a fucking clue – excuse my French – a far from ideal situation, and he asked if I could see anything at all, through all the blood, and he reached out and wiped it from my forehead, like I was a child, and he was very, very concerned about me. He could break your heart, couldn't he?'

Philomena couldn't speak. She felt full of liquid, full of tears, and she was afraid that if she started crying properly she wouldn't be able to stop. She'd become a puddle on the floor, run off into the ground.

'Anyway, shells were landing pretty close and getting closer. One threw a skull into our pit. It landed next to our heads. We saw it when we raised our faces from the earth. There were always bits of buried bodies being relocated by explosions. God knows how many times some people were interred. You could be buried on your side, blown up again, buried on the other side, ad infinitum.'

'Dan wrote to me about that skull,' Philomena interrupted.

'What did he say?' asked Jonathan.

'He said you looked at it and asked if it had a message for anyone back home. He thought that was funny.'

Jonathan swallowed hard. Philomena feared for a moment that she'd thrown him off course. But he swallowed hard again and picked up the thread of his story.

'We rummaged around the recent bodies in the pit and came up with a few usable bullets and loaded them into spare magazines. Dan told me the plan. "Right sir," "Yes, sir." "This is the plan, sir," he said. "Plan?" "Yes, sir. Climb out of shell hole, crouch down, run like fuck, firing wildly." "Textbook, an excellent plan! I'll try not to shoot you if you promise to try not to shoot me." And Dan said, "I promise to try not to shoot you, but if I do shoot you it will be by mistake and I apologise in advance."

'The plan was executed. And that, more or less, is the basis of why I believe what I believe. My beliefs are based on my first impressions of Dan, particularly how he could rub people up the wrong way. I can see that you don't understand what I've just said. But I have to ask you now, for something. If I tell you any more it can only be after you've given me your solemn oath that you will never, ever divulge that you heard it from me. Can you do that?'

Philomena pondered this for a moment. 'You want me to give you my oath that I'll never let on that you told me what you're about to?'

'I'm not going to tell you unless you give me your oath,' said Jonathan.

'I, Philomena Bligh, give you my oath.'

'That was too easy,' said Jonathan. 'Look, if I tell you, you might be enraged, and you might want to do something, and in that frame of mind you might forget, or choose to set aside your oath to me. What I'm asking is that you do whatever you feel you have to do, but that you're careful to ensure that I could not be your only possible source.'

'Do you want me to say that I've never met you?' she offered; whatever it took to make him go on.

'No, that lie would be too easily apprehended,' said Jonathan. 'What I mean is I need you to make it as difficult as possible for anyone to know that I'm your source, because what I'll tell you, if I tell you, is disputed, and denied, and so far unprovable, and I've been threatened by a top-top lawyer with a slander suit and gaol if I repeat it verbally, and a libel charge and gaol if I ever write it and pass it on. So if I tell you what I might tell you, you mustn't leave this cafe and go straight to people claiming that I've told you. You have to appear to have unearthed it yourself, or been told by someone other than me.'

'I swear,' confirmed Philomena. 'I understand, and I swear.'

'You can swear but you can't really understand because I haven't told you yet,' said Jonathan. He bent his head, indicating that she should bend hers, and, heads almost touching, in a lowered voice, he told her, 'I'm trusting you.'

She nodded, wondering if he was actually mad and there wasn't going to be any import in what he might tell her.

'In Dan's memory,' he added.

They were so close she could feel the heat from his head.

To see his earnest eyes she had to lean away sideways and turn towards him.

'Yes,' she said.

'Okay, then,' said Jonathan, sitting back a little, checking around him. 'A short while later, on the tenth of November to be exact, me and Dan were in a trench lying up. It was a German trench; marvellous construction. We were advancing. Everyone was talking about how an armistice was rumoured for the next day, but nothing was confirmed. Dan and I had managed to arrange things in a sort of unacknowledged way so that we knew where each other was most of the time but didn't mention it. You didn't want to get too close to anyone. Well, you did and you didn't. You wanted friends but they had a habit of dying, so you didn't want them. He'd been hinting about the rift with his parents; he wasn't going to take over the shop, was he?'

'No,' said Philomena, 'he didn't know what he was going to do.'

'I was lucky,' said Jonathan. 'My parents could afford to keep me in school, then I got a scholarship. Despite that I wasn't clever.'

'You must have been.'

'No, I worked hard, feverishly so, because of what my parents sacrificed to invest in me.'

'You're clever now.'

'If I am, I've been trained to be,' said Jonathan. 'A lot of it is learning the accent. Contrary to what they would have you believe, the way the people who run things speak is an accent, rather than the "right" way. This accent lends authority and gives the impression of intelligence. Anyway, from down the trench we could hear someone barking "ATTENTION". It was a sergeant acknowledging a new officer, a captain. He looked a bit sheepish, this captain. Right uniform, right stance, but not completely at home in it.

'We'd got used to slouching about when it was quiet. We could have stood up and greeted the captain, but we didn't. We did sit up a bit straighter, though. There was a boy, a private, carrying his luggage. An old trunk. I could see it had labels: Cape Town, Shanghai, Khartoum. Me and Dan took an interest in Captain Anthony Dore, for it was he.'

Philomena leaned forward, anticipating that he was about to give an explanation for his extreme reaction last evening to Anthony Dore's name.

'We weren't rude to him, apart from not getting to our feet on the very fine German duck boards, which wasn't rude as such; more informal. But he and Dan took each other the wrong way from the start. Dore introduced himself: "I'm Captain Anthony Dore," and I stood up, but Dan didn't. Dan said "Congratulations," and left a little pause as if that's all he was going to say, as if he was congratulating Dore on being himself, or on remembering his own name. It was a real moment of uncertainty until Dan followed his potentially sarcastic congratulations with, "on joining the best bit of the line, sir." Which just about saved it, but still managed to point to the fact that Dore was the new man. I noticed too that Dan had coarsened his accent and I knew that this was because

Dore was so posh. "You are?" Dore asked Dan. "Second Lieutenant Case, sir," said Dan, then added, "promoted in the field"; which again could have been interpreted as a bit of a dig at the captain; i.e. "I've earned my commission whereas you are just posh."

'I could see that they'd got off on the wrong foot so I introduced myself to Captain Dore much more politely but, I have to confess, I did play my native accent up a bit so Dore knew where we all were. He asked me if I was the senior officer present, which I was, along with him – but when I jokingly said "apart from you" he took it the wrong way, and he asked: "What are your orders, at this moment?" – knowing that we definitely hadn't been ordered to slouch in a captured German trench. There must have been some orders to be actually getting on with, something to do with winning the war.

'Anyway, I caught Dan's eye in the corner of mine and I felt like I was in church: the vicar's paused in his very long sermon, it's deathly quiet, and the old lady in front lets go a fart. In short, I got the giggles. Dan, in an effort to make me laugh out loud, said, "Standing orders are to win the war, Captain Dore." And I could barely hold it in, and Dore thought it was about him, which it was in a way. I managed to speak, to say that there had been a skirmish earlier, that is, explained why we were lounging about now; we were knackered. But Dan kept going, and said something stupid – with a completely straight face, like "They defend, we attack; we attack, they defend," declining defend. "I attack, we attack, they attack."

'Dore interrupted but didn't look at him and he asked me who held the ruin that was the only thing you could see from our trench. It had once been a farmhouse but now it was just bits of wall. The enemy had it that day, but it had been ours several times, I told him, and I saw something change in Anthony Dore and he said that we were going to make it ours again in the morning. I told him we'd left it because they'd brought up a captured tank and he asked whether "retreating" had been good for our morale. He was suggesting we'd given in a bit too easily, that we lacked backbone, but I tried to stay calm as I explained that the decision to retreat hadn't been anything to do with morale, it was a strategic decision taken higher up, but he cut me off saying that we had new orders to press on and occupy as much ground as we could because the Kaiser had abdicated. Now this was potentially very good news. It definitely meant the war might be about to end. But Dore wasn't celebrating. When I looked deep into his eyes I could see he was a mess. I'd seen that look before, many times. His nerves were shot. He didn't like me seeing that. It made him turn away from me to Dan and he said, straightforwardly: "You may be a good soldier, but some people could take you the wrong way."'

Philomena assumed, because he'd got Dan off to a tee, that the way Jonathan transformed when giving Anthony Dore's contributions was an accurate impersonation of him: the heightened accent, the clipped vowels, the angle of the head.

'At this point Dan could have accepted this half a peace

offering and things might have ended up differently, but Dan was being bloody obstinate by now as well as borderline insolent, and he replied, "Some people shouldn't try to take me at all." I winced, and, not for the first time I thought to myself that one day Daniel Case was going to land me right in the you-know-what. Dan gave Anthony Dore his biggest grin as if to say that the whole episode had been a joke and assured him that everything would be all right. He told Captain Anthony Dore that he loved fighting armoured vehicles with his bare hands. It was clear Dore didn't know what on earth to make of Dan. He didn't have a clue how to handle him. Which was how Dan liked it. Lastly, Dore made another attempt at making things the way he thought they should be. He said, in a way that a friendly captain would say to a subordinate officer, which Dan was but I wasn't, "Let's have dinner tonight, on me," indicating that his trunk contained victuals. When Captain Dore moved on I turned on Dan, but he wasn't having it. He did apologise later. He thought I was too much in awe of men like Dore.'

Jonathan looked at Philomena for a long while and seemed about to say something else. But he didn't, he said: 'D'ye want more tea?'

She shook her head.

'I'm going to have some, and a bacon sarnie,' he said, briskly.

'Okay then,' she said, changing her mind.

The extraordinary detail of his story made Philomena uneasy. Why could he recall so much of that encounter? The cafe had emptied a little and there was no longer a queue at the counter so he was able to catch a woman's eye and shout the order before continuing in full spate.

'So me and Dan were treated by Dore that night to a hamper of the finest tins of this and jars of that and bottles of the other, and we were all a bit merry. The conversation wasn't flowing as easily as the drink, but the atmosphere was at least convivial, and I could see that whilst Anthony Dore wasn't at ease with Dan, he was drawn to him. And when Dore said that regarding the next morning's planned attack of the ruin, "We must continue to impose our will on the enemy," I could tell that he was inviting arguments against the attack and that it wouldn't have taken much for him to agree that it was a bad idea and to go to whoever ordered it and tell them so, especially if the war was ending. But before Dan or I could give Dore the answer I think he would have liked another man entered the dugout. A Major Chiltern.

'We knew him quite well; he was about our age. He was also posh, but he didn't care what we were like with him off duty as long as we drank with him and played cards. Anthony Dore changed when Chiltern arrived. The latter helped himself to some choice pieces from Anthony Dore's hamper – without asking first – and said: "Only a captain, eh?" There was obviously something going on between them. I later found out that they'd been at school together and hadn't got on. They'd been in opposing factions. I've never found out any exact details, but it was obviously something that Anthony Dore was embarrassed about. He was a jolly drunk, Major Chiltern. Fleshy, you know, and florid. Looked much older than his years. The opposite of Anthony Dore. Anyway, Major Chiltern banged his pack of dog-eared playing cards down on the table and we fished around for all our pennies and started playing. It was dealer's choice and when it came to Dan he chose three-card brag, which Anthony Dore hadn't played before. It shouldn't have been a problem because it's the easiest game in the world.'

Jonathan broke off whilst the teas were delivered. He took out a hip flask and poured what smelled like rum into his. 'Want some?' he offered.

'No thank you.'

'It keeps out the chill.'

'I'm not cold.'

'You're a proper northerner,' he said, putting his flask away, 'whilst I am only an ex. So Dan explained the rules of three-card brag, with a bit of help from Major Chiltern, and we played a couple of hands – d'you play?'

'I've seen it played. It's very common.'

'Do you know the rules?'

'Three cards. Bluffing, betting. And you can play blind.'

'Indeed you can,' said Jonathan. 'Your cards are dealt face down and you bet without seeing what your hand is.'

'Someone playing open against someone playing blind has to double the blind man's bet and they can't call a blind man,' said Philomena. 'They have to wait for the blind man to call.'

'That is true but not material in this case. You do know the rules.'

Philomena shrugged. 'And I know cribbage, whist and rummy.

But I only play for matches; spent matches at that.'

'Did Dan gamble?'

'Not when he was with me,' replied Philomena, defiantly.

Jonathan pursed his lips and nodded. She watched him pour additional rum into his tea. She wasn't surprised. She knew men who had left for war teetotallers and returned hardened drinkers. But for all she knew, Jonathan had drunk like this before.

'We'd played a few hands when Major Chiltern had to go outside, during which time we heard an incoming round. All three of us in the dugout stiffened and did the mental reckoning vis-à-vis incoming – the calculations you make based on the sound, pitch, trajectory, speed of approach, and a bit of guess work. Dan and I concluded that it wasn't going to directly threaten us. Anthony Dore, however, went under the table. Now, I'm not saying that he was a coward – it crossed my mind to go under the table, too. Even then things might have been all right – he could have got up and resumed his seat and nothing would have been said. Except while he was still under there Major Chiltern came back in and asked where Dore was. He saw where he was, or where he was emerging from, and I could see an ugly gleam in Chiltern's eye. Anthony Dore sat back down in his chair and tried to pretend nothing had happened. He was suffering, though. Shaking. You couldn't miss it. Dan took pity on him, I did too. And Dan said, really quietly: "I thought it had our names on it, too." But Anthony Dore took it the wrong way and accused Dan of condescension. Dan protested that it wasn't, and I backed him up, and Anthony Dore told me to shut up, whereupon Major Chiltern deliberately made things even worse by asking Captain Dore if he remembered flunking at school. Flunking what, he didn't specify, but it was a horrible thing to say at that moment. You could see Chiltern and Dore transported back in time, to school, where it had evidently been merciless. Men can be horrible to each other. They can be bullies and they can be bitches.

'The upshot of this exchange was that Dore was clearly riled. You could tell by his glower that he wanted to do something to Major Chiltern. Dan and me were being swept up in something beyond our control and I wish we'd just walked out and left them to it.

'Anthony Dore clenched his fists and declared that in order to prove who was brave we should play one hand of this three-card brag, all of us blind, betting everything we had. I think he meant at first everything we had on us,' said Jonathan, 'but, because Dan said that playing a game of blind three-card brag wouldn't prove who was brave, the situation escalated. Dore misunderstood him again, I think. To my mind Dan was trying to say there was no need for any proof of bravery, but Dore thought Dan was saying that the stakes should be higher. The atmosphere was very heated. We'd been drinking, there were obvious conflicts between us, we were frightened, and it was nearly over – the war, I mean. An inflammable combination of elements.

'Major Chiltern said he wasn't playing anymore, which gave Anthony Dore something to crow about. That left Dan and me. He turned to Dan and demanded to know what Dan owned. To which Dan replied that he owned nothing. Dore demanded to know what Dan would inherit. What did his family own? The lease on a shop, the stock, which he might not even inherit, Dan told him. Dore said he was an only son of a wealthy family and stated that he'd bet everything he was going to inherit against everything Dan and I were. I said I was out of it and I suggested that we all shook hands and forgot about it, but Dore started scrawling his pledge on a bit of paper. Major Chiltern said it was going too far and tried to leave with his pack of cards but Anthony grabbed them so Chiltern left without. I could see Dan was getting riled by Dore so I said aside to him, "Just walk away," and I think he might have, except Dore seized on my wording and said, "Yes, Dan, why don't you just walk away?" That is, act like a coward. And Dan wouldn't do that. They pledged everything, and the cards were dealt, and—'

The bacon sandwiches arrived. Jonathan bit ravenously into his but Philomena couldn't face hers. She was feeling sick. Jonathan continued talking with his mouth full.

'Anthony asked Dan to remind him of the value of hands in three-card brag, which are, in ascending order: highest card, then highest pair, then a run – ace, two, three being the highest, then a flush, then three of a kind – the highest being three threes. Yes?'

Philomena nodded gravely. So this was it. Dan had lost all his family's possessions in a card game.

'Two hands. Three cards each, blind. Dore threw his pledge

into the pot. Dan was about to do the same, when he hesitated. Dan was about to speak, perhaps to call it off, but Dore ignored him and turned his first card over. The king of hearts. Dan really couldn't walk away now. He turned his first. It was the two of clubs. Anthony Dore was winning. He turned his second. The jack of hearts. He's definitely winning. Dan turned his second. The five of spades. He's going nowhere. Dore turned his last card. It's the ace of spades. He had three picture cards but only ace high. Dan turned his third card and didn't look down at it. I did, and Anthony Dore did. It was the two of diamonds. Dan had won with a pair of twos. He still didn't look.'

Philomena frowned and sat back sharply; so what was the point of the story if not that Dan lost everything at cards?

'Nobody spoke,' said Jonathan. 'I have to say I was glad that Dan had won. Are you going to eat that?'

She hadn't touched her bacon sandwich. She pushed it towards Jonathan, who took it up and bit into it. Chewing, he went on:

'After a while Dore stood up and walked out. Still Dan hadn't looked at his last card. He asked me: "Did I win?" I told him that he was an idiot. He saw his hand and grunted: "It's just a game, just a fucking game." He took Dore's pledge and pinned it to a beam with his knife. You're still under oath that you won't let on to anyone that I'm telling you all this.'

Jonathan took another ravenous bite. For a few moments she watched him chew. When he'd sufficiently cleared his mouth he said, 'Anthony Dore came back in. He tried to smile. Dan was standing by Dore's impaled IOU. Anthony said something about a chap taking a joke too far and Dan said he wasn't a "chap" and what joke? Anthony tried to make out that the game had been a bit of fun, but Dan wasn't having it. He asked him exactly how much he'd won off him and Anthony turned on his heel and left and I said to Dan that the situation wasn't at all funny.'

Jonathan's face contorted. 'Dan was stupid! I told him to just give the pledge back to Dore. It would never be honoured! But he just turned away, and we got on with ignoring each other for a while. The next time I looked, the IOU wasn't pinned to the beam. I don't know where they went.

'So. Unbeknownst to us at the time, the next day the Armistice was signed at five a.m. Paris time. The attack was for six a.m. It was put back, which made us think we would be spared, then put back again, until nine a.m. when we stood-to – got ready, that is – and we were told that an armistice would come into force at eleven a.m. At that time we should stand fast and must not fraternise in any way with the enemy. That would be treason. Naturally, we still hoped for the order to attack to be rescinded, but it wasn't. Major Chiltern, Anthony Dore, Dan, me, sergeants, corporals, privates; husbands, sons, brothers, lovers; good and bad. We waited, we waited; we attacked. Pockmarked terrain; you could see men for a few moments then lose track of them for a while. I knew where Dan was mostly, and occasionally I glimpsed Major Chiltern, and very occasionally I saw Anthony Dore.

'I could see Major Chiltern walking into trouble. Two of

their lot had caught him in a pincer movement that he was totally unaware of. I tried shouting, but he couldn't hear me. I gestured to Captain Dore – whom I could see – that he must go to Chiltern's aid. I don't know what he did do, but it wasn't that. So Dan and I started trying to have a pop at Chiltern's stalkers, but before we succeeded we came under pretty accurate fire ourselves and we had to skedaddle. We became separated at that point. When I could look again I saw that Chiltern had spotted one of his stalkers and was taking aim. He winged that one but the other one shot Chiltern several times, killing him. I shot that one, then the winged one. When I got him in my sights I realised he might only be aged fourteen or so, but he had a gun, and he'd used it, and was making as if to do so again. I was nearly at the ruin by now but another of their lot jumped me. A big man. We fought on the ground. It was pretty nasty. He started shouting at me to listen! Listen! And there were voices ringing out. "*C'est finis*! *Der Krieg ist vorbei*! It's over!" When I looked there were men from both sides gesticulating hopefully, some waving bits of cloth in lieu of anything white. It was eleven o'clock on the morning of the eleventh of November. The sounds of battle began to subside, bar the shouts that it was over. There was almost silence, and I was looking into this pleading man's eyes, suddenly feeling completely different about killing him, wondering if I could trust him not to kill me if I let him go, when a shot, and another rang out—'

Philomena's hand went to her mouth.

'And I knew it was Dan. I just knew. And I ran towards

the sound. He was on the ground, barely conscious. Badly wounded. Anthony Dore was suddenly by me. He said: "I got the Hun who did it." I looked where he indicated and there was a boy, a dead German, on his back, clutching a rifle almost as big as him. I looked into Dore's eyes and . . . It's hard to describe. It was like watching a child who has done something wrong try a little bit too hard to look as if they're surprised that the thing has happened at all. I saw him make a deliberate attempt to appear to be innocent. Dan went into a spasm and he died in my arms.'

Jonathan stopped speaking. He didn't look at Philomena for a while. She stared blankly out of the cafe window, into the night. Her mind struggled to accept what she'd just been told. It held the image of Dan spasming in Jonathan's arms just after the war had ended, but it wouldn't take on the implications of his description of Anthony Dore.

'I made an allegation which was denied and investigated and I withdrew it,' said Jonathan. 'Gave my consent that it should be withdrawn. By not pursuing it.'

'You believe that Anthony Dore killed Dan?' Philomena tried to say, but it only came out as a broken whisper.

Jonathan listened hard, nodding as if he understood. 'All I will say is that I looked into Anthony Dore's eyes and saw what I said I saw . . . I'm not saying anything more,' said Jonathan.

But Philomena couldn't let him rest there: 'There was an investigation?' Again her voice broke as she tried to speak.

'Dore said that there was no card game, which is actually

very clever. He of course denies that he shot Dan, but to deny there was ever a card game is very smart because – in the absence of the IOUs – it removes the motive, too. And what with Major Chiltern having perished, it's my word against his.'

Philomena thought, this story can't be right, can it? There must be holes in it. Yes, here's one: 'But what about the IOUs; they would have proved—?'

'I don't know what happened to them,' said Jonathan. 'I think either Dan had returned Dore's to him and hadn't got around to telling me yet – but then why kill him? Or Dore stole them, either off Dan's body before I got to him, or afterwards, from his belongings, while I was reporting him.'

'But you told Dan that the IOUs would never be honoured. Anthony Dore would have known that, too, wouldn't he?'

'I said that in order to persuade Dan to relent. They were legal,' replied Jonathan. 'Notwithstanding Dore's lawyers would have tied it up for ever. Nothing would ever have been paid except lawyer's fees. The full force of Anthony Dore's family would have been brought to bear on Dan and he would have had to give up any claim or be crushed.'

'What does Anthony Dore stand to inherit?'

'Up to a million,' said Jonathan. 'As far as I can tell.'

Philomena allowed herself a moment to imagine being the wife of a millionaire. That big house. A motor car. But they were only flat pictures of worldly goods. She had no feelings about the money.

'But if Dan had returned Anthony Dore's pledge, what happened to his own?'

'Dore stole that, too. They're both evidence of a wager; a wager implies a game,' said Jonathan, fiddling with the crumbs on his plate.

Philomena studied the top of his head, wishing that there were some infallible way of truly knowing another human being.

'Dore denies everything, and in the absence of any witness or any proof, he must be regarded as innocent. But you can see why I had to tell you.'

Would she ever have learned of this incredible possibility if she hadn't come down to London? For the first time in a while she noticed that her hands had fluttered into life and were making new shapes in the air. An officer murders a subordinate on the battlefield? She didn't know whether to believe Jonathan. But why make such a story up? Why make up this whole story if it weren't true, or if he didn't believe it was true? She felt sure that he'd been close to Dan, but close friends fall out, don't they? But how would a falling out lead to this story? She needed to get another view of the situation before she would know what to think about Jonathan and his story. She'd only known him a few hours. Less.

She thanked him, which felt strange – but what else could she say? His effort had been immense. She stood up. Jonathan looked quizzically up at her then also stood. She thanked him a second time and left the cafe. Jonathan didn't try to persuade her to stay, or follow her. She didn't care that she was walking the streets alone in the dark.

CHAPTER SIX

In her bed, during what remained of the night, Philomena couldn't sleep. Too stirred up. Her hotel creaked and groaned hideously anyway. In the pre-dawn quiet the unfamiliar background London noise – continuous motor engines, horses, trains, trams and hawkers, and the hum of millions of humans – was reduced, and all the hotel's sounds came to the fore. The footsteps above, the creaking bed next door one way, the snoring that rumbled in from next door the other way, or from above. There were also the pipes that roared alarmingly every now and again – the waste pipes that is, that ran vertically down the corner of her room. But all these external sounds were themselves only the background to the thoughts swirling in her mind. Jonathan Priest, whom she knew to be Dan's friend because Dan wrote to her saying that he was, was suggesting that Dan was murdered by a superior officer just after the war ended. And she'd sworn that she wouldn't go running to anyone to ask if any of this was true. Well, she hadn't quite promised exactly that, had she? She'd promised to not say that Jonathan had told her. And she wouldn't. But she had to try and verify Jonathan's story, didn't she? If there had been an investigation, there must be a record. The army were sticklers for all that, weren't they?

She took out one of her letters. It was short. In it the author offered his sincere condolences. He'd only just met Daniel. His death was 'a tragedy, no, a crime'. This letter was signed Anthony Dore . . .

Would he have written such a letter if he were Dan's killer? He was, as he stated in the letter, a superior officer 'with him when he died', so a letter would be normal, wouldn't it? To not write would be abnormal, wouldn't it?

Would someone else turn up with another story that told a third version of Dan's death? Perhaps even one in which he wasn't dead at all. He'd been horribly disfigured. Or he'd lost his memory – she reined in her imagination. Dan was dead, that was certain – or was it, now, now that everything she knew had been placed in doubt? But how should she feel about the possibility that Dan might have been murdered? She didn't feel like she thought she should. She imagined that she should feel angry. But she just felt confused.

She lay down and made a mental list of possible next steps.

1. Go back to Major James and fish for information without dropping Jonathan in it. Major James, who had written her the official version of Dan's death.

2. Drop Jonathan in it. Jonathan, a man whom she had witnessed striving for justice in the case of the one-armed veteran, and whom Dan said was his friend –

who'd told her a wildly different version of Dan's death, but one that she was not allowed to quote from.

3. Seek out Anthony Dore. Anthony Dore, a man she'd never met, who wrote her a slightly different version of Dan's death, and had been accused by Jonathan of actually being Dan's murderer.

4. Quiz Jonathan, testing his story.

5. Go home and think about it.

She tried to sleep, hoping that when she woke she would have the answer.

The morning sky was gunmetal grey, rendering The Daphne drabber than before. In the bathroom down the hallway there was a pair of clean knickers sitting tidily on the floor in front of the sink. Philomena had a vision of the owner stepping out of them and leaving them there. Had she been alone? She had a sudden vision of sex with Dan. She didn't chase it away. She let it last as long as it wanted then washed herself, thinking again about Jonathan's story, about Jonathan's character, about what she felt about Anthony Dore in advance of ever having set eyes on him. She told herself to guard against pre-judging him, then went out in search of some breakfast.

She re-introduced herself to Major James' aide and asked if it would be possible to see the major for a few extra moments before she caught the train home. This was an untruth in the sense that it made it sound as if her train was imminent when in fact she didn't intend travelling home immediately, but it wasn't a downright lie.

There was a mirror in the waiting area. She saw that her eyes still displayed the bright dilation of the grieving and the scared. Everyone must be familiar with that look through the war, and now, in the aftermath. Big eyes in shrunken faces. The points of light on the tips of her irises were pronounced that day. She realised Major James was watching her look at herself, a wary look in his eye. Was he sneaking about or had she been preoccupied? He ushered her into his office. As before, she sat on the creaky seat and he perched on the front of his desk, but then she saw that he changed his mind and took his seat the other side, as if the necessity had occurred to him to be more formal.

'Thank you for seeing me again,' she said.

'I'm pleased that I am able to,' Major James replied, showing his practised smile.

'There is something that I meant to ask you yesterday, that I forgot to.'

'Oh?' said Major James. 'Fire away.'

She steadied herself. 'I received several letters of condolence from military sources,' she said. 'One of them puzzled me at the time because it referred to my fiancé's death as a "crime".'

'A crime?' asked Major James. 'Really?' He was acting as if he didn't understand. 'Did they elaborate?'

'No.'

'They shouldn't have written that. Whoever they were.'

Philomena ignored his oblique request for the identity of the writer.

'But something did happen? Something unusual?' she asked.

He mused for a few moments. It was obvious that Philomena knew that something had happened. She hoped that he wrongly assumed – as she intended – that he knew who had written to her that Dan's death was a crime.

'There was an unfounded allegation of a crime, made by a man who couldn't substantiate any of it. No evidence of a crime. No witnesses. That's all.'

'Was there an inquiry?' she asked.

'Yes,' said Major James. He winced and seemed to lose his nerve: 'Look, I really can't tell you anything more.'

'Was it a crime or wasn't it?'

'It was an accusation. Whoever wrote to you was out of turn in bringing it up. I'm afraid that I am very pressed for time,' he said, rising suddenly from his seat.

'Let me tell you what I know,' said Philomena, also rising. 'I shall be very brief. Please give me just one more minute of your time.'

'I have nothing to say except this,' said Major James. 'Pursue it and you'll end up in court.'

'Please, just confirm for me, was there an allegation that my fiancé's death wasn't at the hands of the enemy? Please!'

Major James paused, nodded several times to himself then once to her. She felt herself shiver. Last night Jonathan's story had seemed slightly dream-like, but now it was solidifying.

She said: 'One officer alleged that another officer had killed my fiancé?'

Major James nodded.

'Over a gambling debt?'

Major James nodded.

'But he didn't witness the crime and nor did anyone else?'

Major James nodded.

'The man making the allegation claimed that the gambling debt arose from a game of cards?'

Major James nodded.

'But the accused man denied that any such game ever took place?'

Major James nodded.

'And the pledges, or IOUs, were never found?'

Major James nodded.

She guessed: 'The accused made it clear to all concerned that the allegations shouldn't be repeated.'

Major James nodded. That meant he had been warned off by Anthony Dore?

'The accused was Anthony Dore,' she said.

Something in Major James baulked at confirming this. He neither nodded nor shook his head. She tried a different question.

'The accuser was Jonathan Priest?'

Major James began to move crab-like to the door. 'Your time is up, I'm afraid. I'm sorry about your fiancé,' he said. 'Being the last to die is especially poignant—'

'Yes,' she interrupted, 'you didn't tell me that he was killed after the war ended.'

'It wasn't after, as such. It was contiguous.'

'What does that mean?'

'The war didn't stop dead on eleven a.m.'

'No,' she bristled, 'for Dan it stopped "dead" a few moments after, whilst men were stopping fighting and deciding not to kill each other anymore. That much is true, isn't it? That Dan was killed whilst other men were acting as if it was all over?'

'It is extremely difficult to end a war. Especially when not everyone wants to. And for men in the midst of battle, it's impossible to know the overall picture. They can only deal with what's in front of them. It's very hard to trust that if one stops fighting the enemy will do the same.' He was becoming strident. 'To make any kind of accusation stick you require a witness or physical evidence. Anybody who doesn't have these should tread very carefully, very carefully indeed, and think more than twice before repeating any allegation that a particular crime has been committed.'

'I think that you are thinking something in error,' she said. 'I haven't misled you but you have assumed that you know the identity of the person who described Dan's death as a crime. It was Anthony Dore. He wrote to me that Dan's death was a crime.'

Major James was speechless for a moment. His eyes flicked to and fro.

'Captain Dore wrote that to you?' He looked aghast.

'Yes,' she confirmed.

'Anthony Dore wrote to you?'

'Offering his condolences.' It struck Philomena that it was significant that Major James didn't think that it was at all appropriate for Anthony Dore to write to her. Which told her what? That Major James thought that Anthony Dore had been in some way impertinent to write to her, or brazen, perhaps, or just plain wrong.

'You don't think that it is quite the thing for Anthony Dore to have done, do you? The letter is the reason I thought that Dan and Anthony Dore were friends. Here it is.'

She handed it over without waiting for an answer and watched Major James read it. Outwardly he gave very little away.

'I really have to get on,' he said, handing the letter back. 'I've told you all I can.'

Philomena wondered if he cared. She liked to think that he did.

After that second meeting with Major James she knew that she would have to meet Anthony Dore and decide about him for herself. But as soon as Dore knew she was Daniel Case's fiancée then any chance she had of extracting the truth from him would be gone. His guard would come up. And he must have a guard after what he'd been accused of. Instead she decided to seek Jonathan out to tell him that Major James had confirmed that he had made a serious allegation against a fellow officer. Which wasn't the same as saying that Major James had confirmed that Anthony Dore murdered Dan. Not the same thing at all.

She had a cup of tea in an ordinary working people's cafe and settled herself before visiting Jonathan's chambers, where she discovered from Jones what sort of time he'd be back. She decided against going to court again to watch him because Jones said in view of the time it would be too easy to miss him as he left. And she'd begun to feel uncomfortable being in places she wouldn't normally visit, being amongst only men all the time. There were hardly any women in and around the courts. Only the odd mother or younger woman in the public areas.

With some time to kill she wandered north-east. The ancient area of Lincoln's Inn gave way slowly to less salubrious surroundings. A railway line ran above, borne on a viaduct. Underneath, arches housing modest industrial units. The people here were ones that she felt familiar with. Self-employed men and women running their own affairs. There was a cabinetmaker, an upholsterer, and a marble merchant. She noticed one arch had 'Art Gallery' painted in rough brushwork directly onto the brick. The door – the slightly smaller than man-sized one inset in the big one that opened the entire front of the arch – was ajar. She positioned herself so that she could see inside. The interior walls had been whitewashed. She could see paintings hanging on them. What she couldn't do, though, was raise her foot to step over the threshold, despite the fact that she wanted to. She'd been to galleries before, but big, municipal ones where the paintings hung in ornate rooms and you knew they had to be good otherwise they wouldn't be there and nobody made you feel stupid by finding out what you didn't know about 'art'. That was her main fear, that someone would make her feel stupid if she entered that tiny, intimate art gallery. Someone would ask her if she found a certain painting was like that by such and such, or reminiscent of thingy. And they'd confidently recite foreign names that didn't sound anything like their spelling. She turned to go and nearly bumped into a strong-looking woman coming the other way.

'Crikey,' she said, in a strange accent.

'Sorry,' replied Philomena.

'I thought you were about to go in,' said the woman, in what Philomena guessed was an American accent. She scrunched up her nose. 'It's free entry,' said the woman. 'It's mine, so I should know. Come in. Just look. I won't bother you. I'll leave you alone in the room with them, okay?'

Philomena had just enough time to worry who exactly it was that the American wanted to leave her alone with before she took her by the arm and guided her into the gallery.

She needn't have worried. It was only the paintings the woman referred to. Philomena brought them to mind later as she watched Jonathan make his way down the pavement towards his chambers. There were two pictures in particular that had made a deep impression on her. One was a depiction of a figure, a civilian, lying dead in a street, apparently after an attack. The cobbles had been thrown up and a shutter on a nearby building was dislodged. The rag doll figure lay limp, a pool of blood around its head. She'd looked closer and realised it was a child wearing shorts. The second picture was of soldiers but they were all square and machine-like, in rows. The earth that they were trying to dig into was metallic in colour. Men and metal seemed to have commingled. It wasn't realistic. It looked like the men would clank when they walked, and get rusty if left out in the rain.

Twenty minutes had passed whilst she looked at the paintings. She sought the owner out in order to say thank you before she left, but the woman hadn't seemed to expect anything of her; she'd just waved her away. Philomena tried to place Dan and Jonathan and Major James within the worlds depicted in the art. Mud, blood, metal machinery; masses of men, dead children – the hell they'd inhabited so recently. How much should she take that into account?

She allowed Jonathan to see her before he entered his chambers. He stopped and studied her from twenty feet away. What had he been going through since he'd told her his story? What on earth was she going to tell anyone back home? She couldn't return that night and start telling relatives, friends, that Dan might have been murdered.

Jonathan was still a few feet away when she heard herself say to him, 'It's Dan's birthday, today.'

Then they were in Jonathan's office and he was sympathising with her and saying he hadn't known that and quizzing her about what she'd done that day.

'Here. Have a drink of this.' He was standing over her.

'Oh,' she said, smelling the brandy, 'no thank you.' But she felt so tired and so in need of comfort, and so friendless.

'Go on, yes.'

And in the moment when she took the glass he was giving their fingers touched and recoiled before Jonathan let go.

'Happy birthday, Dan,' she said.

'Happy birthday, Dan,' echoed Jonathan.

They both sipped their drinks. After a few moments she asked: 'What did you hope I'd do after you told me your story?'

'I didn't have a single objective,' replied Jonathan. 'You have a right to know.'

'You wanted me to know so I would have to share the burden,' she countered, firmly.

He neither confirmed nor denied this.

'I want you to meet me when your work is over for today,' she said.

'May I ask what for?' said Jonathan.

'I don't know yet.'

She hadn't known until that moment that she'd stay another night.

CHAPTER SEVEN

She found a cleaner hotel, The Whitehall, in the same relatively inexpensive part of the city. Her room still didn't have much in the way of furnishings, but there was no sewerage pipe running from ceiling to floor. Her view was restricted to, mostly, a tenement block, but at least there was a margin of sky.

She sent a telegram to Jo, apologising for staying another day. After recreating her shrine to Dan she lay down on the bed and allowed her hands the freedom to make unconscious shapes in the half-light.

No rest. She found she'd adopted a new, less elegant habit; twisting the cheap metal band on her wedding finger. She rose and went to the window. Across the way in the tenement block a young, white-faced man in shabby army uniform stared out of his window. Against the dark of his room his face appeared almost translucent. Philomena couldn't tell if the young man was looking back at her. The distance between them, and the angle, and the fact that he was immobile made it impossible to know. She took up her coat and hat and set off to meet Jonathan at the cafe they'd eaten in after their first meeting – The Conduit – the one with the friendly waitress.

'Why do you like it so much here?' she asked Jonathan.

'Did I say I liked it so much?'

'You come here a lot, I can tell. They know you.'

'It's a bit of a strange reason, actually,' Jonathan admitted. 'Some might think it a macabre reason.'

She looked around for signs of anything macabre. It all seemed spick and span and newly decorated. The waitress thought she was looking for her and came over so Philomena had to apologise; they had everything they wanted.

'Are you going to tell me why you like it here so much?' she asked.

Jonathan shifted slightly and smiled nervously.

'It was bombed in the war. A Gotha dropped a bomb on the street.'

'I see.' She thought about Gothas and Zeppelins. Their deadly visits had been front-page news during the war, as had the bombings of German civilians.

'I suppose I first came here to have a look at what remained of the damage. It interested me, the idea that while I was fighting in another country my own was being bombed from the air. I'm not sure that that's ever happened before. I came to the street and this place was open. I came in. I liked it. I've never discussed the bombing with anyone here. I feel at home. I don't know whether that has anything to do with the fact it was war-damaged.'

Philomena looked up and around for any signs of damage. Jonathan's story made her regard the cafe's near-perfect condition differently. The recent decoration had been a necessity, the completion of a rescue.

'How's your new hotel?' he asked.

'Slightly less gruesome than the first.'

Even he didn't know where she was staying, now.

'So you didn't go straight back to Major James or march up to Anthony Dore and blurt it all out and drop me in it,' said Jonathan, trying to grin.

'I went back to Major James. I don't think I dropped you in it. I didn't say how I'd come by the information – I didn't say I had any information, actually. I was a bit sneaky. I said that one of the letters I received about Dan's death described it as a crime.'

Jonathan wrinkled his nose, recalling his letter to her. He certainly hadn't used the word 'crime'. 'Is that an actual letter or one you created?'

'Actual.'

Now he leaned forward, and his voice took on an edge. 'May I ask who wrote it and are they a potential witness?'

'They're not a potential witness, no.' She added nothing, waiting for him to have to ask another question.

'That's a pity,' said Jonathan, sagging. 'It was a general state-ment, that Dan's death was a crime. When they said "crime" they obviously meant what a godawful waste of a life at the end of a godawful waste of millions.'

'I thought so at the time. Until you related your story.'

It took a few seconds for Jonathan to work out who the writer of this letter might be. Philomena saw him arrive at the name and then discount it. He looked to her, a dazed expression in his eyes.

'He *wrote* to you?'

'If you mean Anthony Dore, yes.'

'He wrote to you,' repeated Jonathan, almost to himself. He grimaced. Something perhaps even more horrible occurred to him. 'Condolences?'

She nodded. She could see the anger rising in him.

'I'm almost speechless,' said Jonathan.

He had so much energy churning inside him that Philomena feared he might combust. For the first time she understood how someone can be described as 'beside themselves'. And she felt in danger. The heightened animation she'd previously witnessed in Jonathan on his feet in court inhabited him now, seated next to her. His mouth was open, his eyes blinked and flickered, his brow furrowed deeply. The forces at work here were intense and very powerful. Philomena was being caught up in them. They were threatening to encircle her. She could feel Jonathan's energy pressing her to do his bidding, and Major James also pressing, and Dan, and on the fourth side a shadowy grey energy that she imagined was Anthony Dore. Her hands had lifted and were pressing outwards; the backs were trying to make way for her to pass.

'I can only think of one word to describe Anthony Dore, and it's far too rude to say out loud,' said Jonathan. 'It's a short word.'

'I think I know the word. But his letter proves nothing as far as I'm concerned.'

Jonathan changed, and studied her closely, and she could see he was putting the professional, lawyer part of his brain to work, to assess what she'd said.

'Yes. I can see that,' he said. 'You've no reason to take my word as gospel. I can see that. I've grown accustomed to being disbelieved. At first I thought the force of my belief would carry, but what you eventually come to realise is that it's possible that nobody else feels the same as you about something that you think is the most important thing in the world.'

There was no rancour in his tone, no accusation, no suggestion that he was levelling anything at her. Philomena decided that if ever she was in court accused of anything she would want Jonathan Priest to be defending her.

'Show me Anthony Dore. Point him out,' she demanded suddenly, surprising herself.

'You haven't met him, then?' said Jonathan.

She shook her head.

'Come on,' said Jonathan, standing up.

'I don't want to meet him,' she blurted out. 'I just want you to show him to me, without him knowing.'

Jonathan opened his mouth to ask something, but didn't ask it. He said something else: 'He might know that you're here by now. Someone might have told him.'

'Major James?'

'Or someone in his office, or someone else he has told about you. You can't trust anyone.'

'I know,' she said, shooting him a look.

★ ★ ★

En route she didn't let on to Jonathan that she'd already been to look at Anthony Dore's house. Being less than candid with him felt awkward, but not deceitful, as she was sure that he hadn't told her everything either. She felt that she needed to act in her own interests – hers and Dan's, and if that meant keeping secrets from, or omitting to offer information to even the man Dan described as his 'new best friend', so be it.

They took up watch in the Mayfair square, their backs to the railings around the private gardens.

The side away from Philomena, Jonathan had his hand in his jacket pocket, manipulating a pack of playing cards, his nervous displacement. The Dore house was dark except for the entrance light and two upstairs windows. There was hardly anybody else on foot in the vicinity. For minutes on end all that could be heard were motor engines, horses' hooves, cart wheels. From time to time Philomena asked a question.

'Is he married?'

'No. He lives with his father.'

Dogs in the distance. Ruff, ruff! Ruff! Echoing.

'What else do you know about him?'

'I know his walk, his shape, his rhythm—' Jonathan broke off because a male pedestrian had entered the square. The figure neared. Jonathan pressed back into the shadows, urging Philomena to follow suit.

'Some of his habits,' he continued, in an undertone.

He could see that Philomena expected him to say that this figure was Anthony Dore.

'Is that him?' she hissed.

'No.'

Another pedestrian entered the square from the other direction. Philomena looked again to Jonathan.

'You've been here before, doing this, haven't you?' she asked.

'I've investigated him, yes,' he replied.

A dog snuffled loudly somewhere nearby in the dark. They both feared it would discover them and bark.

'Can you hear that?' whispered Philomena.

Jonathan's answer was to press back against the railings. Their sides came together awkwardly but neither dared move until the danger was clear. The dog sounded as if it was rooting right at their feet now, which was strange, because they still couldn't see it. A pile of last autumn's leaves, trapped against the foot of the railings, moved.

'It's a hedgehog!' giggled Philomena.

'Some spies we make,' retorted Jonathan.

They settled back to watching the house.

'He's an only child now,' said Jonathan, *sotto voce*. 'Mother deceased. Two brothers perished in the war. Anthony's the middle one.'

A man appeared, heading into the square. Jonathan began to tremble. Philomena looked up at him and this time he gave a tiny nod of confirmation. In his pocket his hand fumbled the playing cards.

They watched the figure walking the other side of the road. So this was Anthony Dore? Philomena glanced sideways at Jonathan. His features were set. His jaw flexed as he ground his teeth. She experienced a surge of energy. She wanted to act, to achieve more than merely watch Dore walk the pavement, climb the steps to his house, and enter. Suddenly she found herself moving out of the shadows and taking a line that would allow her to pass him. Jonathan took a step and reached forward to grab her but he hadn't reacted quickly enough. If he made another attempt he was at risk of revealing himself. She heard him stifle a cry then curse her roundly under his breath.

From a distance, but closing, she took in Dore's appearance. Shorter than Jonathan or Dan, slighter than Dan, he seemed a little off-balance. Under the influence of something. She saw him register her presence. He'd seen what? A lower-class sort of a girl, to him. But good posture. Walking alone. Hmmm. Would he be able to hear her heart thumping in her chest? She noted everything she could about him as they closed on each other. Round face, thin moustache, uneven gait. But what she was really looking for was of course not visible. He slowed down, and cheekily raised his hat to her. Philomena became scared that now she was the object of his scrutiny. Her impetuous action started to seem more like dangerous folly. She tried to end the situation by speeding up a little, but couldn't resist – right at the last, just as she passed – glancing into his eyes.

He smiled but she didn't. Did he do lower-class girls? Was that a reasonable presumption? She kept going, fearing Dore might call out something, but he didn't. Behind her she could feel that he had turned to watch her walking away.

'Go home, go home,' urged Jonathan under his breath until

Anthony Dore turned and continued to the steps up to his house. When he had one foot on the lowest Jonathan's impatience to get after Philomena won out. He broke cover to pursue her, but Anthony stopped! Jonathan froze, mid-step, in full view if Anthony looked his way. Out of the corner of his eye Jonathan monitored him – an agonising wait whilst Anthony continued to watch Philomena . . . and watch her . . . and watch her . . . until she was out of sight. Only then did he climb the steps to his house. Unable to wait for him to get inside, Jonathan sneaked away, and as soon as he felt that he was in the clear, he ran after Philomena.

'What the hell are you playing at?'

'I wanted to see him,' she replied.

'Did he have "I murdered Daniel Case" tattooed across his forehead?'

'You're being ridiculous,' said Philomena.

'Listen to me—'

'Why?' demanded Philomena, her voice rising. 'Why should I listen to you?'

'Because I told you about this.'

'You told me that something terrible had happened but there's nothing being done about it; that's what you've told me. And we're in the street.'

'So?' he demanded.

'The way you're acting anybody watching is going to think I'm under threat from you. I didn't know I was going to get that close to him. I didn't plan it. But I don't see why you're so steamed up about it.'

They stood there for a few moments, their hot breath showing in the air. Jonathan's like a stubborn animal, she thought. A goat. Are we just going to stand here?

'What if he ventures out again and comes this way?' she suggested.

They began to walk, side by side, a wide space between them, but not an empty space. The very first public house they came across, by mute consent, they entered. Philomena said what she wanted to drink and he made the purchase while she found an empty table. In a mirror she watched him grimly knock back a large whiskey chaser whilst the proper drinks were being poured. The shot seemed to sort him out. When he sat down he'd become much more reasonable.

She said: 'Tell me the next bit of the story. What happened when you made your allegation?'

'Hmm,' he said. He looked straight at Philomena, warning her that he wasn't going to spare her. She nodded her consent.

'I don't know how long I'd knelt on the battlefield holding Dan's body. Someone – a stretcher-bearer – eventually gently prised him away from me. I was covered in Dan's blood, though didn't realise it at the time. I stumbled back to our dugout to find that it appeared to have been visited by someone intent on searching his possessions. Whoever it was had been in a hurry because Dan's kit was scattered all around. I knew instinctively that the searcher had been Anthony Dore, looking for the pledges, and later I assumed that he'd found them; otherwise why make it the first line of his defence that there had been no card game? If the pledges ever turned up the first line of his defence would be destroyed and the rest of his lies exposed.

'Still bloody, I went out and sought the location of Dan's body. I found him covered in a blanket, on a stretcher, outside a medical tent. I gently searched him, but the IOUs weren't on him. He felt cold, already. Nobody could tell me if Anthony Dore had been to visit him.

'Major James might have had a few, but he listened attentively to me, and made notes. At the end he grunted a few times then silently contemplated me for what seemed like an age before saying, "Get cleaned up while I look into this," and I realised how bloody I was. I found some water and had a dab at the worst of it, and waited irritably for any word. I tidied up Dan's possessions until I was called to return to Major James' dugout.

'It was empty, so I waited. Footsteps behind me warned that someone had entered. Major James started speaking before he reached his seat. He was brisk: "Priest."

'"Sir."

'"At ease."

'"Sir."

'"Your allegation."

'Major James opened a file. I tried to read upside down the official letter on top of the papers in the file. It informed someone that someone had died in action. It was accompanied by a B104–82A notification of death.

'"I've taken it seriously," said Major James, "because of your personal standing, but the bullet that killed him is enemy –

we dug it out; Major Chiltern's dead so no one can corroborate that there was a card game—"'

Jonathan looked around to make sure no one in the pub was eavesdropping. 'I said to him, "Is Captain Dore saying that there was no card game?"

'"Yes, he is," confirmed Major James.

'"Oh," I said, "But these are the cards," dumbly holding them out.

'Major James took them from me, turned them this way and that. "That is a pack of cards, yes." He gently returned them to me.'

'You had the cards?' exclaimed Philomena.

'Yes, they were in our dugout. When I stumbled on them, for a moment I was elated. I was excited that they were evidence – was halfway out of the door to show the major – but he was right. It was only a pack of cards. You see, I thought that Dore would deny he'd murdered Dan, but it never occurred to me that he'd deny the existence of a card game. Clever bastard. Anyway, the other reasons Major James gave for not pursuing my allegation were compelling: no sign of the IOUs, no witnesses to the death. I didn't even see it myself. Regardless of which— "I believe that Captain Dore murdered Second Lieutenant Case, sir," I repeated.

'"I advise you to be very careful about voicing that allegation," said Major James, chopping the air with his hand. "I've conducted this unofficial enquiry very hush-hush, so that it can't rebound on anyone—"

'"Dan was trying to tell me something," I countered.

'More footsteps entered the dugout. Major James leaned in towards me. "You know how it is," he confided urgently. "He was probably asking for his mother."

'Anthony Dore was standing alongside me and I barked, "Where are those IOUs, Dore?"

'"Captain Dore," said Major James, correcting me.

'Dore turned to Major James and opened his palms as if to say, "You see, what can I do?"

'"Second Lieutenant Case was your friend, wasn't he, Captain Priest?" asked the major.

'I remained silent. I was having to stop myself leaping sideways at Dore. I'd viciously elbow him in the ribs to double him up, grip his head, pull it down and smash my knee up into his face. I'd wipe that supercilious grin right off it. He wouldn't have a mouth left to grin with by the time I'd finished.

'"Was he your best friend?" Major James continued. "How long had you known him?"

'"Six weeks," I replied.

'Major James raised an eyebrow. Dore looked sideways at me and his lips parted and he inhaled, and for a moment I thought he might challenge my claim. I bristled and clenched my fists and I knew if I ever did hit him I wouldn't be able to stop. Sensing an impending explosion Major James put himself between me and Dore, his back to the latter. "Look at you," he said quietly to me, "you're all in. We're all in. But also 'up'. Exhilaration plus relief plus exhaustion plus everything else."

'Major James stepped away to a distance from which he could address both me and Dore.

'"Captain Dore's letting this go, aren't you?"

'"Yes sir."

'"As long as you never make such an allegation ever again," added Major James.

'I turned to Anthony Dore: "I saw the look in your eye and I know the truth and you know that I know."

'And Anthony Dore turned to me and said – he explained, patiently, kindly, as if tolerating unruly behaviour from a misguided minor – that if I did repeat the allegation to anyone he'd have to instruct his lawyers.

'I bridled and was about to snap when Major James again stepped in. "Captain Dore knows that you're a hero, and that Daniel Case was, too."

'At which I walked out. Without saluting. Or permission. Anthony Dore was posted to another zone soon after—'

A surge of laughter from a far corner of the pub had made Jonathan break off. Philomena watched him swill the dregs of his drink, stare into the bottom of his glass, his mood altering.

'I detest being dominated by these thoughts. I don't like the no-sleep no-rest life I've found myself in. Some days I feel like I died, that I'm a ghost, a wraith, muffled from the humans teeming this city, moving much more ponderously than they. Then I see another spectre, recognise another spirit wading, head down as if into a headwind, having to think where to plant each step, with what degree of force to grip the ground, drive on; someone else flexing the joints consciously, aware of the effort to do the simplest, taken-for-granted things, and I avoid them, not wanting to be like them. I force myself to wade out of that viscous air that I so easily slip into. I'm normal again for some, impossible to predict length of time. Normal? No, not normal; normal was before.'

He got up and went to the bar, saying: 'Same again?' not waiting for a reply.

Philomena sat stunned. That last speech of his had been like watching someone strip to their soul. She didn't have to ask him 'What's your life like?' He'd told her. But he hadn't looked nor sounded as if he were asking for sympathy. That was what made it so moving. He was describing a much more eloquent version of her walk with a black dog in a long dark lane. Again she watched him down a chaser whilst the drinks were poured. When he returned he sat and said, 'Sorry about all that.'

'Don't apologise,' she said. 'No need.'

'I just go on,' he said.

'Who do you go on to?'

'Myself. Self-pity: ugly, weak, repellent. Never talked like that to anyone before. Won't do it again. Don't know what came over me. Usually just blather on to myself. First sign of madness, they say.'

Philomena puffed her cheeks and blew a stream of compressed breath out in order to indicate that she couldn't possibly know.

'But there again,' he continued, 'they say that if you think you're mad then you can't be. Only those who don't recognise they're mad can actually be mad.'

Philomena watched a muscle twitch in his cheek near his mouth. His eyes turned darker.

'If I could be certain. Verification; proof . . . If I was . . . I've sometimes thought that if I could be certain I'd . . . And he knew I was, he knew that I was . . . He'd have to know I was . . .'

'Yes,' said Philomena.

'Yes, what d'ye mean, yes?'

'I know what you mean,' said Philomena.

'What do you know from that incoherent ramble?'

She looked around and lowered her voice. 'If you could be certain that Anthony Dore murdered Dan you'd do something. You've often thought you would, but he'd have to know you were doing what you were doing in revenge for what he'd done to Dan.'

They looked candidly at each other for a long time. Jonathan felt no hostility from her; however, he still wondered if he should deny that physically avenging Dan was what he'd meant. No. If she ever accused him of making that threat he'd just deny it. He'd play Anthony Dore to her Jonathan Priest. He was never going to *do* anything, anyway. He'd just continue to fester.

The publican reached for their glasses and said, 'Time.'

Jonathan grabbed his back and drained it. When they were alone again he grinned and said: 'Now we've established that I'm potentially unhinged, shall we go on somewhere?'

Yes, thought Philomena. There's plenty more to know about all this.

He took her to an underground club – you had to descend some iron stairs to enter it. Once inside, Philomena looked around the place a little anxiously and he guessed she felt ordinary and provincial in comparison with the strikingly individual people at the bar and tables. For instance, someone who might have been a woman but who was in a man's suit greeted them. She had a light man's voice or a raspy woman's, whichever way you chose to look at it. Jonathan was known there. Nobody paid much attention to him and Philomena beyond a few glances. They sat and ordered drinks. A pianist played a baby grand in the corner. Dreamy music, with spaces between the notes.

On the wall behind their table hung a large photograph. It looked as if it was of a porcelain urinal. Philomena craned to see it. Yes, it was a photograph of a urinal. She looked around to see if anyone was laughing at her for looking at it. Jonathan smiled and said what sounded like 'dooshom'. She was stumped for a moment. Jonathan pointed and again said, 'Dooshom – it's a picture of the dooshom.' She gathered he was voicing the artist's name. There was a title to the photograph of a urinal – *Fountain*, it said. She now understood that the urinal was some sort of a joke. Anyway, she mused, the world had gone to hell in a handcart so why not hang such a photograph on a wall.

They watched the pianist.

'Satie,' said Jonathan, 'one of the new lot.' He looked at Philomena and she nodded, believing he was supplying the player's name. He realised the misunderstanding. 'Satie's the composer.'

Philomena watched the pianist not called Satie for a while longer. The drinks arrived and she asked a question she'd been saving. 'How do you know whether your clients are inn—'

'If they tell me that they're innocent, I proceed on that basis,' interrupted Jonathan, obviously weary of the question.

'But do you believe them?'

'I proceed as if I believe them. My job is to give them the best possible defence so that the justice system can—'

'When I watched you in court, that man—'

'What man?' demanded Jonathan.

'The war cripple, yesterday.'

Jonathan inhaled sharply. She'd just let slip that she'd watched him, prior to meeting him. He felt his heart quicken. What was the significance of this? What should happen now? He should ask why she hadn't mentioned this before. She didn't appear to be about to say anything more about it. She looked distinctly unembarrassed. But he could hardly accuse her of keeping secrets, could he?

'Do you think he was guilty?' she asked.

'It doesn't matter,' replied Jonathan.

'It mattered very much to him what you thought. He was terrified when you ignored him after the innocent verdict was read out.'

'Did you speak with him?' asked Jonathan.

'No.'

'Then how do you know that about him?'

'I could see it.'

'You mustn't judge by appearances,' said Jonathan. 'They can be very misleading. Have you learned anything from seeing Anthony Dore?'

She looked away.

'Nothing,' said Jonathan, answering his own question. 'It was neither misleading nor revealing.'

They listened to the music for a few moments.

'In court yesterday, did you notice the judge?' Jonathan asked her.

'Yes.'

Jonathan seemed about to add something but instead he returned to a previous subject. 'That war cripple yesterday. I don't think your reading of him is right. It isn't that he wanted me to approve of him; I think he hoped that I could sort everything out for him, perform magic, turn back the clock so there had never been a war, he hadn't lost his arm, wasn't on the bread line, in limbo. Our victory is pretty sour for young men like him. Plus, of course, the relief of being found not guilty, not going to gaol must be . . .'

He tailed off. There was suddenly a heavy weight about him, and he looked sunken beneath it. Philomena wanted to ask what he was thinking about, but that was too intrusive, and he'd told her enough about his inner workings, hadn't he? Light from a wall lamp caught his downturned head. His premature grey hairs glinted. The pianist ended the Satie and there was respectful applause. He burst out into some energetic jazz, and a few patrons of the club whooped. Philomena's hands came to life with the music. Jonathan sat up straight. She caught him smiling at her hands. Jonathan, embarrassed, looked away. She watched something take him. His eyes filled up and for a moment she dreaded that he might break down, but he didn't, and they both waited for the difficulty to pass.

'Dan would have liked it here,' she ventured.

'Would he?' said Jonathan, perking up.

'I don't know,' she admitted. 'I was just speaking for the sake of it.'

'He was game for most things,' said Jonathan. 'I thought of Dan as the free spirit I'd've been if I hadn't been always studying.'

She looked steadily at him. He returned her gaze. Her heart fluttered as she recognised that the bond between Dan and Jonathan was authentic and powerful. She remembered when – was it only yesterday? – Jonathan, at their first meeting had said, 'I didn't know him very long, but—' and been interrupted. She knew he had been about to say that he and Dan were very close, or like brothers, or whatever men said when they meant that they loved another man. She felt a rush of jealousy and tears pricked her own eyes. Jonathan graciously pretended nothing awkward was happening.

'I wonder what he would have ended up doing with his life,' he said, taking a swig of his drink.

'I was hoping he'd do me,' she said, and Jonathan snorted his drink out of his nose.

He looked at her and they both roared with laughter. They were so loud that even the pianist playing the jazz looked over. It was a relief to laugh. They were laughing at the pun and the snorted drink but they also laughed because it released all sorts of emotions that up until then had had no outlet. For a while they couldn't stop laughing. They realised that it was starting to become a little trying for the other patrons, but the pianist looked over towards them and smiled, telling everyone that it was all right.

On the back edge of their laughter Philomena asked Jonathan: 'Do you act?'

'Me? Act? You mean amateur dramatics? No.'

'You perform in court.'

'Do I?'

'You know you do.'

'That's not the same as acting. I imagine actors on a stage are there purely for pleasure. Do you act?'

'I help out with costumes at my local amateur dramatic society.'

'Did Dan act?'

'Yes.'

'Any good?'

They properly got the giggles.

After another drink Jonathan insisted on escorting Philomena to her new hotel. Standing outside it saying goodbye was awkward. They'd both taken alcohol, and it was late, and there was nobody else about. Philomena still didn't even know if Jonathan was single. If he had a wife or sweetheart Dan hadn't mentioned it, and neither had he. It didn't feel to her that he had anyone waiting for him at home or anywhere else.

What's the appropriate parting between a man and a woman, both of whom are drunk and grieving her fiancé, whom the man has claimed was murdered?

To avoid a potentially graceless goodbye she turned to him and said, 'Thank you,' with finality, hoping that this covered everything.

Glowing inside, Jonathan wanted to prolong the evening, which had turned into the night. He thought to ask what Philomena was thanking him for in the hope that this would lead to conversation, but in the street at that hour it could only be a brief exchange, so instead he held out his hand and her hand met it lightly for a moment. He wanted to ask her what she was going to do now about the whole business; he wanted to ask her how long she was staying in London; he wanted to ask her if he'd see her tomorrow. But he didn't.

They parted, and Philomena entered The Whitehall. Jonathan loitered, his energy seeping away. He ached with loneliness.

Philomena nodded to the night porter and didn't care what he thought of her as he reached for her key. She climbed the stairways to the fourth floor. The carpet ran out after the second floor, so she was careful not to clatter her shoes on the painted floorboards and disturb her fellow guests. Passing one door she could make out male and female grunts in the same rhythm, and the squeak of a bed, which made her think of a whore and a client. But it could be a couple in love; why not? A married couple, even. She listened for a few moments until she became envious. She moved on, up to her floor. The corridor was empty of people but it somehow felt emptier than that. She shivered a little as she arrived at her room, although she wasn't cold, and she turned the key in the lock. For some reason she pushed open the door without stepping into the room and waited a few moments before entering. Her sheaf of papers was on the table. All appeared as she'd left it. She entered and shut the door behind her. In the dark she threw her hat down on the bed and unpinned her hair. When it dropped around her face she caught the unfamiliar odours of London trapped within it. Too tired to even think of washing it she took up her brush and bent over, allowing her hair to stream down. As she turned her head to one side a horrific sight framed in the window caused her to let out a scream.

Across in the tenement block she could see the white-faced young soldier standing on a chair, placing a noose around his neck. Before she knew it she'd thrown her window open and shouted 'No!' The young soldier hesitated for a moment. 'Don't do that!' she shouted before the young soldier kicked the chair away and flailed in the air, his hands instinctively gripping the noose around his neck. Lights came on in the nearest buildings and windows were thrown open. People were shouting 'What? What is it?' She leaned out of her window and called down into the darkness: 'Jonathan! Jonathan!'

Down below he was already running. He sprinted back to the entrance to the hotel and sped past the porter and raced up the stairs. Outside, police whistles pierced the night. As he reached the first landing Jonathan realised he didn't know what room Philomena was in. He ran back down the stairs and shouted to the porter: 'This is an emergency! Philomena Bligh, what room?'

'Four oh seven,' replied the porter, startled by the command, 'that's the—'

'Fourth floor, yes!' Jonathan shouted as he sprinted up the stairs to the first landing. As he began the second stairs he met Philomena coming down. She barely stopped to say: 'There's a man killing himself.'

Philomena ran on down the stairs with Jonathan trailing behind. They raced out of the hotel and she looked up at the tenement block. An onlooker high above in her hotel shouted: 'It's that one!' Inhabitants of the tenement, drawn by the alarm, leaned out of their windows.

Philomena shouted up to them, 'How do we get in?'

Jonathan took her arm and urged, 'Around the side!'

They entered the tenement and ran up the first two flights of stairs. Bewildered-looking people were opening their doors.

Jonathan asked Philomena: 'Which floor?'

She looked around. 'I need a window to get my bearings.'

An old lady who stood in her open door waved them in. From in there Philomena quickly deduced that the angle to her window opposite meant that they needed to go up at least another floor. They ran out of the old lady's and up the next flight of stairs and when they met more bemused tenants on the next landing she cried, 'Is there a young soldier on this floor?' Someone indicated a door and Philomena tried the handle and it was locked.

Jonathan stepped back and kicked it and the door flew open and the young soldier was in front of them twitching on the end of the rope. Philomena went in first and wrapped her arms around the dying man's legs, held him up to ease the pressure around his neck while Jonathan rummaged in the kitchen drawers and came up with a sharp knife. He stood the chair on its legs and climbed up on it and sawed through the rope. The young soldier's entire weight was suddenly in Philomena's grasp but she anticipated this and made sure that they landed without him striking his head by slipping a hand underneath to cushion it before it struck the floor. For a moment she was face to face with his twitching body, holding him. She untangled herself and turned him onto his back. Jonathan listened for his heart. He thumped the young soldier's chest with the heel of his clenched fist. Philomena began giving the kiss of life. The first policeman arrived.

When it was over Philomena felt her whole body begin to quiver uncontrollably. She put up a hand to steady herself, finding Jonathan's shoulder. He recognised her condition for what it was.

'Philomena,' he said. She didn't respond. Seeing her eyes lose their focus he clicked his fingers at the bridge of her nose, once, twice, roughly. She blinked and he brought his hand to his own face, making her follow. Her eyes met his, zooming in and out to find the range. 'Philomena, it's mild shock,' he said. 'I'm going to get you to your room. You just need a few moments in your room. Yes?'

She nodded. A strange gap had opened up between her and him. When he began to lead her she knew she was next to him, being touched, guided, but she felt absent, hollow. Nevertheless she could walk back to the hotel, in through the door on jelly legs. As they passed the night porter she knew that he coughed theatrically and Jonathan snapped at him: 'She just saved a boy's life.'

Later, she sat in her chair and he leaned by the window. She looked across to the now-empty room. They hadn't been speaking much. She'd been wondering if the sensation she'd had, holding the young soldier's twitching body, was similar to what he'd felt when holding Dan as he died. She knew that she could never ask him that question.

Jonathan had been looking around. He'd seen her shrine to Dan. It had given him quite a shock. He'd too easily become unmindful of the fact that she was Dan's fiancée. The reminder had deflated him. Now he was in a familiar mood.

'One theory,' said Jonathan, continuing in public a conversation he'd been conducting alone, 'is that we kill ourselves when there's someone else we really want to kill, but we are unable to see it through.'

She looked sharply at him. Was that a confession? Jonathan looked like – she imagined – she got a glimpse of him as a small boy blinking back tears brought on by an injustice. But then his shields went up to protect that boy, and adult Jonathan was snarling, 'I already wish that I hadn't told you that story about Dan and Anthony Dore.'

'But you have.'

'That story just causes trouble. My trouble hasn't halved since I told you. Now I'm worried about you, too.'

'So that is why you told me. It was to relieve your burden, not to actually get anything done – or perhaps it was; tell it to someone else and see if they do anything, rather than just fret. It strikes me,' she added spitefully, 'that once outside of court where you are performing, you are a bit of a worrier.'

'I wasn't ever going to tell you the story. I wasn't ever going to write it to you or come and find you. It is only because you turned up here unannounced that I told it to you.'

'So it's all my fault?' she said, raising her voice, exasperated.

'What's all your fault?' retorted Jonathan, fuelling the argument.

'You were going along nicely down here until I turned up?' she snapped.

'I don't know that Dore did kill Dan, I really don't—'

'Yes you do!' She was emphatic now. 'Why go through all that you have, tell me all that you have in the way that you have only to turn around and say—'

'I've given the wrong impression!' He was almost shouting now. 'I *suspect* Anthony Dore, yes. *Believe* he did it? Yes. Am I *sure* he did it? No. *Certain* he did it? No.'

'You are, you are!' returned Philomena, striking the side of her chair for emphasis.

'Are you telling me that on the basis of what I've told you and one sighting of Anthony Dore you are unequivocally *certain* that he murdered Dan?' challenged Jonathan.

She bit her lip.

'How can you be certain? How can you be sure? It's only my word against his. No witness, no evidence – Dan was too reckless; he should have taken more care; he shouldn't have riled Dore. Dan was an idiot, a stupid—'

Philomena turned away from him and stared at the floor, cutting him off. She wouldn't look at him, wouldn't look at him ever again. After a few moments, still with her eyes averted, she went to her door and opened it. In the corner of her eye, Jonathan sagged. Sighing, he picked up his hat and took a few faltering steps.

'I'm sorry,' he tried.

She gazed resolutely ahead. He took a few more steps until he was in front of her, side-on on the threshold.

'I hope the young soldier survives,' he said, fiddling with the brim of his hat.

She swallowed. Jonathan went out through the door. She closed it after him. He stood outside in the hallway cursing himself.

She lay down on her bed. It all felt impossible. The dawn was arriving. She willed peace to enter her body.

CHAPTER EIGHT

On the second ever morning that Philomena awoke in London she was recalling a play that she'd made costumes for in Saddleworth. She sat up, wondering if clothes, costume, was a good idea. Could she be like that girl tutored by the professor, but doing it to herself? Clothes and a bit of pretending. Was that all that was needed?

Hurriedly she began to dress. She looked at Dan's photograph, hoping he'd comment on her plan. Such as it was.

But she hadn't time to make everything; she needed it all that day, for goodness' sake. And what of the cost? And how much more time could she afford to spend on this mission? For that was what it had become. Two more days, she hoped, after which she really had to get back to the business. Now she wished she had brought some work with her, but she'd had no idea, had she?

But meeting Anthony Dore might prove impossible. She would have to find him, first. And talk to him. She knew that if she asked him anything that even barely resembled a leading question he would be immediately suspicious. Especially if he'd been warned about her. Would Major James do that?

She couldn't decide. She didn't know what pressures he was under. She had no idea if Anthony Dore would be expecting her.

Clothed, she parted the threadbare curtains. Looking out of the window, there was no sign of life in the young soldier's room. So she had something she wanted to achieve and a mad notion of how she should go about it. Breathe deeply, Philomena; breathe very, very deeply, she said to herself. The last thing she did before leaving the room was pick up her felt flowerpot hat.

At reception the day porter, a pleasant individual, smiled at her: 'I hear there was some trouble in the night.'

'Trouble?' asked Philomena, uncomprehendingly.

'You saved that young soul. Everyone's talking about it.'

Oh yes, remembered Philomena, there was all that. 'It was nothing. Anyone would have done the same.'

Still smiling, the day porter shrugged as if to say he wasn't sure about that.

Philomena privately disagreed. If anyone wouldn't have done the same, that was a disgrace. 'And I didn't do it alone,' she said.

The day porter dipped his head, saluting both her deeds and her humility, and got on with his work.

Philomena moved on, out of the hotel, recalling Jonathan's decisive actions to save the suicide. He'd quickly understood what was wrong and what needed doing. He hadn't asked any questions – in fact she couldn't remember him speaking, apart from 'Around the side,' and 'Which room?' He'd fallen in and co-operated. She could see why Dan would have liked to be shoulder to shoulder with him in the war. But what a complex and infuriating man he could be! One minute solid and simply getting on with things, the next threatening to erupt. And there were the dark, heavy atmospheres that suddenly emerged, threatened to envelop; his self-confessed tendency towards melancholy and worse. The drinking wouldn't help that, would it? Why didn't he reduce it or stop?

At a post office she sent yet another telegram to Jo explaining that she had to stay on for another day. From a directory she noted the name and address of a likely-looking dress agency and made her way to it. On the way she practised making her accent a little more southern, rehearsed sounds in her head and listened intently to anyone speaking nearby.

On the threshold of the dress agency she paused for a moment and a pair of women of about her own age in smart clothes brushed past her on their way in. They behaved as if she didn't exist, which caused her to ask herself what on earth she thought she was doing. She tried to answer 'nothing wrong'. She wasn't about to attempt a deception for any financial gain, but if 'caught' by Anthony Dore, what might the consequences be? If he had murdered Dan would she be risking her life? No. Dore wouldn't have any motive to kill her, would he? Yes, if she'd acquired proof. Which would be? She didn't know, yet. If she ever got proof she'd get away from him and the authorities could do the rest.

Changing her mind about entering the dress agency she instead went to drink a cup of strong tea. And she had a sugar in it to settle her stomach. Where would she meet Anthony Dore? And how? These details would determine how things went. Should she keep her protective wedding band or remove it? Get a better one to go with the clothes she imagined she'd need? She could be what – a widow?

Just live now, just do the next thing; you can't know what will happen next – death teaches that.

She finished her tea and walked back to the shop. This time she pushed the door open without allowing herself to doubt. Once inside she felt more comfortable because she was surrounded by things she understood; rows of shelves and rails of clothes. The two women who had been oblivious to her were still in there chattering brightly as they half-examined various pieces. They appeared to be just browsing, unlikely to actually purchase anything. Philomena moved nearer and homed in on their manners and their speech and deportment, telling herself that what she planned was just a girl's dressing-up game. Once she looked right and was speaking differently why would anyone think that she was in disguise? They'd take her at face value, wouldn't they?

She began to notice a refrain of the two women: 'What fun!' 'What fun!' they kept saying. But the rules of 'What fun!' were difficult to apprehend, because the women seemed to use it arbitrarily, whether discussing clothes they'd seen, what they'd had for breakfast, (kippers, kedgeree, coffee), where they might go for lunch, people they knew (Tilly, Monty, Freddy, Bunty). They headed for the exit. With them gone the shop would be empty. Philomena chose some items to try on and entered the communal changing room. She didn't want anyone to see her undergarments, which were clean, but practical, not decorative; cotton, not silk. Without looking at herself in the mirror she knew that her cotton underwear really didn't work under these sorts of dresses. She'd have to buy some that did. But as bad luck would have it, the two women entered just as she was slipping on her first dress, a sleeveless black crepe de chine with silver trim. They both stared for a moment then smiled and proceeded as if she was there for their benefit – an audience for them. There was something juvenile about them, wanting attention from strangers in that way.

Only one of the women had anything to try on. That dress looked outlandish on the hanger and ridiculous when she got it on. It wasn't even clear which was the back and which the front. The two of them were in fits of laughter over it and Philomena couldn't help smiling. The one who wasn't trying the dress on called over for Philomena's opinion. She said that she agreed that the dress was slightly unorthodox. That word made the women think for a moment. Wide-eyed, they laughed some more.

'That's a perfect description of this dress,' hooted one of them.

'That's a very good word,' agreed the other. 'Let's use it

as much as we can today. Let's have an unorthodox day.'

For a moment Philomena worried that they were belittling her. But they weren't. They examined her openly.

'I wish I had your figure,' said one.

'That dress looks marvellous on you,' said the other.

'Thank you,' she stuttered.

'Is it a special occasion?' inquired one.

'Yes,' she said, timidly.

'It's a *man*, isn't it?' exclaimed the other.

'It *is* a man, isn't it?' squealed the first.

'Well he's a *goner*,' said the second woman.

'He'll want to *eat* you,' said the first.

Philomena blushed deeply as an image of sex flew into her mind.

'If he hasn't already,' cackled the second woman, setting her friend off.

Only after they left did she slip off the dress and her underwear and put the dress back on to see if she could get away without anything underneath. She was slender enough to carry it off. Not skinny, though. She had hips, and a bottom. The dress was pretty much straight up and down but too thin. She felt too vulnerable without underwear. She was going to have to buy a silk slip.

She knew this way of dressing was going to make men look at her. It would be wrong to entrap a man to trick him out of money, but if you needed to get near to one in order to find out if he'd done something to someone you loved, or to clear his name for him if he hadn't, she thought it was justified.

She laid out the items that constituted her new evening outfit and calculated the cost of hiring them for one or possibly two nights. She was haemorrhaging her cash. She couldn't afford a complete daywear outfit too. But she'd have to add a coat to cover the marvellous dress in the day. She also had to have a hat for eveningwear. And a hatpin; hers was too plain. Her hair was unfashionably – for this sort of girl – long but she'd keep it pinned up. It'd do, without cutting, if she could manage to roll it around her ears. And she'd rent a little handbag. But there was another problem. She'd only come to London with one pair of shoes, rather sensible ones. Of course not right for this. How much would shoes be? She slipped her own coat over the agency's sleeveless dress and went out into the shop to look for some, finding a pair of high Louis heels that looked right. She also located a green velvet coat with raglan sleeves, and a neat velvet dress hat. In the changing room she tried it all on once more, then returned to her hotel, via a haberdasher's for underwear – a slip, knickers and silk stockings, and in her room she put it all on. She practised walking, standing and sitting. She felt like an exotic owl caught in daylight. Lord knows what the surly porter would make of it all when he saw her. It would confirm that she was a woman of a certain type, probably. In the event, when she exited the hotel, she didn't see him, but she could feel eyes upon her.

Philomena's next problem was make-up. She didn't own anything remotely suitable and didn't want to splash out on stuff she'd never use. In Selfridges she browsed the make-up counters. She'd always imagined herself in Selfridges if she ever visited London. She could remember the opening adverts ten years previous: 'London's New and Wonderful Shopping Centre Dedicated to Women's Service.' It certainly served her. She found an assistant whose own make-up appealed; subtle but glamorous at the same time. She hovered until the assistant greeted her, and had a little lie prepared. Speaking in her new voice modelled on a girl from home, the eldest Osbourne, plus those two women at the dress agency, she said: 'I've been caught out, rather. I've borrowed this outfit but none of my make-up works with it.'

The assistant understood at once, and gestured that she should sit, offered to coil her hair, bless her, and started chatting. Philomena couldn't be taciturn given that she was receiving a favour so she had to make up things about her new self as the need arose. She said her home was in Saddleworth, which it was; that her name was Philomena, which it was; that she was going to meet a man, which she was, she hoped; that she was excited at the prospect, which she was. It all seemed to pass muster. But the thing she was not satisfied with was her name. Using her own, jarred. She couldn't pretend to be someone else if she retained her own first name.

From the make-up counter Philomena made her way to the ladies' rest room to examine herself. Only one cubicle was occupied. She stood at the washbasins and looked at herself, forthrightly, in the bevelled mirrors. She was in costume, now, and needed to learn what other people would see. A painted Philomena – beyond her means to sustain and completely unnecessary for her real life – which felt not only miles away but also years ago. What was her real life, now?

She had been walking up on Pobgreen only three days before. Alone, as usual, recently. At her favourite spot. Dove Stone Moss is behind you and if you just edge forward, Yeoman Hey reservoir is revealed down below. But this time it was different at her favourite spot. She had had unpleasant feelings there, peering down the precipitous drop. She'd had a dark impulse to step out . . . Nothing would survive that fall. But she didn't seek death; that wasn't it. She craved weightlessness. Giving in to that would end in death, of course, so she'd resisted. To succumb to weightlessness – that had been her desire.

The lavatory in the occupied cubicle in Selfridges in London flushed. Philomena pretended to be washing her hands as she slipped off her inappropriate wedding band, concealing it in her hand. A woman exited the cubicle and came to the hand basins. In the mirror Philomena watched her walk. She was very elegant. Philomena tilted her pelvis forward slightly in an attempt to emulate her. She watched the woman wash her hands and check her appearance. She caught Philomena looking, and smiled. Philomena was horrified for a moment then she returned the smile, much more confidently than she felt. The smile worked because the woman seemed entirely at ease as she left the rest room.

Alone, Philomena practised walking like her. She could see her whole self in one mirror. 'What fun!' she said out loud to her reflection. She closed in on her image saying her name in her new voice, but exaggerating the accent even more. It felt strange, naughty; even rude. Perhaps Philomena wasn't such a bad name after all if you said it in a certain way. When she arrived in front of the mirror again she shortened it: 'Phil. Phil. Philly.' She sounded too posh now, too exaggerated, and like she was calling a horse, dog, or henpecked husband. 'Philly! Philly!' Approaching caricature. She toned it down. 'Okay, Phil? Having fun? Isn't this fun? Phil . . . Felicity.' Why did she say Felicity? She stood still, looking into her own eyes wondering if she really knew herself.

'Felicity?' She greeted her reflection. 'Felicity? Hello, Felicity. Okay, Felicity? Having fun, Felicity?' The wedding band went in her pocket.

After lunch she practised being Felicity in a post office whilst searching the directories until she found a telephone number, which she rang. A servant confirmed that Anthony Dore was at home and was asking the caller's identity when Philomena replaced the handset on its cradle. Her new voice hadn't alarmed the servant. He'd acted as if the owner of the voice was legitimate. This was good. But what now? She knew where he lived, knew what he looked like; needed to speak with him without alarming him. She drifted towards his address. Dusk arrived early, and with the sundown came chill, and new doubts about how implausible and vague her plan was.

As she arrived in view of the front doors to Anthony Dore's

house they began to open. She walked on as swiftly as possible to a place where she could turn to look. But Anthony wasn't to be seen. Instead an older man was descending to the pavement. She thought that she had seen him before but couldn't think where. A grand motor car pulled up at the bottom of the steps. The driver smartly alighted and opened a passenger door. The older man entered the car and it drove away. This speculative spying on Anthony Dore's home was useless if all she was going to achieve was sightings of other men.

But then Dore himself emerged, a little furtively, and descended the stone steps. Philomena turned and walked away a few steps in the opposite direction from the one he seemed set upon.

He made off on foot and she turned and followed him, first to a restaurant, opposite which she took refuge in a cafe, where she sat staring out for nearly an hour, deflecting any friendly overtures. He visited a pub where he stood at the public bar, whilst she nursed a drink in the lounge. Two women in couples surveyed her with suspicion and put themselves between their men and her. In neither place was she being Felicity. In her clothes but not being her. Now Dore entered a murky passage between two tall, scruffy, nondescript buildings.

Philomena waited to see if Anthony re-emerged from the passage. When he didn't, she crossed the road and looked into it. Seeing no movement, she checked behind herself, took a deep breath, followed, making as little noise as she could – trying to silence her footfalls yet not creep on tiptoe. She walked slowly past the door that had the only visible light showing around it, looking for any sign that might tell her what lay behind. There was nothing except a spy hole. She kept walking, further into the passage.

She didn't like it down there. Didn't like it at all. She could make out different kinds of blackness but that was about it. That shade of black might have been a pile of rubbish, that one might have been something moving – and now she could hear sounds. Breathing, and perhaps the scratch of a shoe on the ground. Beginning to panic, she swore that if she got out of the passage in one piece she'd go home. In desperation she reached for her hatpin. It had a very sharp point and the shaft felt strong, but it was difficult to get a decent grip on. It would only give her a very little time to get away if she was attacked. Aim for eyes or privates.

She backed up the passage until level with the mysterious door. A closer look still revealed nothing of what kind of place it was. For a few moments all that she could hear was the erratic thumping of her own heart. One fear out here, another fear about what lay in there. Which to choose?

To knock on the door and try to gain admittance required more courage or recklessness than she possessed – she turned and walked forwards as fast as she could, into the lit street, across the road, and attempted to calm herself, still keeping a tight grasp on the hatpin. A group of people, young, bois-terous – five women and two men – came into view. This group was obviously in a party mood. One of the men limped badly and had an eye patch, but this didn't stop him having his arms around the waists of two of the laughing girls and kissing their necks, each in turn. The other man rapped on the door and the party was admitted instantly. That they were inside reassured her.

Then her decision was made for her. The hairs on the back of Philomena's neck stood up and she knew that she was being watched. She turned her head a fraction. She could just make out the shadowy shape of a man standing completely still a few yards away. No movement. No acknowledgement. No greeting, no gesture of any kind. His silhouette told her that he had his hat pulled low, his hands in his coat pockets. Seconds ticked by whilst she watched him and knew he watched her. When he moved a foot and shifted his weight in her direction this impelled her across the road and into the passage and up to the door just at the same time as a pair of women arrived slightly ahead of her. Philomena quickly assessed them. They were dressed expensively but both had on gaudy make-up – eyes too black, lips too red. They raised their faces for inspection via the spy hole. The door opened and the two women entered without speaking. As she tremblingly crossed the threshold in their wake Philomena heard a man's cheerful Cockney voice say: 'All right, girls. You're early. No show tonight?' The two women answered, in slightly posher voices: 'Thank God.' The man looked over their heads towards Philomena and frowned a little. He was big, but not threatening, unless, she imagined, he chose to be.

'Gotta new friend?' asked the doorman of the two women.

The women turned to look at Philomena. She had to say something or go back out, where the threatening man might lie in wait. She made her decision, and spoke in public as Felicity for the very first time:

'No, I'm not with them.'

'No?' said the man, and he cocked his head slightly, inviting her to explain herself.

'I'm supposed to be meeting a friend,' she said, shocked at the sound of her own words, fully expecting any of the three to slap their thighs and hoot at her fake accent. But none of them did.

'Where are you supposed to be meeting this friend, miss?'

'Why, here,' she said, as Felicity.

The doorman smiled. 'Where is here, miss?'

Of course she didn't know, so she tried to flutter her eyelashes. And she mined that accent, mined that voice, that sounded at once lazy and authoritative, for all it was worth.

'We're supposed to be having some fun. He told me to come here.'

'What's his name, please miss?'

Her mind raced. Before she could stop herself it was out of her mouth: 'Daniel.'

'Daniel, don't know him, don't know any Daniels here. But that might be only one of his names. And how are you known?' he asked, still friendly.

She was losing her nerve. 'I've made a mistake,' she said, turning to go.

The pair of women were still watching.

'Not necessarily, miss.'

Philomena stopped.

'You know what kind of place this is?' asked the man, raising an eyebrow slightly.

'I think so.'

The man shot a sideways look at the pair of women and they headed for the interior. When they were gone he peered out of the doorway left and right, before turning back to Philomena. 'I'm not saying that you look like a matron, miss – the opposite, in fact, but you're not working undercover for the police by any chance?'

'The police? No.'

'Are you working for anybody? A newspaper, for instance? A gossip writer?'

'No. I'm not working for anyone,' she replied, absolutely truthfully.

He cocked his head and pursed his lips. She shrugged and spread her hands, gestures she hoped would say 'What else can I do?' and 'Are you going to let me in?' and 'I'm not really bothered whether you do or not. '

'I'll tell you what,' he said. 'You are just here to have fun, I expect, so I'm going to let you in, and if you do have fun, that's all to the good, and if others have fun because of you, likewise, and if Daniel turns up, you can have fun together.'

If only he could turn up, she thought. 'That's very kind of you,' she said.

'What's your name?' asked the man.

'Felicity.'

'Let's hope you live up to it,' said the man. 'My name's St Peter; I definitely live up to mine. If anyone bothers you just let me know,' and he stepped aside, inviting her to enter wherever it was. A place of entertainment, which was something of a secret, where the clients used aliases and which didn't want the police, the press, or the law to enter. If St Peter was on the gates, what was the name of this place? Heaven?

Philomena left her velvet coat at the cloakroom. She could hear what sounded like American jazz being played quietly upstairs. In a room on the first landing there was a trio of Negro men playing piano, double bass and a dreamy clarinet to an appreciative audience seated at tables scattered around the room. The musicians made her think of the Commonwealth soldiers and airmen who'd appeared in Manchester during the war, multiplying the black population. She scanned the audience for Anthony Dore, but he wasn't there. She turned a circle, feeling a little obvious, and looked in through the open doors into the other two rooms off the landing. One room was a bar in which people sat on high stools at the thing itself, chattering away ten to the dozen, whilst the other had an empty dais and one or two denizens waiting for something to begin. He was not in either, master Dore, so she climbed the stairs to the next landing. On the way there was an alcove with a curtain partly concealing a sofa on which a man and a woman were locked in an embrace. Philomena had to study the man for a second in order to ascertain whether he was Anthony Dore, thinking that if it was him he was a quick worker – he'd only been in the place a few minutes. She was shocked to see that the woman had her hand busy inside the man's trousers. Philomena wasn't prudish by any means but she'd never seen that sort of thing in a public place before. Had had her hand inside Dan's trousers numerous times, but as far as she knew they weren't being watched at the time.

As she moved on up to the landing proper she was getting a pretty good idea of what sort of girl Anthony Dore might expect to bump into here. Trying not to think too much about the notion of behaving in a deliberately alluring way with the man who may have murdered Dan, she came across more fellow patrons engaged in playful exchanges. They were being sexual, but it wasn't dark. It was dark in that there was little illumination, but there was not a feeling of darkness. She was being scrutinised, of course. Frank attention. She told herself that if she didn't look a man straight in the eye there was no good reason for him to approach her.

Then she saw him. Anthony Dore was sitting in an easy chair, engaged in conversation with a waitress. Philomena paused for a few moments to give herself one last talking-to before she moved into his eye line and sat where he could see her. She let him have a very good look at Felicity. She crossed her legs one way, then the other. She presented her profile, one side then the other. She could feel him watching. She wished that she smoked cigarettes so she'd have had something to do with her telltale hands. She ordered them to be still, placing one on her thigh and the other on the arm of the chair. This felt too posed, so she played with a wisp of hair. The waitress delivered a drink to Dore then came to her.

'What would you like?' she asked. She sounded European, like some of the refugees that had travelled on the trams. Almond eyes.

Philomena had planned to ask for a lemonade but suddenly, very badly wanted something stronger. 'A rum, please. With a dash of blackcurrant, and water.'

The waitress nodded and moved away. As she passed near Dore, Philomena saw him beckon to her. She went to him, listened, bent her head and concentrated hard on what he was saying. It looked to be something complicated, in sections, that she had to repeat back to him, that she had to learn. She returned to Philomena, who sensed some impatience from her but there was no attitude in her voice when she recited: 'That gentleman inquires whether you are alone and if so whether you want to be.'

This was it. The opportunity. The thin end of it. Should she grasp it? Or could she say that she did want to be alone and walk right out of there? Part of her very much desired to do that. She could go back home and – what? Go back home and what? Feel terrible. Sew. Sew for the rest of her life knowing that she'd been told something, told by someone she tended to believe, and she'd done nothing about it. She could go back home and sew her own shroud and climb in and lie down and wait, for twenty years or thirty years or however long her natural span was destined to be.

Or she could make some kind of reply to Dore's overture. She realised that her hands were describing shapes so she clasped them together.

'That gentleman,' she replied, as if it could have been any one of several.

'That one,' confirmed the waitress.

Philomena looked over to Anthony Dore and made eye contact for the first time bar the glimpse in the street and he smiled, then looked away. She was surprised. She'd expected him to be more assertive.

'Do you know him?' she asked the waitress.

'He is here last night, but that is my first night,' the waitress said, in her accented English.

Philomena stole another look at Dore and felt a rush of apprehension.

'If you ask me,' the waitress offered tentatively, 'I think he is probably all right, and from look of him he got money. And he's young man and there aren't many of those about. And he has no bits missing, that you can see.'

Philomena looked at the waitress, wondering what event had led her to make that last observation; she had known a man who'd seemed complete whom she'd subsequently discovered was not?

'I wouldn't go so far to say suck it to see,' continued the waitress, 'but you might do worse.'

Philomena saw the twinkle in her eye. Accept the drink. Why else would a girl be in this place? Grasp the opportunity.

'Tell him to come over.'

There was a moment when the waitress and she held each other's gaze. Underneath their smiles, shades of sadness.

'I'll keep an eye for you,' said the waitress. 'To see how it is done.'

Philomena watched her go to Anthony Dore and relay her answer. He looked as if he was trying not to smile too broadly. She tried to imagine him cowering under a table in a dugout as an enemy shell exploded and reminded herself to remember to speak in Felicity's accent.

So, there she was, on her own in a strange London club pretending to be someone called Felicity, wearing hired clothes, about to have a drink with the man who might have killed – who'd been accused of killing – her fiancé.

Dore rose from his seat. He'd previously picked up a few women in this sort of place. Some were showgirls who were really prostitutes; some were prostitutes who said they were really actresses. All the ones he'd had sex with, bar one, had been prostitutes of one sort or another in that they'd afterwards accepted gifts of money. Not streetwalkers, any of them, nor difficult to approach, but capable of declining. They had to be won.

Whatever intimacies ensued were superficial in two respects. Firstly, no commitment was anticipated. Secondly, Anthony concealed nearly all of his true self from the women. From men, too. Had done for years. He'd laid down layer upon layer of protection – not regular and even like undisturbed sedimentary rock; twisted and turned in upon itself like upheaved igneous strata.

Recently he hadn't felt able to let his defences naturally evolve. They'd needed an accelerant. Yes, to Major James he'd denied absolutely everything regarding his involvement in the death of Daniel Case, and been believed. But he felt that this had been achieved on a wing and a prayer, inspiration, in fact. To say that there had never been a card game had been an audacious stroke that had beaten the initial accusation. Now came the long haul. Fearing that one day he could be accused again of shooting Daniel Case, Anthony Dore had sought help. In order to learn how to rehearse his innocence, he was secretly visiting a psychiatrist. That is where he had been this teatime, engaged in lying on his couch and lying to him. His reason to be there, and continue to visit, he maintained, was that he irrationally feared other people would accuse him of some terrible action. What people, what action? probed the psychiatrist. No idea; someone as yet only shadowy, wielding lies about some heinous crime. The psychiatrist had enquired from whence this fear might stem and Anthony had again had no idea. The psychiatrist had nodded sagely and droned on about childhood this and repressed that and the 'unconscious'. Sometimes Anthony listened, sometimes not. When in sessions it was his turn to speak he'd discovered how easy it was to paint himself as an innocent victim in his own history. He polished memories of himself until they reflected the story he felt most favourably revealed him. He presented evidence that showed he was a sensitive soul, too sensitive, perhaps.

Anthony found solace in the fact that he had proved himself to be an accomplished dissembler because the psychiatrist – an expert, surely – had failed to see inside him to the truth.

Walking over to this green-eyed girl tonight, he was reminded of another woman, the one who wasn't a prostitute, who'd told him not long into their conversation that she wanted to stop talking because she had a thing about sex with strangers. After they had done it Anthony would have liked to see her again but she had argued that he couldn't be a stranger the second time. He'd heard a foreign accent in her English, had a vision of her visiting every seedy nightclub in London, and perhaps Paris, and all the other capitals, having sex with strangers again and again, not for money. Could she have pursued her existence if the war hadn't happened, if pre-war morality had continued? Or would she have been a maverick in any era? Was this emancipation? He had really very much wanted to see her again. Not as a commitment. She was unsuitable in every social respect. A secret mistress, perhaps. He had needs, of course he did, for companionship, and sex, and other cures for loneliness. So here he was, hopeful once more. He sat down opposite this one and said: 'My name's Anthony.'

'I'm Felicity,' the girl said.

'How do you do?' said Anthony.

He tried to keep his face turned towards her. He smiled.

She was very attractive, but he couldn't quite read her: actress, prostitute, good-time girl, free spirit? Strong body. Arresting face. Sparkling eyes. Good luck to me, he thought.

CHAPTER NINE

Immediately Philomena feared that she was about to be found out – she didn't even know the correct reply. She didn't really know enough about how a woman like Felicity spoke or lived or ate when mixing privately. She had no proper idea about any of it. The girl playing the girl in the play had had lines to recite and weeks of rehearsal. Felicity could hardly say 'What fun!' in response to everything Anthony said.

'I'm okay,' she risked.

'"Okay." How American,' said Anthony.

'Everybody's saying it, aren't they?'

'Not everybody's saying it, no,' said Anthony. 'But there are lots of things that not everybody is saying.'

What did she think about Anthony so far? He was almost handsome, and very posh, but there was something brittle underneath; he wasn't quite balanced. What stopped him being handsome was that he wasn't quite tall enough, nor broad enough, and his mouth wasn't right – too wide, and his eyes were pinched in the corners. It wasn't a list of calamities but, assembled in this one person, with what he gave off, it added up to a sense of not quite rightness.

The waitress arrived with the drinks; Felicity's rum and black and his Scotch. After she'd gone there was an awkward moment whilst Philomena and Anthony searched around for conversational re-openers.

'It's my first time here,' she offered, as Felicity.

'What do you think of the place?' asked Anthony, sounding a little like he was claiming responsibility for it.

'It seems okay,' agreed Philomena, and she summoned a smile to let Anthony know that she was teasing him in saying okay again so soon.

'How did you hear about it?'

'Oh. You know,' she said, buying time – wondering whether to make up a name of someone, immediately deciding not to because it could lead to a whole series of other questions. 'Gossip.' To engage both hands, she rolled her glass between her palms.

'They don't make it easy to find, do they?' said Anthony.

'Well you can't be too careful, can you?' warned Philomena, taking a big sip of her drink, and thinking, this is 'okay'; Felicity's a tease. She's enigmatic.

'You can't, can you?' said Anthony, widening his already wide mouth in a smile, and she got the feeling that he was trying to play but it wasn't quite coming off.

'Not everyone deserves to be admitted,' she said, artfully raising an eyebrow. 'And St Peter's on the gate.' Immediately she kicked herself hard – she risked being found out because she didn't know the name of the club they were in.

'D'you think Peter is the doorman's real name or one he's

adopted for The Gates of Heaven?' said Anthony Dore, pleased with his wit.

The Gates of Heaven, thought Philomena, thank you. And her broad smile of relief was misinterpreted by Anthony as an invitation to move in.

'What do you do?' asked Anthony. He'd leaned forward slightly, and he had a new expression on his face. He'd put a bit more emphasis on the word 'do' than was strictly necessary, trying too hard to be suggestive. Philomena imagined he wanted Felicity's reply to be something along the lines of 'anything you like'. He was looking at her hands for the first time as they encircled her glass. Ladies' hands don't have scrabby nails and rough pads to the fingers, evolved to resist the pricks of sewing needles and pins.

'I'm an artist,' she blurted out — it sounded so to her - inventing Felicity's occupation on the spot.

'I bet you are,' said Anthony.

She placed her glass on the table next to her, folded her hands in her lap, said: 'I know, it's ruined them,' before catching on that he was being lascivious. For a moment he looked perplexed.

'A real artist?' he asked.

'Yes.'

Anthony was disappointed. He'd thought she was saying she was another sort of artist. In bed. He rallied, asked: 'What sort of art?'

What sort of art? He might be an expert. The rich all had the odd Old Master hanging on the wall, didn't they?

'I don't categorise it, really.'

'Modern stuff,' said Anthony.

Philomena felt truly, deeply up to her neck in it. The door was to her left; she could make it in four swift strides.

From somewhere she dredged: 'Well, yes. I am making it now, so it is modern. What's your line?'

'I suppose you could say I'm in business.'

'Which is . . .'

'Business. Stuff. Money.' He waved a hand dismissively.

'Stuff?' asked Philomena.

'Too boring. How would you describe your art?'

'How would you describe your business, stuff, money?'

Anthony paused. Very well, she needs certain reassurances. 'More than sufficient,' he replied. 'That's how I'd describe my business, stuff, money.' He widened his eyes and inclined his head, warning her that that was all she needed to know. 'So, your art; describe it.'

'I express myself,' Philomena said, as Felicity, petrified behind her smile.

'Oh yes?' he teased.

'I let my secrets out.' There, she'd introduced the idea of secrets.

'So you don't have any secrets,' asked Anthony, grinning.

'Oh, I do,' said Philomena, flaring her eyes.

'But you let them out, you said,' said Anthony, hooked.

'There's an endless supply. My secrets are replenished on a daily basis.'

'Better out than in,' said Anthony, shifting in his seat, hoping she might say something like 'better in than out' and they could proceed from there.

'Is that your motto?' she asked, deliberately leaning forward slightly, wetting her lips with a quick flick of her tongue.

Anthony also leaned forward, mirroring her. 'Where did you go before you found this place?'

'Somewhere else that I liked,' she fired back.

'This sort of place?' he asked, lewdly.

'What sort of place is this?' she asked, mock innocent.

'Uninhibited. Illegal,' said Anthony.

'It's terrible that it's illegal to be uninhibited,' she replied, revelling in her lasciviousness.

'Isn't it just,' said Anthony, smiling broadly. 'Where are you from?' he asked, looking Felicity square in the face, and Philomena immediately panicked that he'd heard a trace of her true accent underneath her rapidly evolving alter-ego's.

'That's a secret,' she said, trying to keep the flirtation alive.

'Where do you live?' asked Anthony.

And whereas Philomena thought that this question also indicated that Anthony Dore had smelled a rat, in fact he was enquiring if she had a place to which they might retire in order to have sex.

'That's a secret, too,' she said, suddenly feeling absolutely disgusted with herself, and him – though she couldn't blame him for thinking Felicity might be willing – and disgusted with the place they were in, and for a moment she considered telling him the truth about herself and putting him right on the spot simply by asking him directly if Jonathan Priest's allegation was true.

'Are you really an artist?' he asked.

'Yes. No.'

Instead of looking bemused by her contradiction, he seemed to take it as evidence that the game of 'will we do it?' continued.

'Which?' he begged, and Philomena loathed him. And she knew that when Dan and he had met they would have loathed each other.

'I have to go,' she said, suddenly standing up.

'What?'

She didn't answer him – she gathered herself and began to walk away without any sort of farewell and without looking at him.

Anthony realised that he was also on his feet, and that the waitress was watching him, frowning. Felicity was already at the top of the stairs, beginning to descend. Anthony resisted the urge to run after her. What the hell happened there? he asked himself. Other people were looking at him. They must be thinking he'd said or done something, but he hadn't. That Felicity should come back and finish her drink and then they'd know that he hadn't done anything. What on earth was going on? They'd been getting along famously, enjoying a terrific time together, and now people were staring at him! He prepared to hurry down the stairs after her but the waitress cried: 'Your bill, sir!' and he had to stop to pay the bitch.

Philomena was on the first-floor landing, on the way down to the entrance, trying not to attract attention to herself but moving more quickly than is normal. St Peter glanced up and saw her and looked immediately concerned. Realising that she wouldn't be able to avoid a short exchange with him, Philomena glanced back to make sure Anthony wasn't following.

'Did you find Daniel?' asked St Peter.

She glanced back again for fear that if Anthony Dore was following her he could have heard that.

'No,' she said, trying to sound not too disappointed.

'Is everything all right?' asked St Peter.

'Oh yes,' she said, brightly. 'I'll be back another time, if that's all right.'

'You had fun?'

'Oh yes. What fun!' Did that sound too shrill?

'You haven't collected your coat.'

There she was, trying to act as if nothing were wrong, about to leave without her coat. She tried to compose herself as she walked back to the cloakroom where the attendant had retrieved her garment and now helped her on with it. St Peter smiled and opened the front door for her and she walked out, resisting the urge to run. When she heard the door close behind her she quickened her step to the road. A taxi was passing so she threw up an arm and it stopped. When it rolled away from The Gates of Heaven she sank back in her seat and deliberately exhaled because she hadn't been breathing freely for some time.

The streets were dark, sparsely peopled. They passed a row of shops. In a little garden or square off to the side she saw the flames of a bonfire, and men, like statues, warming themselves at it. They looked mostly young, dressed in military uniforms. Nearby at a night kitchen, hands holding ladles dished liquid into mugs offered up. For a moment she thought she glimpsed the soldier she and Jonathan had cut down – she almost called for the taxi driver to stop – but when she saw the boy's face clearly in the flickering light it wasn't him but one similar: another young, gaunt and pale.

Was she in peril from meeting Anthony? She didn't think so. He had no idea who she really was. Should she find Jonathan to tell him she'd met Anthony Dore and her opinion of him? What was the point of that? She was never going to meet Anthony Dore again, either as Felicity or herself. Failed plan. Objective not achieved. It wasn't as if she could make him tell her anything, was it?

As she entered The Whitehall, exhaustion washed over her. The porter barely acknowledged her whilst handing over the key. He was a surly one; greasy, spotty, who despite his obvious deficiencies arrogantly tried to give off that he shouldn't be here as he was too good for the place. Philomena idly wondered if night staff were chosen for their disagreeableness, or if the unnatural world of nocturnal work had made this one the way he was. Dropping her key in her hired bag she began to climb the stairs, wishing she were going to her own bed, using the hand rail as an aid to lift her tired body.

Anthony watched Felicity from outside the front doors. He hadn't arrived at his vantage point in time to see if she'd retrieved a key or spoken to the staff. Was Felicity staying there, or visiting? It was a rather shabby place. The porter moved out of Anthony's view and didn't reappear. Anthony decided not to make inquiries about Felicity. He'd simply follow her, corner her, and demand to know why she'd walked out on him so abruptly. He slipped in through the entrance doors, swiftly crossed the foyer, and started up the stairway.

Almost asleep on her feet Philomena was taking the last steps to her room when a figure stepped out of the shadows, startling her. She stifled a gasp.

'Phil?'

'Jonathan . . .'

He stood back and looked her up and down. 'Gosh. You look . . .'

'I went shopping,' she said, truthfully, feeling somewhat guilty, then telling herself not to feel that.

'Didn't you just!' said Jonathan, no hint of disapproval in his voice. But there was a question.

'It's all hired.'

Flustered, she rootled in the folds of her unfamiliar bag for the key. She wasn't sure how she felt about finding that Jonathan had been waiting for her; checking up on her. She remembered to remember that he didn't know about Felicity, or about her having met Anthony Dore.

'My key,' still rootling.

'You've lost it?'

'I can't find it.'

Jonathan watched her search in her bag, relieved that she hadn't just told him to get lost.

She'd forgotten her intention never to speak to him again, and she knew she looked fantastic, if a little jaded. She thought that he must have been wondering where on earth she'd been to that time, dressed like that. It must have looked as if mourning Dan was quite low on her list.

A stairway down, Anthony Dore could hear the soft noises and the occasional sound from two voices, a man's and a woman's. He heard the woman distinctly say 'got them' and the man mutter something. Anthony heard a key in a lock. Believing they were about to enter a room, desperate to see if it was Felicity and a man, he inched towards the corner of the landing.

'Can I come in?' asked Jonathan, on the threshold. 'There's something I need to tell you, that I wasn't quite straight about last night.'

'I don't know,' she said.

He held his hands up to show he presented no threat.

'How long have you been waiting?' she asked.

'Not long really,' said Jonathan. 'I wondered if you wanted supper. I could tell you about this thing.'

'It's too late for supper, now.'

'Yes, but it wasn't when I first thought about it.'

'Very well.' She opened her door and stepped in.

'Thanks,' said Jonathan, following her inside.

★ ★ ★

Anthony peeped around the corner, just glimpsing the man's heels before the door shut behind him. He waited, went to the door and listened from a few feet away. He couldn't hear anything from inside room four oh seven. He didn't even know if it was Felicity in there.

Inside the room Jonathan stood awkwardly, unsure where to put himself. Philomena perched on the edge of the bed, removed her shoes, rubbed her feet, wondering whether she should tell Jonathan anything of her adventures. He looked out towards the shabby young soldier's window, and said: 'I was wondering about the boy, the young sol—'

'I don't know,' she said, meaning she didn't know what had happened to him.

'Oh, I do,' said Jonathan. 'He'll survive, they tell me at the hospital.'

'You went to see him?'

'Yes.'

'Good. I'm glad.' Glad the boy would survive and glad Jonathan went to see him. It hadn't crossed her mind to do so.

'His name is William Rust. He's nineteen.'

'I thought he was about that age. Did you find out why?'

'No. He's not speaking yet. His throat, you know. And they didn't find a note.'

'Poor lad. I thought I saw him earlier, in the street.'

'I'm going to try and get him off. No point in charging him with attempted suicide.'

She nodded. No, no point. There was something familiar about Jonathan being there. It was quiet.

'Do you mind me being here?' he asked.

'No,' she replied, surprised he asked that. Had she been telling him she did mind without meaning to?

'Look, I should go,' he said. 'You must think I'm mad. I wondered if you wanted supper and then I lost track.'

'I would have liked supper with you,' she said quietly, almost to herself, watching Jonathan's eye fall on something. He stopped moving towards the door and dipped his head towards the photo of Dan smoking a stick.

'This is good.'

'Isn't it,' she said, not wanting him to go. 'But you said there was another reason other than supper you wanted to see me.'

Jonathan patted his pockets. 'I've got something of his, somewhere.'

Outside the room, Anthony Dore could hear the man's voice had moved closer and he could almost make out a few words, but he could also hear footfalls coming up the stairs. He was going to have to move away – and fast – if he wasn't to be caught snooping. He took off in the opposite direction from the approaching feet. As he walked further down the corridor he could tell that they had left the stairs and were walking behind him. Accelerating as much as he could without breaking into a run, for that would advertise his guilt, he saw a door marked exit that he pushed open, hoping that it looked as if he knew where he was going. Behind the door lay an uninviting service stairway. He gave in to panic and began to run down, on the verge of tripping, taking the steps two, three, or even four at a time.

Inside four oh seven Jonathan's hand emerged from his pocket and Philomena was astonished to see that it was holding a photograph of her. She had been about to reach out her hand to take whatever it was that Jonathan had of Dan's but now she didn't know what to do. Jonathan twitched the photo back and forth as if unable to decide what to do with it, either. He tried to joke: 'I expect you know what you look like.'

'That's me in a previous life,' she said.

Jonathan carefully placed the photograph of her on the bedside table next to the photograph of Dan.

'Was that the thing?' she asked, suspecting that that photo couldn't have been the thing he'd said he hadn't been straight about last night.

'Cognac!' said Jonathan loudly, flourishing a hip flask. 'Fancy one?'

She shook her head. Jonathan took a big swig then reached in another pocket for something else. It was a pack of cards held together in a plastic band.

'These are the cards,' he said.

It took her a moment to catch on. 'The cards from the game?'

Jonathan nodded. 'The alleged game. I didn't let on last night that I still had them.'

Philomena immediately wanted to touch them, hold them.

With great reverence, Jonathan handed the pack to her. 'You can remove the band.'

Philomena slipped it off and around her wrist, then didn't know how to hold the cards.

'You're thinking about fingerprints, aren't you?' said Jonathan. 'There aren't any. I stole Dore's to test them. Got them off a glass in a bar. But these cards are too battered and sweaty and scarred to give a reliable result.'

'That's a pity,' she said with feeling. 'That's a damned shame.'

'He would have claimed any fingerprints were from another game, on another day,' said Jonathan, resignedly.

'But you said he and Major Chiltern hadn't met before in the war,' said Philomena, countering his apathy.

'My word against his, again. He would also have argued that I couldn't prove that Major Chiltern had always owned the cards, so he, Anthony Dore, could have played a hand with a previous owner. Or that Major Chiltern had lent them to another man with whom Dore played cards. Basically, if it isn't possible to trace the pack from new and prove that they had only ever been in Major Chiltern's possession then even a crystal clear set of Anthony Dore's prints on them wouldn't suffice.'

Philomena felt more guilty that she wasn't telling Jonathan about meeting Anthony. To cover it she fanned the cards and said: 'Everyone plays brag. It's not a proper game like poker or something.'

Jonathan glanced at her for confirmation that this was a non sequitur.

'Yes, there's no strategy to brag that I can see,' he agreed. 'Once the cards are dealt it's just bloody-mindedness.'

At which Dan had excelled, thought Philomena. Jonathan took another swig of cognac from his hip flask.

'Damn Major Chiltern. If only he'd mentioned it or written to anybody about the run up to that card game. Dore couldn't have known that he hadn't when he lied that there wasn't a game. Lucky bastard. I put an ad in the *Times* – anonymously. Asking for anyone who'd spoken to Major Chiltern on his last day, or received any letter from him, to reply – also anonymously if they wished.'

'Anthony Dore's lack of guile might indicate that he isn't using any, that he has no need to,' said Philomena.

Jonathan studied her, his eyes piercing hers for once. 'Are you playing devil's advocate?' he mused. Before she could answer he added, 'You're right to be sceptical.'

She didn't know what more to do with the cards so she replaced the elastic band and handed the pack back to Jonathan. Both resumed looking out of the window. A distant door banged shut. Faint footsteps.

'Can I ask you something?' she said, warming to a subject that had been nagging at her.

Jonathan looked at her, scared. But: 'Yes,' he said.

'How seriously did you think about killing yourself?'

Jonathan glanced out towards William Rust's window. Then he couldn't return Philomena's gaze. He gulped some cognac. 'I'm still here.'

He looked hounded, cornered, did something, fought it, made some shift inside, shrugged.

'After my allegations were dismissed I went on a bit of a bender. I wanted to do something, to act, but there was no clear thing to do. The war had ended, the guns were silent, there were no more explosions, but I felt all that was still going on inside me. I tried to write you a letter but I couldn't get the wording right. I know I sent you one eventually but it was very much diluted. By the way, may I have a look at Dore's letter to you?'

She knew exactly where it was so it only took a moment to find and hand over. Jonathan read it, shaking his head.

'The next day,' he went on, 'I went to Dan's makeshift grave where it said, "killed in action" and I thought, this just won't do, this just isn't on, this is a lie.' He handed Dore's letter back to Philomena. 'I looked for Major James but he'd already packed up and gone. I didn't even know if anyone else was aware of my allegations. But soon I had a visit from a chaplain named Gillies. It didn't go well. He offered me comfort; I asked him what he thought was the truth about my allegation. He said he didn't know what I was talking about. He'd heard I was in difficulty. I think he knew that I'd made an allegation, but not what it was. He told me that I should tread carefully – I should know that, especially as I had been a barrister before the war. I asked him what he was before the war, a man of God? I started swearing a bit I'm afraid. I said, "You fucking believe me though, don't you, God-man? I can see it in your eyes. Even though you might not know the sordid details, you know that what I alleged is true." You can see how far gone I was, how close to the edge. He swore back at me; "I dinna fucking will inything, actually," he said. Fair play to the chaplain. He was Scottish. I can't do a Scottish accent. But he said: "The fucking war's over and I'm going to go home and forget aboot it and if I wis you, I'd do the same. Forget it, drop it, or you will ruin your promising career." To which I inquired if the chaplain had been offered a nice little tenure somewhere. I was just being out and out rude by now so he turned on his heel and muttered something about praying for me. I remember shouting at his back: "I'm going to tell God about you!"'

Jonathan tutted and shook his head as if to say: What was I thinking of?

'Next thing, I found myself almost arrested for fraternising with the enemy. The military police had to prevent me from sauntering over to the German lines to inquire if any of them were witnesses to Dan's death. I don't know,' said Jonathan, scratching his ear. 'When I was sitting one night, a bit tipsy, back here in London, thinking about . . . It's huge emotions with no outlet . . . Anyway, I didn't do it. Here I stand before you, as proof. Nor did I tell God about anything. I would have done, once. I used to argue with atheists who challenged me to prove the existence of God. No one can, of course. Prove it. Now I feel the same certainty about Anthony Dore's guilt that I used to feel about the existence of God. I know it's true but I can't prove it. Perhaps one day I'll stop believing in Dore's guilt, too.'

Jonathan drained his cognac and confirmed the flask was

empty by holding it upside down. Philomena could see that the large quantities of spirit taken in such a short time were acting as a sedative. He reached in a pocket and withdrew another flask that he proceeded to open.

'Don't,' she said. 'You're killing yourself this way, instead,' she admonished. 'Lie down.'

'Hmm?' mumbled Jonathan, his eyelids becoming heavy.

'You're almost out. Lie down on the bed.'

'I gotta go,' mumbled Jonathan, stumbling.

'Lie down,' she repeated, laying hands on him.

Jonathan had no strength and no balance. He couldn't resist being steered to the bed. It was a very awkward manoeuvre. Both parties were anxious to avoid over-familiarity. Jonathan lowered himself down to sitting on the bed and proceeded to lie down. He tried to keep his feet on the floor, which meant he was twisted, his back on the bed, his thighs and calves to the side. Philomena, in a businesslike fashion, slipped his shoes off, lifted his legs onto the bed so he could lie straight.

'Might you be sick?' she asked.

'I hope not,' said Jonathan, attempting a feeble smile. 'I need all the alcohol to enter my bloodstream.'

She helped him wriggle off his coat. Almost out, he tried to speak: 'Promise me . . .'

'Promise you what?'

'You must never . . .'

She bent closer and believed that he said, 'not all his fault' but she couldn't be sure.

She stood looking down on him for a good while until sure he was asleep. She went to the chair and pulled it up to the window. It was a still night. Her hands moved slowly in the air, circling.

A bit later she tried to sleep in the chair.

A bit later she lay on the bed alongside Jonathan, making sure they couldn't touch by placing a pillow between them.

Later, still unable to sleep, she was propped up on one elbow. In repose Jonathan's hair had fallen off his forehead, revealing a scar. She traced the straight line of it in the air, just above it, thinking that it might be from the wound he received when he met Dan. After a while she fell asleep.

Jonathan woke, bleary-eyed, mouth familiarly furry. Warm breath was kissing his ear. Shocked, he sat up and looked down on the slumbering form nearly next to him. A pillow separated Philomena's body from his.

He carefully extricated himself, easing himself down the bed between her and the wall and off the end. He took up his coat and hat and slipped on his shoes without bothering to do up the laces. He looked down on her. Her stomach gently rose and fell. When he went in closer to her face, he could discern a tiny feather that had escaped the counterpane. It vibrated as she inhaled and exhaled. The privilege he felt being able to see her asleep filled him with tenderness.

'Sleeping beauty,' he breathed.

★   ★   ★

When Philomena awoke she was alone. The photo of her was still lying there, next to Dan's and the sheaf of papers. Jonathan hadn't taken it back.

She rose and removed Felicity's clothes, put on her dressing gown, went down the hall for a wash and came back to her room and dressed as herself. Downstairs at hotel reception she booked another night in the same room.

She went to a cafe and ate breakfast, relieved to not be the only female so doing. She tried to think clearly about what she most wanted and how she might achieve it. Outside in the street a coalman's wagon threatened to shed its load because the horses had taken fright. A motor car was trying to reverse out of the range of the animals' flailing hooves. Philomena thought of Jonathan: infuriating, a drunk, and damaged; but also intelligent, attractive and humane. She thought of Dan. There was a glass of water by her on the cafe table. She drained it and put it upside down on the table, her index finger upon it. She asked Dan if he'd been murdered by Anthony Dore. If the answer was yes she asked Dan to move the glass. To make the glass move . . . It didn't. Was the wet on the glass a hindrance? She tried with a dry glass . . . Still nothing. She shook her head, looked around, thinking that if anyone had witnessed that display they'd be entitled to think her deranged.

CHAPTER TEN

When Anthony entered Felicity's hotel and approached reception he had a box of chocolates tight under his arm. He smiled at the porter – not the one he'd seen the previous night – and asked for Felicity by forename. 'Surname?' the porter asked. Anthony didn't know. The day porter frowned and said that as far as he knew there wasn't a woman by that forename in the hotel; he didn't generally know guests by their forenames. Anthony asked if it was possible there was a young female guest with green eyes. The day porter's eyes narrowed. He was clearly suspicious. Perhaps this woman was in room four oh seven, ventured Anthony, closely watching the day porter's expression for any sign that he was right. Did sir believe that a woman named Felicity, in possession of green eyes, stayed in room four oh seven? asked the day porter. Anthony had to reiterate that he didn't know. So let me get this straight, said the day porter. There's a woman. She's named Felicity – is sir sure of that? Yes. Felicity has green eyes? Yes. Sir's not sure she stays here, but thinks she might be in four oh seven. Why did sir think such a woman might be in that particular room?

What could Anthony reply to that? I followed her but lost her then eavesdropped on a man and woman entering that room? Better to say nothing. The day porter tapped a fingernail on the desk, took up a pen. What was sir's name, first name and surname? Anthony felt his confidence drain away. There was no question of giving his real name. It was all he could do to look the impertinent fellow in the eye. Upping his accent a couple of notches Anthony gave the porter a false name, and himself a title. The day porter's eyes narrowed further and he wrinkled his nose, sniffed, as if fraud was an odour. It was clear that he wasn't going to give this obvious conman anything. Would sir care to leave a note and the chocolates in case the day porter discovered a guest was named Felicity and she had green eyes, and if so, she was the Felicity with green eyes to whom sir referred? Anthony Dore stared at the impudent cur for a few moments without seeing any sign that he might crumble. He left without a word. The day porter shook his head.

Philomena stood, smiling, on the raised triangle of pavement in the centre of Piccadilly Circus, enjoying the sunshine on her face. She closed her eyes and it felt warmer. In her ears the roar of circulating motor traffic, the clip-clop of horses, the grinding of cart wheels on the road, the verbal buzz made by crowds of strangers. Feeling the wind rise, she opened her eyes. Angry-looking clouds, off-white and slate, sped in from the north and crossed the blue-grey sky. When they passed in front of the sun the temperature immediately dropped. She shivered. Three young soldiers seated on the top deck of an omnibus doffed their caps to her. She blushed and turned away, and felt guilty that she'd been caught standing still, dreaming. With purpose in her step, she set off.

The American woman's art gallery was in a part of London that looked similar to parts of Manchester but felt quite different. The capital had a sense of vast spread, of mass, but no topography, hills that Philomena could either see or sense, no natural features or boundaries bar the river. In London, she had no sense of how long she would have to walk to get out of it. By the open door of the art gallery hung a hand-painted sign proclaiming 'Participation Event' in large letters. She lined herself up so she could see inside. A handful of people looked on as others wrestled with something at floor level. She drew closer until she could make out that they were fashioning a sort of relief out of brown clay. She didn't see the gallery owner until she heard the American voice inviting her in. 'Come and have a look,' the woman called, completely unselfconsciously. A few members of the audience looked up towards her and smiled. They were dressed arty, the men in soft suits, the women in Romany colours. Philomena timidly entered.

There were three people wrestling with the clay: one middle-aged woman and two young men. They were on the clay and in it. Moulding it, tearing it, shaping it. It was a kind of landscape. Philomena could see that the woman was guiding the young men, but they were instigating what emerged. She took that it was a depiction of a battlefield, with trenches and chewed up ground, and lumps, little lumps everywhere on its surface. As she bent closer she was startled to realise that each was recognisably a figure of a man. She looked to the American woman.

'It's great, isn't it!' she enthused.

One of the young men began to drive his heel into the clay, grinding something down. The mood darkened. The other soldier joined in with him and the energy levels leapt. They couldn't grind or stamp hard enough. All the spectators took a few steps backwards. One of the soldiers hurt himself he was stamping so violently – he clutched his leg. The other went to him and put his arm on his shoulder and they stood there, chests heaving, like beasts that had been running.

After she left the gallery Philomena headed for Jonathan's chambers. She wanted to tell him about the clay landscape. From Jones she discovered that he was in court. When she seated herself in the public gallery a man was in the dock, mid-speech. Jonathan was in his seat, and the other barrister, the prosecution, was on his feet, nodding as the man in the dock went on: 'So then I went round. I admit I went round there but that's where their story and mine diverge because their story is a story whereas my story is the truth.'

Jonathan looked up towards Philomena. He had a brightness in his eyes. He looked at the man in the dock and back to Philomena. He gestured with his hands, mouthed something. She cupped her hand to her ear and gestured, 'What?' Jonathan made a weighing gesture with his hands and she guessed that he was asking her if the man was being truthful. She watched the man properly for a bit longer.

'They say that when I went round or from their point of view came round I was in a rage; they said in fact that they expected me to be in a rage, which indicated that they thought I had some justification to be in a rage—'

Jonathan looked up and she gave the thumbs down as her verdict on the veracity of that individual.

A powerful voice boomed out: 'Is this going anywhere?'

She looked towards the owner of the voice, the judge. The smile fell from her face and she half rose from her seat. She recognised him, from two previous sightings; in court, presiding over Jonathan's previous case, and he was the older man she had seen leaving Anthony Dore's address. Jonathan raised his palms towards her and patted the air, a 'stay calm' gesture, and he was mouthing, 'Wait for me.'

In the area where public and professionals mingle Jonathan sat down beside Philomena and confirmed that the judge was indeed connected to Anthony Dore. He was his father. And previously, he had been Jonathan's mentor.

'What?!' was all she could say.

Jonathan ran his hand through his hair and bent forward to lean on his knees as if he had belly cramps. He started saying something else that only came to her as a mumble. She had to incline towards him in order to hear: 'I was in judge Dore's chambers before the war. When I met Anthony Dore that day in the trench I guessed he must be my mentor's son.'

Her mind was racing to assimilate the ramifications of all this new information.

'If I'd revealed at the time that I knew his father, it might not have happened. There were several times when I almost managed to get it out, but the moments passed. Anthony Dore is nothing like his father – that's why I didn't say anything to you. Why bring the father into it? It didn't seem important – if Anthony Dore killed Dan, his father had nothing to do with it.'

'Does he know about your allegation?'

'I don't know,' said Jonathan. 'If he does he's never let on.' He shrugged and spread his hands. 'What difference does it make? Judge for a father or no judge for a father, there isn't any proof against Anthony Dore.'

Irritated that Jonathan had not only withheld relevant information but was also telling her how to interpret it, Philomena snapped, 'What were you trying to say last night when you fell into your self-pitying drunken stupor?'

Jonathan looked sharply at her. 'I was too drunk to remember.'

'Something about me promising to never something. Not his fault or something.'

'Did I say that?'

'That's what it could have been.'

'I've no idea what I was saying. When I'm drunk, there are doors in my mind that aren't open when I'm sober.'

They turned away from each other.

'What else haven't you told me?' she snarled sideways.

Even though nobody had called for him, Jonathan stood and said that he had to get back. There followed a wretched moment when either he or Philomena might have reached out, but neither did. Jonathan walked away. Philomena felt like weeping, or smashing something.

Jonathan entered the private areas of the courts and sank down onto the first available bench. He leaned forwards again, his head in his hands. He hadn't any dope on him. He couldn't have a drink. He was miserable. Someone halted by him.

'Everything all right?' asked Judge Dore.

Jonathan sat up and rose to his feet.

'Yes, sir.'

'Are you sure?'

'Yes, sir.'

The judge searched Jonathan's face, unconvinced.

'We're due in. I should sort yourself out.'

Jonathan nodded and the judge smiled and moved on. But something occurred to him and he came back.

'Is it a problem at your new chambers?'

'No, sir,' replied Jonathan.

'Shame, we might have tempted you back.' A mischievous twinkle came into the judge's eye. 'In that case, in my experience, there are only two things in life that can induce that sort of abject misery in a man: women and money.'

'It's a bit of both,' said Jonathan, hoping that that would be an end to it.

'You have my sympathy,' said Judge Dore, ploughing on.

'If I can be of any assistance, let me know.' The last he said cheerfully – too cheerfully for Jonathan.

'I wouldn't want any of your money. It's not about the money.'

Judge Dore's brow furrowed. Jonathan had sounded truly angry. They stood looking at each other for a few moments. Jonathan imagined telling judge Dore about his son. When the judge said, 'What the hell are you talking about, Priest?' for a moment he feared that he had told him.

'I meant that I didn't need you to help me with money, sir,' he stuttered.

'I wasn't really offering to, Priest, it was just a manner of speech. I wasn't offering you money any more than I was about to offer to supply you with a less troublesome woman than that which you are plagued by.'

'I'm sorry. I misunderstood.'

Judge Dore softened. He wasn't a bad man, Jonathan thought. 'It was a mutual misunderstanding. And there's really no problem with your new chambers?'

Before Jonathan could reply a clerk appeared.

'See you in there,' said Perceval Dore. 'I'll hold them off for two minutes. Use the time.'

'Yes, sir. Thank you, sir.'

As dusk fell again Philomena set foot on the southern approach to Waterloo Bridge. The many boats and barges plying the Thames had begun to show all their lights, yellow and white. Stretched reflections rippled on black water. She'd walked miles, criss-crossing north and south, killing time. Weary and hungry, her feet hurt. The evening's rising damp gave wet thickness to the air. This little added resistance, she was convinced, further hindered her already laborious progress.

Leaning against the wall of the bridge she felt empty, run out, and that it wouldn't matter if she tipped over into the depths below. She again had a strong desire to experience a fall through space – a few free, weightless moments. A boat underneath, sliding under the bridge, pulled at her and she leaned over more. White faces angled up, their hands going to their mouths, and she sent her weight backwards.

After that it took her she didn't know how long waiting, doing absolutely nothing, barely breathing, before she recovered the strength necessary to walk on to the Strand, where she gratefully caught a bus travelling in the direction of her hotel, alighting once in order to purchase suitable make-up.

A transformation later, St Peter smiled broadly and bowed low as he ushered her inside The Gates of Heaven.

'Have you found Daniel?'

'Not yet, but I've an address for him now. "The Lion's Den".'

'Our sister club,' replied St Peter, quick as a flash.

On the first floor Anthony came directly over to her. 'I'm so pleased to see you here again, Felicity.'

She was momentarily wrong-footed by the warmth of his welcome. 'Oh, hello, Anthony.'

'Are you meeting anyone or are you free to pass the time with me?' he said, steering her to some seats.

Almost recoiling from Anthony's touch she masked the impulse and let him guide her.

'Would you like a drink?'

She asked for a lemonade.

'That won't make you very relaxed, will it?' quipped Anthony.

'That might not be my aim,' she said, as Felicity, trying to summon up a hint of flirtatiousness.

'Yesterday evening you were about to tell me whether or not you really are an artist,' said Anthony.

'Does it matter?'

'I don't know,' replied Anthony.

'I am an artist. That's *all* I do.'

Anthony looked to see if she was making some kind of joke by putting so much emphasis on the 'all'. No, she was clearly making a point.

'Oh,' he said. 'Then why are you here?'

'Because I like it here.'

'Oh,' repeated Anthony, at a loss. 'It was pretty odd the way you got up and left last night.'

She shrugged as if to say, 'That's me.'

'Did I say something?' he asked, clearly irked.

'No.'

'Did you suddenly discover that you disliked me?' He was trying to remain level but his eyes and mouth were fixed. Philomena felt a flash of danger from him.

'No,' as candidly as she could.

'It was nothing about me?'

'No,' direct to him again. Would that settle it?

'Have you a neurosis that causes you to behave in that manner?'

'Do I have a what?'

'Do you know what a neurosis is?'

'Not exactly.'

'It's an irrational anxiety or obsession. Did you suddenly become anxious last evening?'

Why wouldn't he shut up? She was going to have to give him a better answer than just saying 'no' to everything.

'To tell the truth,' she said, 'I did become anxious, suddenly. That I was doing the wrong thing with the wrong man in the wrong place.'

'Go on,' said Anthony, less aggressively.

'I've never been anywhere like this before,' she said, slipping a needy undertone into her voice.

'Ahhh.' She was a novice. Now he understood.

'But I am lonely,' now inviting his forgiveness.

'I know what you mean. But people who saw what you did, they must have thought I had said or done something.'

'I'm sorry for that.'

'You're sorry for it?'

'Yes.'

She watched him suddenly brighten. This was a different Anthony, lighter, more alive. Antagonism sloughed off him. It was as if he'd been enveloped in a thick coat of it and now that it was cast off he could come alive.

'All right, I forgive you.'

'Thank you, Anthony, that is sweet of you.'

'Don't mention it. It's the war, isn't it?'

'What's the war?'

'It's set us a few problems. How to live, that sort of thing.'

My God, thought Philomena. Is this the same man? He seemed so in earnest, so genuine, so likeable.

Across the room Jonathan had stopped mid-stride and his mouth was wide open. He was unable to believe his own eyes. Philomena, sat chatting with Anthony Dore? Them laughing together? He retreated before either of them saw him, pressing himself to the wall. He wanted to become flat, to merge with the hard plaster. He stole a look. Dore was leaning forward to touch Philomena's arm and she was letting him and they were both smiling – no two ways about it – they were flirting! Philomena was flirting with Anthony Dore! Jonathan had to get away.

There was a drape to his left – slide behind it – but it concealed something; his head struck it. An electrical fuse box. Did it have an on/off switch?

'You know, Felicity,' confided Anthony, 'I've been thinking about you a lot today.'

His cold hand on her knee.

'Get your hand off there.'

Anthony looked at her for a moment before lifting his hand. Smirking, he placed it on her thigh.

'Get it off there or I'll hurt you,' she told him.

'Promises, promises,' said Anthony, a steely glare in his eye.

Fear rose from Philomena's belly. Suddenly the lights went out.

There was panic as people in mid-movement collided with each other. Some screamed. Men and women called out the names of those from whom they were separated, and 'I'm over here!' 'Where?' and 'Someone put the lights back on!' and 'Ow!' and 'Help!'

Philomena seized the opportunity to extricate her thigh from Anthony's hand. He, however, seemed to think that the surrounding mayhem and the darkness was his opportunity to take a better hold of her. She felt his hands on her waist, her breast. She tried to punch his face in the jet blackness but her arm was trapped against the chair by a falling body. Other bodies rolled into her and away. More screams and names called in terrified voices; panic infecting, spreading like a virus, other voices crying, 'Stay still! Stay still everyone! Don't move!'

She tried to protect herself by getting to her feet but Anthony followed suit. Now they were being buffeted by humans on the verge of stampede, desperately searching for a way out. Someone could die in there, crushed, trampled to death underfoot and Anthony was still trying to take a hold on her. She freed an arm and reached for her hatpin. Some of the more self-possessed patrons fired their cigarette lighters and held them up so there were glimpses of people's heads. She felt a hand again on her waist, sliding down towards her buttocks – she didn't like it at all and called: 'Anthony?' He replied, 'Yes!' and she tensed her muscles to stab him when a hand gripped her arm, stayed her blow. Jonathan's voice in her ear hissed: 'Don't.' Again: 'Don't.'

In the darkness she submitted and slackened, allowing Jonathan to guide her away from Anthony, moving against the herd. Anthony grabbed for her and tried to latch on again, calling 'Felicity, is this you?' She felt him brush her bare arm, seize it and for a moment she was in the grip of both Jonathan and Anthony, in the dark, in the panicked crowd. She snapped her wrist and twisted out of Anthony's grasp, and went with Jonathan.

They pressed their way through the crowd that was pouring down the stairs like water that had suddenly found a fall until he glimpsed his dope supplier and her guard pushing a side door open. They would have a nifty way out. He headed after them and found the door led onto a fire escape. Jonathan let go of Philomena once they were on the iron steps. The two ahead descended to the safety of the ground, but Jonathan strode up the escape. Philomena could tell he was furious. His back was rigid. He turned his head once to make sure she was following. She could understand Jonathan being shocked to find her in there with Anthony Dore, if he saw her before the lights went – he must have done; he never would have found her in the dark without knowing she was there to be found. Except he was there in The Gates of Heaven too, wasn't he? They both had some explaining to do.

Up ahead of her Jonathan stepped off the top of the fire escape onto a flat roof and half-turned to wait. As she neared:

'I go there to buy my dope,' he said curtly, leaving her to explain her presence.

A brooding silence. She wouldn't be bullied by him, or cowed by his anger.

'I was trying to gain Anthony Dore's confidence, in the hope that I could verify what you told me,' she said, trying to make it sound the most reasonable thing in the world.

'How did you meet him?' asked Jonathan.

'I followed him.'

'That didn't look like a first meeting.'

'Second.'

'He thinks you're some sort of tart?' followed by, slightly less aggressively before she could protest: 'He thinks you're a particular kind of young woman from the way he was touching you.'

'I didn't like him doing that. I told him to stop.'

Jonathan's jaw flexed angrily.

'What is that in your hand?'

'My hatpin,' she said, deliberately not looking down at it, as if holding it like a dagger was normal.

'What was your intention?'

'As you correctly read; I was intending to stab him.'

'Stab him dead?'

'Stab him just in his hand or arm.'

'You thought you could be that accurate?'

'Just a little jab.'

'Somebody falls against you, jogging your arm, or forcing it, so your four-inch hatpin enters not his hand, but his heart.

He's dead. Or you stab someone else entirely – in the eye for instance – did you consider that?'

'But none of those things happened.'

Jonathan now was frowning, puzzling something out. She felt that in his mind he'd moved on from her impetuous stabbing attempt. 'Who does Dore think you are? I mean, you couldn't have told him your real identity.'

'I've told him my name's Felicity. He thinks I'm an artist. That's all he knows. I created her in order to meet him.'

'Felicity? That's why he was calling it.'

Philomena laughed: 'Did you think he was expressing great happiness?'

Jonathan looked rueful: 'It was all a bit of a blur.'

'I can't believe that you thought he was shouting for joy!' scoffed Philomena.

'I wouldn't put it past him. People going mad in a dark room might be his idea of a good time.'

'Oh, come on.'

Jonathan turned his head towards the parapet, a serious look on his face.

'Do you think anyone's been hurt?' he said.

'It'd be a miracle if they weren't.'

'People didn't need to panic in that way.'

'Why not? It was terrifying,' she said. Now she thought about it, he hadn't shown any fear in the panic. More evidence of his dual nature; decisive in a real physical crisis, nervy otherwise?

'And she's an artist?' he asked, turning back to her.

'Spur of the moment. It explains my unladylike hands.'

'What do you think of Dore? Have you got anything out of him?'

'No.'

'Do you think you would have if the evening hadn't been interrupted?'

'I don't know. It wasn't going the way I wanted it to.'

He pondered this for a few moments then seemed to lose interest. He went to the edge of the roof and inclined his body over the parapet. After a while she did the same, but several feet to his right.

At that moment the power was restored to the club because light suddenly spilled from the open door, revealing dozens of people milling below.

'There he is,' said Philomena quietly.

From their precipitous vantage they could see that Anthony Dore was searching – presumably for Felicity, amongst the patrons who had made it out of the building. He was moving swiftly between groups, checking the women.

A wind came up, a gust, rippling Philomena's flimsy dress. She crossed her arms and shivered.

Out of the side of his mouth Jonathan asked, 'Where did Felicity come from?'

'I just made her up. There's a girl in a play we did, and a professor—'

'*Pygmalion*,' interrupted Jonathan. 'Eliza Dolittle and Professor—'

'Higgins,' she interrupted back.

They were still looking down at Anthony Dore.

'You should have let me stab him,' said Philomena.

'If you had done you'd be in the wrong.'

'I wouldn't have killed him with this thing,' she claimed.

'You don't know that.'

'You *want* him dead,' she goaded, 'but you can't bring your-self to kill him so you tried to ki—

'I didn't actually try to kill myself,' interrupted Jonathan. 'And I only want him dead *if* I can be certain he killed Dan.'

'You *are* certain.'

'Not certain enough to *do* anything.'

'Certain enough to tell *me*.'

Jonathan shrugged. She bristled, grabbed his arm and pulled him around to face her. 'What am I supposed to do now you've told me?' she accused. 'It would have been better if you hadn't!'

'Damned if I did, damned if I didn't. I never anticipated that you'd be quite as aggressive as you are – perhaps aggres-sive is the wrong word – no, perhaps not, looking at you now, and knowing what you've been—'

'You thought Dan's fiancée would be a wallflower?'

'No, but dressing up to trick Dore into—'

'I think that when you wrote to me you wanted someone to take charge because you're *incapable* of—'

'It's true. I've done *everything* I can.'

There was a few moments' pause. Their spat had had the effect of reeling them in nearer to each other. Their faces were close, his inclined down, hers up. She got fresh booze, waning eau de cologne, perspiration, male skin. He was slightly taller than Dan.

'So,' she said quietly, 'that's why I was in there.'

'I buy cocaine there. Dope helps you stay awake, alcohol helps you to sleep. Learned that in the war,' said Jonathan.

'The war, the war, the fucking war. Did Dan take dope?'

'A little. Until it was outlawed Harrods ran a line of nifty gift sets: "A Welcome Present For Friends at the Front". Cocaine, heroin, a syringe, needles. I use powder these days. Easier to carry. You have no vices, Philomena?'

'No addictions,' she said.

'There's plenty of time. Plenty of time.'

A bell began to chime the hour, slightly ahead of another. They listened. Not looking into each other's eyes. Jonathan licked his lips. Philomena shifted backwards slightly. They weren't so close anymore. Now she couldn't smell him.

'I'm going home tomorrow, which is today,' she said. 'I should be there now.'

'Come and see my home,' said Jonathan, matter of factly.

Yes, thought Philomena. There's more to say, more to know. And time to fill. 'Why not?' she said. 'But I have to get my coat.'

They looked down again and saw Anthony Dore striding away. He turned a corner and was out of sight.

'Do you think he's gone?'

'Looks like it,' replied Jonathan. 'Which is worse, me bumping into him, or you?'

'If I bump into him I'll have to talk to him,' said Philomena.

'It'd be awkward. I'd have to play along.'

'But if I go in for your coat,' said Jonathan, 'they know me. We don't want anyone making the connection between us. The man on the door doesn't miss a trick.'

So Philomena slipped into the club to retrieve her coat. When she emerged Jonathan slunk off ahead of her, right then left down narrow streets, then at a wider one they risked entering a taxi together.

It wasn't over. The investigation by Felicity could continue, if desired, with Anthony Dore still ignorant.

CHAPTER ELEVEN

Worried about Felicity, Anthony entered The Whitehall, the hotel he thought was hers. Making a snap judgement of character, he offered the night porter cash in exchange for the answers to some questions. Yes, there was a woman registered in that room, four oh seven. No, no man, but the night porter wouldn't be surprised if she'd had a male guest. Oh? What was the night porter saying about her? Nothing, beyond that. A man had visited her last night and stayed for about two hours — beyond that, he couldn't say. What did this man look like? asked Anthony. Taller than sir. Dark hair and eyes. And in the morning there had been reports of stains on her pillowcase that seemed to be a gentleman's hair cream. No, she wasn't in now. Her key was here.

Anthony decided to push his luck. He explained, man to man, that he'd rather fallen for Felicity without knowing much about her; she was that kind of girl, you know? The night porter did know. He shared Anthony's belief that they were discussing a loose, attractive woman, probably a liar who cheated men. The night porter added helpfully that the gentleman had better get a move on with 'falling for her' because she was due to check out in the morning. What name had the gentleman said he knew her by? Felicity, said Anthony. That began with an F, didn't it, mused the night porter. Well, she hadn't registered as an F, she'd registered as a P. That's a common trick – using a false name with a gentleman. She's P. Bligh.

Bligh, Bligh? That rings a bell, thought Anthony.

'Is Felicity a nickname, perhaps?' inquired the night porter. Ironical perhaps? Or cynical?

'You know,' confided Anthony, 'you're right. I'm now feeling distinctly uneasy about her because she told me her name was Felicity.'

The night porter understood this, and didn't blame him. He voiced his hope that the gentleman hadn't lent her any money, and understood that the extra coin that had appeared in the gentleman's hand was payment for the lend of the key to Felicity's door, just to have a quick look. And for an extra consideration the night porter agreed to come up and keep a lookout, and give a warning should it be necessary, whilst the gentleman was inside Felicity or P. Bligh's room, engaged in establishing her bona fides.

Thus Anthony found himself waiting whilst the night porter quietly opened the door to room four oh seven before standing aside and conspiratorially whispering 'two minutes'. Anthony entered and nudged the door halfway shut behind him so that the night porter couldn't see directly in. He went to the window, as he always did on entering an unfamiliar room. He had a look out towards the tenement block opposite, then turned to look into the room and began to search. There was very little hanging in the wardrobe – a sign of a tendency to leave in a hurry? A small suitcase on the floor was empty. As he neared the bedside table there were photographs and what looked like a bundle of papers. The night porter coughed in the corridor. Anthony hurried to see if it was a signal. No, the night porter was just coughing. Anthony turned back into the room and looked down on a photograph that was lying on the bedside table. It was recognisably Felicity but not exactly her. It could have been of Felicity's plainer sister. Anthony looked at the other photograph, the one in a frame, and he almost gagged. It was of Daniel Case! Felicity knew him?

Anthony's heartbeat shot up and his breathing came in short gasps. His palms were instantly damp with sweat inside his gloves. He only became aware that he must have emitted a strange sound when the porter stationed outside enquired, 'Everything all right?' Anthony tried to reply but his mouth was so dry his tongue stuck to the roof of his mouth. He furiously worked his jaw to generate saliva and managed a weak 'Yes.' He took out a handkerchief and shakily wiped his brow.

Returning to the wardrobe, he feverishly rummaged in the clothes, finding a jacket that bore a nametag that read Philomena Bligh. He explored the bundle of papers on the bedside table. Flicking through them he found his own letter of condolence that he'd addressed to Philomena Bligh, November last. As the night porter fidgeted outside and began to whistle tunelessly under his breath Anthony scanned several of the other papers in the bundle. Extracts from letters Daniel Case had written to his fiancée leaped out at him. Anthony speed-read, his eyes racing to take in as much as possible. He glimpsed the name Jonathan Priest and 'my new best friend'. Also, towards the end of the same missive, 'My darling, my darling, my darling'.

Philomena and Jonathan's taxicab pulled up a little to the west of Marble Arch, at an apartment block of several floors. Very London; she'd never seen a building like it before arriving in the capital. It had large rectangular windows – more like a department store – and a glass entrance. There was something maritime about it. Only five or six storeys, yet it had a lift. Jonathan pressed the button to call it. They kept well apart as they waited for the lift to descend to the ground floor and maintained their distance once they were inside. The floor they alighted on – the fifth – had the same wooden parquet floors as the foyer. It absorbed sound, unlike the bare boards at her hotel. Jonathan stopped at a door and inserted a key in the lock, opened the door and stepped back to allow her to enter first. She hesitated on the threshold then entered.

First impressions were that it was clean and spacious, and spare, and modern. No heavy wallpaper, no aspidistras, and no tables on which to stand any. Jonathan led her down the hallway indicating rooms as they passed them: the lounge, the bathroom, master bedroom, guest bedroom, dining room, and the kitchen. They entered the last, which was large enough to accommodate a small dining table. A gas cooker! Fancy. Jonathan pulled out a chair for her. She sat. He opened a cupboard and pulled out bottles: whisky, rum, vodka. He asked what she wanted and poured what she told him. He didn't sit.

'I want to discourage you,' he said, 'from taking any further action against Anthony Dore.'

'Why?' she asked.

'Because there isn't any more that you can do.'

'Neither of us knows that.'

'I'm not arguing that there shouldn't be justice, or revenge—'

She interrupted: 'What are you arguing?'

'You've tricked him, yes, you've got inside his guard, but you're going home tomorrow so all this is academic anyhow.' He flapped his arms dramatically.

Philomena narrowed her eyes. What lay behind his objections? 'It looks bad to you, doesn't it? Me dressed up with Anthony.'

'Not my place to say.'

No, but you are saying it, aren't you, beneath your words. She wasn't having him thinking that about her. Did he really believe that? 'You don't know what passed between us.'

Jonathan tried to ignore the rising taunt in her voice. 'Where did you meet him the first time?'

'In that same club.'

'It's full of bachelor girls, notorious for its goings-on. There was a scandal: a girl who frequented the place died from taking dope she probably got there.' There, he was saying, that was why I thought what I did. And, you don't know what you've been doing. You don't know the true nature of the place you were in, what context you are being judged in, therefore what signals you are giving off, what other people would reasonably be concluding about you. But Philomena was keeping pace with Jonathan's thoughts. If she was reckless being in The Gates of Heaven in that way, then so was he.

'In that case you in particular are taking a big risk going there.'

'Yes, I am,' said Jonathan. His defiant, slightly sulky tone and his jutting chin made Philomena pause.

'Are you saying that you want to be caught there?'

Jonathan's head inclined down; his voice lost its brittle edge.

'I acknowledge that it's potentially rash. Perhaps part of me does want to be caught. Perhaps part of Anthony Dore wants to be caught – hence his letter to you.'

'Or he thinks he's very clever,' suggested Philomena.

'Not so clever. You've tricked him.'

'Yes, I have.' Now she was emphatic; her means justified the end. 'He doesn't know who I am and he doesn't know what I want so I have a huge advantage—'

'Until he realises that you're not going to give him what he wants,' said Jonathan, challenging her. 'He will be assuming certain things about a single girl he meets in that club.'

'Yes, yes, you've already said that,' said Philomena, impatiently.

'And what have you got from tricking him? What have you actually got? You were about to stick a bloody great pin in the man—'

'He wouldn't do something,' she snapped.

'You two looked quite cosy.'

Philomena opened her mouth to continue the spat, then closed it. She frowned. Was there a little bit of jealousy behind those sarcastic words? A new thought struck her about Jonathan.

'How *long* did you watch us?'

'I wasn't *watching* you, I saw you.'

Philomena could smell a little mendacity; a whiff.

'How long?'

'Only briefly.'

'How briefly?'

'I glimpsed you just before the lights went.'

A guess: 'Were those lights anything to do with you?'

'No,' said Jonathan, meeting her inquisitorial gaze. He didn't blink. She changed tack, sat back.

'We need the truth about Anthony. Felicity might find it,' she said.

'It's only justice if he is caught, and punished, for the crime of murdering Dan; there's no point otherwise – it's not justice otherwise. You can wish the worst on him but you'd feel forever uneasy if you do something before you're certain that he killed Dan.'

'I agree.' She flared her eyes and pushed forward her head, marking an end to that line of argument.

Jonathan sighed with his mouth closed, impatient with her,

and with himself for allowing their exchange to become adversarial. But it was unfinished. He decided to come at it more wisely.

'But what can Felicity find?'

'I don't know, yet. He likes Felicity.'

'That much is obvious, but your Felicity can't find any evidence because there isn't any. She can't find a witness to the card game because they're dead. So she's getting under the guard of the suspect for what, a confession? Something incriminating?'

'You've been thinking about this longer than me,' she said, making it sound as if Jonathan's will was weak.

He sat down opposite her and kneaded his scalp with both hands. He sighed. A twinkle returned to his eye.

'How does Felicity speak?'

'Like this.'

'Say a bit more.'

'I can't think what to say.'

'The quick brown fox jumped over the lazy dog.'

As she said it as Felicity, she couldn't help smiling. Jonathan smiled, too.

'Do you know the story of Hamlet?' he asked.

'We read it at school.'

'The man who knows what he should do but can't do it. The man who's been instructed by a ghost,' said Jonathan.

'Does Dan's ghost instruct you?' she asked.

'No, not literally, not like Hamlet's father.'

He got up and paced the kitchen.

'This is how I see my life: I became a barrister by accident. When I was born no one would have dreamed of predicting this future for me. I was supposed to work in a mill or something. But I got here. But I'm here under sufferance, I sometimes feel. They tolerate me and others like me so they can say that anybody can progress and improve themselves if only they try hard enough, therefore society is fair. If Dan had had the help I've had he might have been in my position. This makes his death even more enraging, because he was killed by a man with no talents, a man who has had everything served up to him. A weak man in a powerful position. Which is what I see about me, every day, and it makes me sick.

'What happened to Dan added to grievances already kindled in me. There's another incident that drives me. In the war, earlier, there was a young lad, Irish, one of those who the government knew was under age but they turned a blind eye because they needed the numbers. He was sixteen when he enlisted, just seventeen when he got shell shock, still just seventeen when he was court martialled for leaving his post – he wandered about behind our lines, incoherent – not deserting, not what I'd call cowardice. And he was seventeen when we executed him. The firing squad wouldn't pull their triggers. The officer in charge had to shoot him.'

Philomena twitched as if she'd been slapped.

'That wasn't me,' added Jonathan. 'I defended him. I was his failed defence counsel.'

'It doesn't sound like there was much you could do.'

'But it was wrong!' He turned away from her, picked up

a bottle of Scotch, made to dash it against the wall, thought better of it, poured some into a glass instead, drank it down. Silence.

'Another thing about Hamlet is that he thinks about killing himself,' Philomena said quietly.

Jonathan drained his whisky and poured himself another generous helping.

'Where does the name Pygmalion come from?' she murmured, trying to get him to speak.

'It's a myth. Pygmalion's a man. He avoids women. He's a sculptor. He makes a beautiful sculpture of a female. He falls in love with it. Venus hears his wish that she be real, and makes it so.'

'And they live happily ever after?'

Jonathan shook his head, still facing away from her.

'Do you think about stories all the time?' she asked.

'My clients tend to fit certain recognisable types, with variations. In certain situations human behaviour is quite predictable.'

'What's your type? And don't say Hamlet; he's a prince.'

'It's quite difficult to say what your own type is,' said Jonathan, still facing away.

'Setting aside the prince bit, you're not all Hamlet, are you?' she said. 'Your father wasn't killed by your mother's lover, for instance.'

'Actually, now you come to mention it . . .' said Jonathan, making her fear for a moment that she'd overstepped the mark – his father might have been killed by his mother's lover for all she knew. But he turned to her and grinned to release her. They both smiled for a few moments.

'What's Anthony Dore's type?' she asked.

'You've probably seen more of him than I have,' replied Jonathan. He winced and flashed another smile to show that that wasn't accusing her of anything.

'He's insecure,' she said, 'but I don't know what he was like before you accused him of murdering Dan.'

'Middle son of three. Fact. Least popular son – speculation, based on anecdote. Elder brother Edward, mentioned three times in despatches, school rugger hero, in the law, doing well, killed in war – facts. Younger brother Albert, generally loved by all, pianist, medical school; enlisted early, also dead – facts. Anthony, middle son, no particular talent, does something in the City. Killed comrade on battlefield because he'd lost his family's wealth gambling with a working-class man, couldn't face the music.'

'Speculation,' said Philomena. 'The music made him more fearful than the consequences of murder?'

'Correct,' said Jonathan. 'Whatever the actual reality, that is how he saw it, in his mind. Or he was just angry, and Dan didn't matter.'

He poured them both another drink. They sat in silence, not looking at each other. The kitchen began to feel crowded, airless. It became so that again they couldn't look at each other, for fear of what might happen. She swallowed hard and often, searched for something distracting to say: 'Ever since Dan's death I've been waiting to do something. To act.

I should feel surprised by my behaviour since I came to London.'

Jonathan nodded to show he understood. 'I should stop taking dope,' he said. 'I only really use it now when I know that after a recess I'm going to be on my feet, presenting my case. I use it to engender the feeling that nothing can go wrong. Having said that I also use it afterwards, too, to celebrate. I'm an addict, let's face it. I'll find whatever excuse.' He went to the doorway and beckoned. 'Come on. I'll show you something.'

She worried he was going to disclose something terrible to do with drugs. 'Show me what?'

'Something.'

She looked alarmed.

'What are you scared of it being?' he asked.

'Everything. Anything.'

'Fear of the unknown. But if you sat there and guessed for a thousand years you wouldn't get it. I promise that it won't harm you.'

'It?'

'Come. Come.'

She stood and let Jonathan lead her back down the hallway to a closed door. It was a room he kept locked.

'This is the third bedroom,' he said, unlocking it.

Bedroom?! She nearly protested, opening her mouth.

'Not in use as a bedroom,' Jonathan reassured.

He opened the door and stepped in and switched on the light. She gasped. Jonathan turned and gestured for her to enter beside him. It had once been an ordinary room. Now, every wall was painted and re-painted with images and frag-ments and slashes of colour, reds and browns and oranges. The splashes on the ceiling testified to the violence of the person responsible. Some of the individual images were of men dying and being brutal, killed and killing in various ways. There was a recurring one of a pair of figures locked in what could only be a fight to the death. The whole wasn't composed in any ordered way that Philomena could make out; it looked like it had been done at different times, in different moods. There were pots of paint and brushes strewn about the floor. There was one easy chair, ruined by paint. It had also been slashed. A kitchen knife was embedded in it. The room brought tears to her eyes.

'All my own work. I'll have to do it up and replace the chair before the landlord comes around,' said Jonathan. 'You can have a go, if you like.'

He hadn't known that he was going to suggest that. Philomena looked at him to check that he meant what she thought he did.

'But it's yours.'

He tried to smile. 'You can't make it any messier than it is.'

She felt sick with tension. Jonathan picked up a paint brush and handed it to her. 'There're some overalls over here.'

But all she could think of was that she really wanted to be naked. 'Will this paint wash off skin?' she asked.

'Yes,' said Jonathan, not catching on, prising the lids off various cans.

And without looking at Jonathan Philomena slipped out of Felicity's dress and shoes and out of her new silk under-garments and she was naked. Jonathan saw her and he grunted. She picked up a tin of paint and took aim and threw the contents so hard at a wall that some of the paint splashed backwards, spattering her bare skin. Her eyes shut to save themselves. It was red paint, crimson, so it resembled blood. She felt the paint run down her body, opened her eyes. There was some left in the tin. She tipped it upside down over her head and it poured over her shoulders and down her back, a rivulet, in the groove of her spine, down and down, cold? Hot? Must be cold. She was panting.

Jonathan looked on. White skin, brown hair at armpits and lower down. Green eyes flashing, red paint dripping. Jesus! His instinct was to strip off as well but fatally he hesitated, felt too awkward, too inhibited. And he had an erection.

Philomena incidentally smeared some of the red drips across her blushing skin as she took better hold of the brush and started to drag the paint spatters across the wall, working fast, spreading this way and that before it dried.

Jonathan felt like he was in the presence of Dan. She was elemental like Dan. She raised her arms and her breasts lifted with them. He was unable to resist imagining what sex with her would be like.

But he knew instinctively that she wasn't saying to him let's do it here and now. His experience in law told him that if he did force himself upon her in this circumstance no jury of men would blame him, but that wasn't the point. He needed to think differently. Her nakedness spoke of her trust in him. She was trusting him, yes? She was saying to him: look, this is how intensely I feel and I have faith that you won't abuse it. She was telling him that he was special, just as he had told her she was to him by showing her the paint room in the first place.

He started tugging clumsily at his clothes, taking great gulping breaths in an effort to overcome his fear. It'd be a strange thing not to have an erection, wouldn't it? Philomena wasn't looking at him anyway. When he was naked he took up a pot of orange paint and splashed it on another wall and began to fashion it into garish shapes. Philomena looked across and saw that he was also naked and his erection and she let out a guffaw. She came to his wall and joined in with his vigorous shaping of the orange paint. She felt savage with desire.

She could've just taken him inside her, just had him, fucked some of her unbearable feelings away. Rutted and fucked until she felt normal again. They accidentally touched, just the lightest brush of upper arms. Perhaps not even their skins met but just the hairs standing proud. An electric shock went through them as they worked the paint hard. His body was ready, her body was ready, but the rest of them was not. He had his terrible secret, and she feared, she feared that if she took him inside her now, she feared for her mind.

After she was showered clean of paint and clothed again Philomena wondered what sort of goodbye they would have when she left Jonathan's apartment. In the event it consisted of a look into each other's eyes and an awkward handshake, and Jonathan made a feeble joke about hoping she wouldn't stab him with her hatpin. A Rubicon had been crossed but there was no understanding yet of what new world they had entered. One thing was for certain: there was no going back. Not to innocence. Being naked together like that – they couldn't have done that had Dan been alive. Was it a betrayal of him, as bad as failing to bring his murderer to justice? They were both having these feelings and thoughts.

'Goodbye,' she said.

'Goodbye,' said Jonathan.

She was walking away.

'Look,' called Jonathan, coming after her.

She turned, wondering what he was going to say, recklessly hopeful for a moment.

He caught the expectation in her eye just before she banished it. The moment passed so quickly that both of them only knew it when it was gone.

'I'll come down and get you a taxi cab,' said Jonathan.

They didn't speak whilst they were waiting at the side of the road, and didn't speak as she got into the cab. As it carried her away she felt she was embarking on a huge journey of which the taxi ride was only the first stage, leaving behind someone she wasn't sure she should be leaving.

Oh, Dan, why did you get mixed up in that stupid game of cards with Anthony Dore? And die just as the war ended? I'm not saying that it's your fault if he murdered you, of course not, but why weren't you hiding in a hole anyway, trying to stay alive so that you could come home to me?

Is it better or worse if my next lover is your last best friend?
Or should I be like those foreign women in black in mourning?
Did Anthony Dore kill you?
Must I avenge you?

CHAPTER TWELVE

It was quiet, almost silent, when the sound of the motor died away. She heard the soft click as something landed on the ground near her feet. Instinctively she tried to recreate the projectile's trajectory – looking in the direction from which she calculated it had come. There were only deep, dark shadows. She was on her toes heading for the hotel entrance when the next missile came, the second click on the ground near her feet. She began to move faster, felt something hit her on the back – yelped and protectively put up her hands, scuttled to the hotel doors, forced her way through them. After carrying on into the hinterland of the foyer she turned and tried to see out. The bright lights made her blink. Shielding her eyes she peered from the lit foyer out into the night. Someone was out there. The dark was impenetrable – she could see no one, but knew she was being watched, that the anonymous thrower was still out there. Half expecting an object to smash one of the hotel windows she retreated backwards, further from them, staring from one to another, and to the glass doors, waiting for some ghoulish visage to reveal itself. The surly porter looked on impassively. His lack of alarm made her feel a little insane, as if she was in one world, of turmoil, whilst he was in an adjacent one where there was only indifference.

Shakily she climbed the stairs up to her room. As soon as she stepped inside she smelled danger, but there was no one hiding in there, not in the wardrobe, not under the bed. Neither could she detect signs of anyone having been there. Cautiously she edged towards the window and peered down. No one.

She removed Felicity's clothes and smoothed them, ready to return to the dress agency. Felicity couldn't find out anything from Anthony Dore, could she? Not after he'd groped her like that. If Felicity returned to Anthony he'd assume that his behaviour was acceptable to her. She put on her own night-dress and lay down on the bed. She'd forgotten what it was like to sleep properly, wake refreshed; tried not to make too much of the stone-throwing – if that's what they were – incident outside. It must have been a random event entirely unconnected to her or any situation she was involved in. But she kept coming back to wonder who might want to throw things, not at a chance victim, but at Felicity, whilst simultaneously dismissing that as a ridiculous question, because the only man who knew Felicity and where she was staying was Jonathan.

Before she knew it she'd got up from the bed and was looking out of the window into the darkness. A glow developing in the sky told her that it was nearly dawn. She really had to try and sleep. She lay down again. When she closed her eyes her thoughts were filled with images of Jonathan, naked. She turned her head to look at Dan's photograph.

Jonathan lay on his bed wondering again what it might be like to be Anthony Dore, thinking his way deeper into him. How had his allegation affected Dore? Did he lie awake worrying? Did he wonder who else knew about it? How would he be able to tell if someone knew of it? Would people stop talking when he entered a room? Would he be shunned at his club – his legitimate club, that is? Or could the result of any rumour about him be things Dore was unaware of? For instance, things that would have happened had been prevented from happening: an introduction not made, perhaps, or an opportunity denied him. Jonathan knew that Dore didn't need to work as such, but if someone heard that he was accused of murdering a comrade that could make life extremely difficult for him. Jonathan hoped. Not that he himself was broadcasting his accusation. He was just hoping that someone else was.

He drifted back to the first time he and Dan had been able to talk properly. After they'd met for the first time in that shell hole they'd managed to make it back to their lines, where they'd parted. Later, after Jonathan had hung his mirror to be able to see as he patched up his scalp wound, he spied Dan further down the trench. Dan and he met halfway, warily. This was the start of them seeking each other out, the first of their 'little chats'. Dan had talked of Philomena and it was a description of a complicated, unsentimental love with many downs and ups. A few days later, after Jonathan's dugout was destroyed by a shell Dan suggested he move into his. When the war was over Jonathan expected that their dialogue would cease, and he anticipated regretting that, and he knew that, without it being physically sexual, that he loved Dan – not that he would ever have said as much.

And now Philomena was here in London Jonathan felt less alone, but he had to admit to certain feelings, and hopes, that he dared not . . . He wondered if . . . if *now you're dead, do you know what we're doing? And I don't just mean being naked near Philomena – because of what I did, the thing I did, I am – what is the word stronger than remorseful? Abject? Conscience-stricken?*

What he hoped for was irreconcilable with what he had done.

Philomena was awoken by a knock on her door and someone hissing her name through it. Thinking it was Jonathan she stumbled upright and went to the door to answer it, but when she opened it it wasn't him, it was Anthony Dore and he seemed to be travelling at about a thousand miles an hour, begging her to hear him out, just hear him out.

She staggered backwards without him laying a hand on her, and before she knew it he was fully in her room, closing the door behind him. Through her befuddlement she was asking herself how he knew she was Philomena. How? He was begging her to be calm and to hear him out and pleading with her not to scream – she didn't have to do anything except listen; that's all she had to do.

She put on her dressing gown, trying to ignore Anthony's furtive glances at her body beneath her nightdress. Why shouldn't she demand that he left, or just scream? Was he a danger to her? A physical danger? He didn't look like he was. He was still placating her – his arms out, palms down, eyebrows raised, head nodding.

All right. She had to hear what he had to say – find out how he'd got ahead of the game. Get him by the window and herself by the door; hear what it was he wanted her to just listen to. She issued instructions and he seemed only too willing to follow. She turned her back and adjusted her dressing gown, making it more secure. She took up Felicity's hat and fiddled with it, fingers ready to grasp the pin. She told him to sit in the chair. He smelled expensive. New leather; his gloves, his boots. Polish. How did he know her real name?

How? Again – how?

Major James? But Major James didn't know where she was. Jonathan? Ridiculous. No, Major James had warned Anthony and he'd set some investigators onto her – that was the most likely explanation. That meant there were other men outside? Police, even? Had she broken the law? She didn't think she had. Jonathan had in telling her. Slander. She buttoned her lip. Zipped mouth shut. Didn't know for certain what was going on. Walked into this. Sleep walked.

'You have done nothing illegal to me as far as I know,' began Anthony, gravely. 'As to the morality of your actions that is for your conscience. I know that your name is Philomena

Bligh, and that you were the fiancée of Daniel Case. I wrote to you expressing my sorrow at his death. I also believe, but do not know, that you have been misled to believe—'

It sounded like a prepared speech. Bordering on pompous. Philomena shifted her weight from one leg to another and he stopped speaking. She'd made that happen? She shifted her weight back again, but nothing resulted.

Anthony didn't start speaking again. He watched her. What were the obvious differences between Felicity and Philomena? Philomena was shorter. But that was the shoes – lack of them. Same green eyes, of course. But less eager. No make-up.

'Why did you approach me pretending to be Felicity?'

But surely from what he'd said he understood why? Test this, she thought.

'If you know that I'm Philomena Bligh, the fiancée of Daniel Case, then I think you know why.'

Anthony narrowed his eyes. 'That's your real voice, isn't it?' he said. 'That accent.'

Philomena pursed her lips. Was that all he could think to say?

'Why approach me in disguise?'

She didn't answer that either. She wasn't going to state the obvious, that someone had told her about the allegation.

'To trick me?' probed Anthony.

She wished he'd stop looking at her body. He made her feel that her nightie and dressing gown were transparent, though she knew that they weren't.

'Very well,' he said, 'I know of a story, in which I feature, against my will . . .' He tailed off.

A statement, but phrased in such a way as to invite the offer of information. She wasn't falling for that.

'You said I had to just listen.'

'The story is a story that might cause Daniel Case's fiancée to disguise herself and befriend me.'

Any harm in confirming that? No. She had to give away a little to get something back.

'I have heard a story, yes, that might lead to that.'

'From whom?'

She shook her head. Wouldn't say. Wouldn't do that.

'The story concerns the manner of your fiancé's death?'

She nodded, eking out the most miserly response.

Anthony sighed. 'Am I going to have to make all the running? Is it going to have to be me asking leading questions that you answer monosyllabically?'

Philomena looked steadily at him. Not even a monosyllable this time.

Anthony appeared to lose his patience. 'That accusation, the one I'm assuming featured in the story, although completely unfounded, was nevertheless officially investigated. No evidence could be found and no motive. Or have you been told otherwise?'

She shook her head. She was beginning to get scared. He seemed very confident of his ground.

'Why do you give any credence to it?'

She looked at the floor, then up at him, unable to provide,

to formulate a scientifically logical reply, wishing once again that there were an infallible way of knowing the truth about another human being.

Anthony knew he'd pierced her defence. Something he'd said was working on her. He'd spent a good while outside pacing, trying to get inside her head. She didn't have any more evidence than anyone else, did she? He'd worried in the past that Daniel Case might have told, or fired off a celebratory message to someone: 'Won my fortune at cards!' or something like that.

'All I can do is repeat my defence,' said Anthony, 'my rock-solid defence. There was never any card game involving Daniel Case and me, therefore none of the other details can be true. End of defence. Verdict, not guilty; innocent. I would like to know what I must do to convince you of that. I would like to know what I must do to convince you that I am innocent and that the official findings of the investigation into the allegation were correct. I would like to know, in fact, why there is any suspicion against me, who has been found innocent, whilst my accuser, whoever that is, who is committing a very serious crime in making false allegations against me, seems to be believed.'

Anthony's rational arguments, his indignant tone, made Philomena fear for Jonathan. It suddenly felt as though she and Jonathan had been in a dream together. In it they could think and say and do whatever they liked and there would be no consequences. They'd created an alternate world that had seemed real. Now another world, Anthony Dore's – no, not his, the real world – had come along and shown how delusional their world was.

'Or perhaps the person who told you didn't accuse me, but only related events?' continued Anthony, giving her an opportunity to absolve herself.

'I'm not going to tell you how I learned the story,' Philomena said defiantly, still standing near the door, hiding her shaking hands behind her hat. She could see Anthony looking at it, wondering why she was holding it when she wasn't dressed.

It hadn't occurred to him to question her attachment to her headgear. He was picturing her naked body. What a prize she would be. Beguiling. Daniel Case's 'darling'. In the corner of his eye the sheaf of letters lay on the table, leading him to remember what he'd done when last in this room. He marshalled his features as she began to speak.

'You can see that once I knew the story I had to investigate it,' she started out, trying to sound reasonable, but inside she wanted the whole thing to stop now. She felt like a child again. She'd been going along denying that she was doing something that she knew was unacceptable and now an adult had caught her.

'Why didn't you approach me as yourself?' Anthony chided.

'Because then you'd know what I might be seeking.'

'But what you did is underhand and it goes against the grain of the law. A man must be told what he is charged with before he is questioned, surely? That is only fair, is it not?'

Philomena nodded in agreement but protested: 'I wasn't charging you.'

'But you were going to question me.'

'I hadn't thought that far – I already knew what your answer was. I was trying to verify it,' rallied Philomena.

'No,' said Anthony, pouncing, 'you were trying to corroborate what someone had told you was my answer. You were already biased against me by what someone else had told you. You had prejudged me.'

'It's in the official records,' she said, hoping this was true and it would throw Anthony off.

'I think you'll find that it's *not*,' said Anthony. 'It is not written in *any* official records. Have you seen it on paper? Have you seen it on paper? Have you seen it on paper?'

'No,' she had to admit, partly to shut him up, 'I haven't.'

'That's because it isn't written. Or if it is, someone's for it. This conversation might be a good rehearsal for the legal action I may be forced to bring.'

Philomena's free hand went to her throat. Good, thought Anthony, that's shaken her to her bare feet.

'Then you must leave now.'

'But I do not want to bring any such suit,' said Anthony, telling the truth for two reasons: first, a libel trial would only draw public attention to the accusation; second, he didn't want this dialogue with Philomena to end – except in his favour. 'And I don't think you've been misled by a currently serving officer. No, I think I know who told you. The unfortunate mad man himself,' he said.

Philomena's gaze went inward, reviewing Jonathan's nervy behaviour. That was a fitting description of him – the unfortunate mad man? Was that how he was known? When she looked out again Anthony Dore was studying her with a sympathetic look on his face.

'I can see that you're out of your depth. Can you also appreciate my position? I don't want to say anything against the man I think told you the story that made you act because I believe he is a fine man who was destroyed in the war. But just because he is a damaged person doesn't mean that he can make such serious allegations against another person and, a) be believed and b) go unpunished.'

Oh God, he was right. She had no answer to make, certainly no rebuttal.

'How long have you been following me?' There was a gleam in Anthony's eye.

'I might ask you the same question,' she countered.

'Excuse me, miss, I know that there are women taking up all sorts of positions these days but prosecution counsel isn't one of them.'

'Yet,' she said, reddening. She hated being called *miss* in that way, with *little* a silent preface.

'Am I to take it that you're a suffragette?'

'Am I to take it that you disagree with universal suffrage?'

'We were discussing who slandered me to you,' said Anthony.

Both tetchy, now. He unable to fully hide his personality, she not seeking to conceal hers.

'Did you like Dan?' she asked.

'I admired him.'

'You didn't know him very well.'

'You don't know that.'

'He never mentioned you in his letters and you referred to him as Daniel in yours. And why did you write to me? That wasn't your job.'

'As I wrote: his death was a crime.'

Anthony didn't blink. When he'd written those words in his letter it had been without cynicism. He'd been in an altered, densely quiet, trance-like state in which he wrote and thought as if slightly apart from himself. These days he was different. He knew Case's death was a crime and that he was the perpetrator of it. He knew, and praised himself, that he said things that sounded right to the listener, but meant something else entirely to him. He deployed ambiguity so that it satisfied both their story and his.

'Why do you think anyone would lay a false charge against you?' he heard her say.

'For the reasons I've outlined; their state of mind,' he shot back.

'But why such a detailed allegation?'

'Someone in possession of a febrile imagination inflamed by circumstance; that is who could invent such detail. And because you heard that man's story before you—'

'I did not say that a man told me.'

The fire flared in her eyes. She looked magnificent. Anthony forgave her interruption.

'Whomsoever told you, you have been unduly influenced. In the same way that I could be forgiven for thinking you are one way because I first met you as Felicity in a particular place. First impressions can be all too hard to correct. Can you try to imagine what your reaction would have been to the story if you had already met me? I put it to you that you never had a chance to form an accurate opinion of me, until now – how can I prove that I didn't do something?' Leaning forward in his seat, now. 'I have no alibi; I was there on the same battlefield, I had the opportunity. I possessed a gun – the wrong kind, mind, but I had the means – there were other guns. But no motive! There was no card game! And there is absolutely no proof! No evidence! No man or woman in this country is expected to prove that they didn't do something. The onus is on the other side; those making the allegations have to make them stick. If I sued Jonathan Priest for libel or slander I'd undoubtedly win.'

Philomena concealed any reaction to Jonathan's name. Went on the offensive.

'How did you discover that I'm Philomena Bligh?'

'Luck,' replied Anthony, emphasising the consonants.

Philomena didn't think that it was luck. Was he watching Jonathan when Jonathan thought it was the other way around? Anthony had seen her with Jonathan? Or was he paying someone to watch for him?

'Are there any gaps in my story, in my version?' he asked, sounding disheartened, exasperated; almost forlorn.

'Your version is quite clear,' she said.

He rubbed his forehead, aping a gesture that he hoped conveyed exasperation, fatigue and despair.

'My inability to convince you is testament to my plight . . .'

He tailed off and turned his head away. She looked at his profile and believed that he was absolutely sincere in what he'd just said. She felt sorry for him.

'I've no real friends,' said Anthony, 'no one to stand up for me. There are people I pay to do things for me. Some of us are destined to keep our own company, aren't we? I've always been on the edge of things. At the periphery.' He sighed and shook his head as if he wearied of himself, and looked at her as if confirming that she would be quite justified should she share that view. 'But all that can be of no concern to you.'

He stood. She wondered how to let him pass her without getting too close. She might have to go out of her room before him.

'You can forgive my confusion about what sort of girl Felicity is. In that sort of place you'd expect a sort of girl. And even in respectable places the war has confused matters. Before it I would never have imagined that I'd see a woman in uniform – apart from nurses – or see young women eating out alone. Did you work in the war?'

'Tram ticket collector. Manchester.'

'Before that?'

'Seamstress.'

'A seamstress.'

'Yes, a seamstress.'

She was a seamstress and tram ticket collector and he was having to engage with her as an equal? His temper flared and he forgot that he wanted to seduce her.

'But not an artist, like Felicity. Yes, before the war it was only really prostitutes who walked the streets alone. I can imagine you as one of those new female police matrons – apart from the fact that you're too pretty – poking your nose about.'

Philomena let her irritation show on her face. This dismayed Anthony. It was quite the wrong note to end on. He sought a more appealing register.

'All I ask is that now having heard me out, you judge me fairly. I don't ask you to like me, just give me justice.'

He indicated with his hat that he would like to pass her to leave the room. She sat on the edge of her bed to give him free passage. He stopped by her. Philomena stared down at his shoes. There was a smudge on the shiny black leather toe of one. Someone would fix that for him.

'I liked Felicity. Shame,' she heard him say.

And with that, Anthony Dore left her room, shutting the door behind him, pleased enough with his performance, reassured that no hard evidence against him had emerged. Felicity had been a lure, an enticement. Luckily, he'd spoilt her game. Had Priest set the bait? Was she in a conspiracy with Priest? He hadn't established that. Were they connected? Priest had told her, must have. He'd put money on it. That might need a response. From his lawyers. But Priest had been warned – can't warn him a second time; that would come across as weak.

Anthony descended the stairs. He might have to kill Priest, or have him killed. But the trouble with assassins was that they knew they'd been hired, and could discover by whom.

Kill Priest himself. One of the things that Anthony had acknowledged since he'd become a murderer was that he had felt homicidal before. He'd wanted to kill; he'd muttered under his breath that he was going to kill. Until Daniel Case on that battlefield, motive, opportunity and implacable dislike had never coincided so invitingly; the deed had felt spontaneous. The premeditated murder of Priest scared him. It would have to be a shot. Anything else required being too close – within touching distance. But the noise a gun makes, hard to get away afterwards. And what if it went wrong and he only wounded his target? Priest would be furious. Priest would retaliate, come after, overpower and deliver him up, or kill him.

Anthony reached the so-called hotel's so-called reception. No porter. Good. He crossed the so-called foyer, daring a challenge. As he strode through the exit he thought how he'd seen his labelling Priest 'mad' strike home. He'd bet that Priest was the tall dark man who'd spent two hours in room four oh seven leaving stains on the pillow. Philomena/Felicity was a filthy slut. Jonathan Priest was mad. Let the latter be known.

Philomena had keyed the lock and half-fallen back down onto her bed, exhausted with it all. She'd lain still for a few moments then sprung up and gone to the window where she looked down on Anthony as he walked purposefully away from the entrance to the hotel. His foot made a stone shoot. She heard it scuttle on the cobbles and saw him follow it, aim, and kick it away, hard.

She went down the hallway to the bathroom and washed, then dressed as herself and packed her things. When it was the proper morning she went down and paid the bill and took Felicity's 'costume' back to the dress agency and paid for keeping it the extra day. The woman there asked if she'd had 'fun'. Philomena smiled ruefully and lied that she had. She set off to find Jonathan.

CHAPTER THIRTEEN

Anthony returned to his home. When he entered, his father was preparing to leave. As usual it was uncomfortable between them. Perceval Dore immediately deduced from Anthony's appearance that he was just now coming in from a night out. His instinct was to express his disapproval but he'd privately decided that he would try a completely different tack with his surviving son. He would try to not criticise him, and to treat him as a friend.

'Good morning.'

'Good morning, father.'

'Had breakfast?'

'Yes, thank you.'

There followed a few moments of awkwardness before both moved on. That was all they could find to say to each other.

Anthony climbed up to his apartment within the house, entered his lounge, moved a set of drawers and lifted a loose floorboard. He reached down into the floor cavity and came up with a small tin, which he unlocked. He took out an oil cloth and unrolled it and he unfolded some tissue and there lay his special things: his French pornographic postcards, his photograph of his mother, the letter she wrote to him on receiving his letter – also in the box – in which he'd pleaded to be brought home from school. He read, as if he hadn't himself written it, it was by another boy he once knew, that at school he was 'miserable', subjected to 'cruelty'. A sharp pain entered his chest. He stopped reading his letter to his mother and instead re-read her reply. 'Things are always diffi-cult when you enter a new world but they invariably improve' . . . 'Best not to show your feelings' . . . 'I shan't let on to your father that you're not coping – you know how disap-pointed—' . . . 'endurance is a virtue, also stoicism, determin-ation; these are the qualities that make us so great' . . . 'mustn't be miserable, you are from a great family, a great country, a great Empire' . . . 'when you look back these will be the happiest days of your life'.

Anthony put the special things and the feelings away and performed the sequence with the box in reverse until the room was exactly how it had been when he'd entered it. He sat on his day bed and took out from his jacket the letter he'd stolen from Philomena's room when there alone. He read it through twice, feeling envious that he had never in his life either received or sent such a letter. He slid it in between the leaves of the Bible that his mother gave him when they packed him off to school. He thought back to when he'd searched Daniel Case's possessions for the IOUs. He'd discovered them in an envelope intended for 'Philomena', with an address. Anthony stood and looked in the mirror and practised saying out loud: 'I am an innocent man,' making his gaze stay fixed on himself.

At Jonathan's apartment block the concierge telephoned up to him. When Philomena arrived at his door he was anxiously waiting.

'Can I come in?'

'Of course,' he said.

When they were in the kitchen she took a deep swallow. This was going to be terrible but it had to be done. She sat one side of the table and indicated he should sit the other. She cleared her throat and asked if it was possible that when Jonathan made his allegation he was so very upset that it affected his judgement. That stopped him dead in his tracks.

'What's happened since you got in that taxi?'

'I've had a conversation with Anthony Dore.'

'How did that come about since you left here?'

'He found me in my hotel.'

'How the hell did he do that?'

'I don't know. It doesn't matter, does it? He came to my room—'

'To your room?'

Jonathan was out of his seat, leaning over the table towards her. She didn't back away, looked him steadily in the eye even though her heart was racing.

'He said he knew I was Philomena Bligh and that he'd guessed what I'd been up to and he wanted his chance to put his side of the story.'

'And now you doubt me?' Jonathan struck his chest hard with the heel of his hand. His anger was terrifying.

'I think you genuinely believe your story and I'm glad you told it to me and you're right, damned if you did, damned if you didn't—'

'Damned right!'

Philomena gathered herself to say the next thing.

'But we must stop.'

A look of horror crossed Jonathan's face. Disbelief. 'You—' he began.

Philomena pursed her lips, ready for a tirade. It didn't come. Jonathan fell back into his seat. His mouth moved, faint traces of words, glimpses of his thoughts. He blinked rapidly, his head moving like a bird's, left and right. My God, thought Philomena, what had she done? She should have just gone home and let him gradually realise over time that the pursuit of Anthony Dore was over.

'You're being deliberately cold,' accused Jonathan, his voice low in the back of his throat.

'I'm not being cold, I'm being normal. Anthony Dore's threatening legal proceedings.'

'Let him; he'd have to be in the dock.'

'But he'd win, wouldn't he? He'd continue to deny there ever was a card game and that would be that. You'd lose your career. Would there be damages? He could sue you for damages, and costs and whatever. You'd be finished.' She knew this made sense; she was returning to him his own logic. Was she getting through to him? He still looked stunned. 'Jonathan, we have to find lives worth living for ourselves, and in order to do so we should only pursue those ambitions that are achievable, and proving that Anthony Dore murdered Dan isn't one of those.'

'Setting all that fine rhetoric aside,' said Jonathan, 'did you believe Dore?' Now he looked at her. Dark grey shades had appeared under his eyes, themselves pools of sadness.

'That doesn't matter,' she said, her heart aching. 'What matters is what we can do.'

'Say whether you believe Dore.'

A straight question, flatly asked. She composed her reply with infinite care.

'I believe that it's impossible to prove your story.'

'Did you form an opinion regarding the merits of his truth versus mine?' Voice rising.

'He strikes me as lonely.'

That was not the answer to his question.

'Do you like him?'

'I don't like him!'

'Methinks she doth protest too much.'

'What?' exclaimed Philomena.

'What's the matter?' said Jonathan, level now in the face of her indignation. 'It's perfectly simple. Do you like Anthony Dore? Do you believe him over me?'

'It's not about that.'

'Do you like him?'

'I think he's— no, I don't "like" him.'

'But you believe him over me.'

Now he was after her. The litigator had arrived on the scene.

'I wish you weren't making it about that,' she said.

'But that's what this is about,' said Jonathan.

'Look,' she replied forcefully, 'you told me an incredibly detailed account that was utterly convincing and he refutes it. It's one word against the other. As you've made the allegation it's up to you to prove it, not up to him to disprove it. Is that the law?'

'That's the law, yes,' Jonathan concurred, 'but I'm asking you whom you believe.'

'And I'm asking you not to ask me that,' she said.

'Because you don't want to say the words out loud: "I believe Anthony Dore over you,"' he challenged.

Her heel tapped away under the table. She looked up at the ceiling. She couldn't say it, couldn't take that step. Jonathan shrugged and shifted back in his seat, his point made.

Philomena didn't know what to say or do next to get them out of the knot they were in. Perhaps there wasn't anything. Perhaps this was it; the end for them.

'I'm due in court,' said Jonathan eventually, wearily. 'Are you still going back today?'

'Yes. Now.'

'Please meet me again before you go,' suddenly begged Jonathan. 'Please. Come with me and we can talk in recess. Please, Philomena.'

She really didn't want to prolong the agony, but he had his hands clasped, beseeching her. She felt awful.

'You can leave your luggage here.'

But she emphatically didn't want to have to come back to Jonathan's apartment again, so took her luggage with her.

In the taxi, to break the silence, she asked what case it was he was in court for. In bitter tones that she hadn't heard him use before Jonathan replied that it was the same case – the same judge; Judge Dore, Anthony's father. Anthony Dore was still getting away with it; he'd fooled Philomena, he seemed to be saying. His was the lone voice crying in the wilderness. She felt that she was betraying Jonathan – or perhaps that was just what he wanted her to feel. It was so important, imperative to him that she believed his story. She worried for his safety if he didn't have that assurance.

'Your hands have stopped moving,' he said.

For a moment she didn't know what he was talking about. 'Your hands.'

He meant that her hands had ceased their independent movements.

She spent the session in the public gallery studying Judge Dore, alert for any sign that he knew of the hostile relationship between his son and Jonathan. Would a judge be prepared to have a barrister in his court who had accused his son of murdering a comrade?

The man who'd admitted that he 'went round there' was in the dock again. Philomena didn't know what he was accused of, but assumed a violent act – serious violence if he was being tried here at the Old Bailey. Jonathan glanced up at her several times as if to make sure that she was still here.

She almost, but not quite, regretted stripping off her clothes and painting with him, but it had felt essential. It complicated things, though, of course it did. She didn't make a habit of revealing her body to men she'd known only a few days. Apart from her father and Dan, Jonathan was the only man who'd ever seen her completely naked. Her father also being dead, that made Jonathan the only man alive who had seen her like that.

Judge Dore looked up at her in the gallery and frowned. She looked away from him, unintentionally catching Jonathan's eye and straight away regretted doing so, for she could see Dore Senior had made the connection between them.

On the floor, Jonathan stumbled over his words when he saw Major James sit down behind Philomena. Jonathan's consternation made Philomena turn around to look for its cause. She jerked back. Major James in turn appeared horrified that she was there, and he realised that Jonathan was looking up at him. Looking behind himself, Jonathan saw that Judge Dore was frowning deeper, following the ripples of tension flowing between him, Philomena – now with her head in her hands – and Major James. To an outside observer they must have borne all the hallmarks of characters in a plot that was unravelling.

'Recess,' called Judge Dore, baffling the court, making it rise with him. Major James hastily vacated his seat and made for the door. Philomena looked down at Jonathan for any sign that he might have an explanation. All he could do was shrug. She rushed out of the gallery. Jonathan found her in the public areas. She nodded sideways towards where Major James was receiving directions from an usher. He saw them and his eyes glazed over: he neither smiled nor greeted.

'They've got to him,' said Jonathan, out of the side of his mouth.

Major James was going to have to walk past them. They stood still and watched him. As he passed he looked only at Jonathan and said 'Priest,' quietly and formally, barely voicing the word at all. They turned to watch his back. When Major James made a certain turn and entered a certain door Jonathan was able to inform Philomena:

'He's heading for the judges.'

They stood in silence and tried to think through what this visit might mean. As Major James had appeared in Judge Dore's court, it seemed safe to assume he intended to visit him.

'We don't know if they're talking about Dan, or Anthony Dore, or anything to do with us,' said Philomena.

'No,' said Jonathan, unconvinced, 'we don't.'

In his room, Judge Dore tried not to glare at the nervous military man sat before him. Having introduced himself, Major James now steeled himself to broach the reason for the meeting, a hesitation that infuriated the judge. Get on with it, he thought. The tension was more than he could bear.

Anticipating a violent reaction from the imposing man opposite, Major James wished the girl had never come to see him — no, that's not true. He wished that he'd never given her any hint of an insight into events after the death of Second Lieutenant Case. So now he was doing Anthony Dore's dirty work for him in exchange for what he had been led to believe was immunity from any nasty business. He could discern some similarities between Dore father and son: the colouring, the shape of the nose, but the father gave the impression of being twice the size of the son, and their characters were obviously dissimilar. Judge Dore was looking straight at him, for one thing, and this reminded Major James that Anthony looked slightly sideways at you, as if ready to deflect, or conceal. He hadn't consciously noticed this before; it was the comparison with the father that brought it out.

'I'm going to have to tell you about a disagreeable event,' Major James began, 'involving your son whilst he was in uniform, during the war, at the end, just after the end.'

Following the unscheduled break Philomena occupied a different seat in the public gallery, this time nearer the exit. Major James didn't reappear and the court was kept waiting for several minutes by Judge Dore. When he eventually entered and took his place he looked up to where she was sitting before the recess. He looked away, glanced up – three times towards different seats – until he located her. A shiver passed through her and her skin goosebumped. As the prosecution resumed speaking Judge Dore gazed at her, fixedly, for what seemed like an eternity. Her heart threatened to leap from her breast and her mouth went dry. The enmity flowing up from him was intense.

This was what Jonathan and she were up against. All this in this room; this man, called a judge, his costume, all the other men in costumes, their wigs and gowns and strange paraphernalia. This court, one of many courts, in a magnificent, heavy, historic building, with ushers and guards and policemen, all with their uniforms and codes and paraphernalia. And Latin; Latin words here and there and above. Words that might be about to be used against her and Jonathan, for Major James had surely told Anthony's father about the allegation – Anthony's version of it, too, because Major James would feel more loyalty, or affinity, or duty to a man like Judge Dore than he would to her and Jonathan. And, if push came to shove, Major James, anyone, would be more frightened of Anthony Dore and his father than they would be of Jonathan and her – what had they got? No power! Compared to all this, this, weight. They were nothing. People like Judge Dore owned England; if he decided to crush them, they'd had it. Jonathan might have one foot in their world but his other was still firmly in hers. Judge Dore could just amputate him.

Philomena could see the turmoil in Jonathan. She willed him to calm, to hold himself together, to stop looking at Judge Dore in that way. The two of them down there seemed to be growing less part of their surroundings, to be focused only on each other. And it wasn't just Philomena who noticed it. The prosecution barrister began to act bewildered; the judge appeared to be ignoring him. He faltered to a close and said, 'No further questions, your honour,' as if it were a tentative enquiry. He sat and there was a long pause.

That began to make people nervous. It felt like someone
had forgotten their lines, or, worse, that nobody was in charge
of proceedings. A palpable gust of fear swept the room. Folk
began to look uncertainly about them, like sheep that have
realised they have broken out of their field. Officials began
to make eye contact with one another, urgently signal, and
it became clear to all that something had gone wrong.

From the gestures Philomena deduced that the onus was
on Jonathan; he was supposed to be doing something, now
that the prosecution had finished, and if he didn't, Judge Dore
was supposed to do something. But Jonathan was still in his
seat, in private communion with Judge Dore, the two of them
excluding everyone else.

'Mr Priest?' said the judge, sending a wave of relief around
the room. 'Approach, please, Mr Priest.'

Jonathan rose and went to Judge Dore. From where
Philomena was sitting he looked like a small boy having to
get up on tiptoe to reach a telling off.

He kept his features as blank as possible and so did Judge
Dore. Lowering his voice, so only Jonathan could hear him,
he growled 'If you ever, ever repeat that allegation I shall
make it my business to see that your life is destroyed.'

Jonathan considered this not unexpected threat for a
moment.

Judge Dore added: 'And tell that girl the same.' Certain that
his demand once voiced would be obeyed, Judge Dore indicated that Jonathan should return to his place and resume.

To Philomena, Jonathan looked crushed. She felt utter

despair. Tears pricked her eyes. Jonathan was undone. His steps were shaky, his shoulders hunched; he presented the sorry sight of a proud man humbled.

He'd reached his seat when she caught a spark of something from him that made her want to leap up and cry, 'Don't do that!' It was the same feeling she'd had when she saw the shabby young soldier about to step off his chair, the noose around his neck. She willed Jonathan to look up at her but he wouldn't. Judge Dore indicated his impatience by deliberately clearing his throat.

On the floor of the court Jonathan leaned towards his bewildered prosecution counterpart and stage-whispered: 'Is that it?'

The poor man looked completely baffled.

'I said, is that it?'

The prosecuting counsel looked up at the judge, pleading.

'Mr Priest!' barked Judge Dore.

Jonathan clearly refused to look at him.

'What did you just say to your learned friend, Mr Priest?'

Jonathan ignored him.

'You,' snarled Judge Dore at the prosecution. 'I order you to tell me what he said.'

The prosecution meekly stood, and unwillingly related: 'He said, "Is that it?"'

'Explain yourself, Mr Priest.'

Jonathan, sounding completely reasonable, replied: 'I was referring to my learned friend's prosecution, my lord. The strategy of it, the detail of it, and his execution of it.'

The entire court was agog.

'You're showing contempt for this court, Mr Priest,' threatened Judge Dore.

'I am?' said Jonathan. 'I'm showing contempt for truth and justice? The prosecution has been, to put it politely, limp, and your son is a murderer.'

'No!' Philomena shouted, to a background of gasps.

Jonathan ploughed on: 'On the eleventh of November last year at just gone eleven a.m. on a battlefield in France, Anthony Dore, in the most cowardly manner possible—'

'Shut his mouth, shut his mouth!' screamed Judge Dore, launching various officials. They ran towards Jonathan and he stopped speaking, gestured his surrender – there was no need to physically restrain him.

'Get him out of here! Get him out!' roared Judge Dore, on his feet now, as pandemonium broke out. 'And I'm declaring this session sub judice! Sub judice, you hear me? Nobody breathes a damn word of this or they go straight to gaol!'

Already out of her seat, Philomena ran down into the public area but there was no sign of Jonathan. She begged an usher to tell her where he had gone and was told that he'd left the building – nobody knew where to. Several officials closed on her, so she took a tight grip on her bag and ran for an exit. Once outside she hailed the first taxi cab that came and told it to take her to Jonathan's chambers, where she asked it to wait.

Jonathan wasn't there. Jones, she could tell, wanted to ask questions – he had already heard something of what had happened in the court. She implored him to telephone to Jonathan's apartment. There was no answer. But that didn't mean that Jonathan wasn't at home; he might have just been refusing to answer.

'Oh Jones . . .'

'What is it, miss? What's happened?'

'I've got to find him.'

For a moment she thought of sharing with Jones her fear that Jonathan might kill himself.

'Miss?'

'Nothing.'

'Go to his home,' suggested Jones. 'I'll send word if he turns up. Telephone to me here.'

'But I haven't any more money for the taxi cab!'

'Money? Why didn't you say? Money we can do.'

She 'borrowed' some cash from Jones and told the waiting taxi to take her to Jonathan's address. Once there, she leaned on the doorbell for what seemed like an age until a different concierge appeared and asked, through the glass entrance doors, for her to stop and proceed to the tradesman's entrance.

'I am not a tradesman!' she yelled, and demanded to know if Jonathan was at home. The concierge reluctantly rang up and got no reply. If Mr Priest was in, he wasn't answering.

'I think he's in trouble,' she wailed through the glass, but the concierge only looked dubious and wouldn't admit her.

She had a vision of Jonathan in his apartment; a chair, a noose.

'Will you go and see if he's all right? Please. Please?' she begged, again and again through the glass, until the concierge relented and went up to Jonathan's floor. He soon returned with the news that there was no answer so he'd taken the liberty of letting himself in. Mr Priest wasn't at home.

'Where to now, miss?' asked the taxi driver, who had left his vehicle and stood a few feet off.

Philomena didn't know. She sat in the back of the cab, for a few moments completely at a loss. Then she told the driver to do a tour of all the places she knew Jonathan frequented. But the driver was sure that The Gates of Heaven would be shut at that time. She didn't know the name of the under-ground club. There were several piano bars, the indulgent taxi cab driver imagined, that had a dooshom on the wall. Deter-mined to do something, anything, Philomena ordered him to drive back to Jonathan's chambers, but Jones still had heard nothing. Back in the taxi, she slumped in her seat. The cabbie asked her if she wanted to look anywhere else, adding, sympa-thetically, that you could look for someone for ever in London and never find them. Philomena despaired. The cabbie smiled ruefully.

But there was one place left. She gave the cabbie the address and he drove off at speed, both of them grateful that there was something to do. When she looked in through the window of The Conduit Philomena gave a big sigh of relief because Jonathan was sitting there, calm as you please, tucking into lunch. She looked to the cabbie and they exchanged a thumbs-up.

Inside the cafe she cautiously approached Jonathan's table.

He seemed normal – no, not normal. When she neared him she could see it was an effort for him to look her in the eye and his appearance was terrible: pale, gaunt, agitated. Was he mad after all? Before she could sit he stuttered, 'The th-thing is, Philomena, I'm no good.'

'What are you talking about?'

Their waitress came over. Philomena waved her away, then gestured to apologise that she hadn't meant to be rude.

'Me, that's what I'm talking about. I'm no good. I haven't played fair with you, or come clean. I've landed you in it. I've landed everyone in it.'

'Jonathan, what are you—'

'If you'd let me finish, I'll tell you,' said Jonathan. 'There's two things. The first is that when the lights went in the club the other night it was me. I threw the switch. I saw you with him and I threw the switch to break you two up and I didn't care if anyone got hurt or worse. That's to show you how impetuous, wrong and selfish I can be. The second thing is this.'

She looked down to where Jonathan indicated. The pack of cards had appeared in his trembling hand as if by magic. One-handed he shuffled and cut them, spilling some. He remade the pack and attempted the manoeuvre again, this time succeeding. He did it again. And again.

'See that?' he said.

She was unsure where this was leading, but a lump of pain had appeared in her guts.

Taking the pack in both hands Jonathan performed another

impressive shuffle then dealt two hands onto the table. Two hands of three cards, face down.

'Turn the first card of each hand over.'

Philomena hesitated. She felt herself swaying on her feet.

'Go on,' said Jonathan, impatiently.

She reached down and turned the first card of the first hand. It was the king of hearts. Jonathan closely watched her.

'Turn the other first card,' he commanded.

It was the two of clubs.

'Now the second cards.'

She turned them, feeling a dizzying sense of impending catastrophe. The cards were the jack of hearts and the five of spades.

'Ring any bells?' asked Jonathan. 'Go on, the last two. Or shall I tell you what they are? The ace of spades and the two of diamonds.'

Her mind raced. That's how the hands were in the card game.

'Correct,' said Jonathan, reading her face, 'that's *exactly* how I dealt them.'

'*You* dealt the cards?'

'Somebody had to,' said Jonathan. He retrieved the hands and shuffled them into the pack, dealt the same hands again, this time face up.

'*You* dealt the cards?'

'I rigged the game,' said Jonathan. 'I rigged it so that Dan would win. And I didn't tell him. And I should have. And look what happened. That's why I'm really no good. Perhaps

I should be tried for Dan's death. I *should* be punished. I should receive my just deserts, shouldn't I?'

'*Shut* up, *shut* up,' said Philomena, through clenched teeth.

Jonathan obeyed. His head went down, as if awaiting the executioner's axe. Then Philomena was raining blows down on his head and shoulders, her fists as hard as she could possibly make them. He made no attempt to defend himself; she wished she held hammers. Blow after blow: 'Hah! Hah! Hah! Hah!' Finally, 'Aaaaaarrrrghhhh!' to the ceiling.

Deep breaths. Gulps. Cold fury.

'You idiot. You stupid idiot. You idiot, you idiot!'

Philomena stood over Jonathan, panting, glaring down. She turned on her heel and left him.

CHAPTER FOURTEEN

In a private room in his club Perceval Dore was studying the face of his son, Anthony, opposite him, waiting for the answer to the question he'd just asked.

'I couldn't tell you before because I didn't want to put a question mark over Priest. I didn't want to harm him. I deferred until it became impossible to ignore that he was slandering me, until I couldn't protect him any longer without harming myself.'

'What do you mean, protect him?'

'I thought the episode was concluded; it belonged only to that time and place. Until I discovered he'd repeated it, and it became clear that he's permanently unstable in his mind and in his emotions.' Anthony tried to confine all his twitches to those parts of his body beneath the table.

The elder Dore nodded in agreement. 'And why didn't you tell me yourself? Why send James?'

'Major James investigated and dismissed the allegation, so I thought it best for him to inform you.'

Dore Senior didn't think that was a completely satisfactory answer. He was tempted to follow it up but in his mind he knew the fuller answer and he was ashamed of it. His only surviving son knew that when he'd had two brothers, he was the least favourite. Thus he was disinclined, out of habit, to come to his father for help.

'So the girl is the dead man's fiancée, and Priest is his best friend, and now they're in cahoots,' said Perceval, summing up.

'That's how it seems,' agreed Anthony.

There was an interregnum caused by a waiter entering the room to fuss around the table, open a bottle of white wine, pour a taster, accepted; two glasses, the bottle in the ice bucket. He went out and as the door clicked softly Dore Senior asked his next question.

'You know Priest, obviously.'

Anthony sipped and swallowed, thankful to have something to occupy his hands.

'I'd met him briefly in the field, and we'd shared my hamper together the night before the battle. Suddenly he turned on me. I didn't know that you had any connection with him.'

'Any idea why he turned on you?'

'None. Whatever led him to make the allegation is all in his mind, poor fellow.'

'It's an extraordinary tale.'

'I can only agree,' said Anthony. 'And it's been pretty difficult to live with.'

His father nodded, showing he understood the strain his son must have been under. Anthony grew overconfident and careless.

'I've sometimes wondered whether I received a knock on the head that I was unaware of and that it has given me amnesia and that there was a card game as Priest alleges.'

Wrong thing to say. His father's eyes had narrowed.

'Is that scenario possible?'

'No.' Anthony looked wounded. 'You see,' he went on, 'this is the real reason that I asked Major James to inform you of the situation. I feared that you'd be suspicious of me.'

'I'm not,' assured his father. 'I don't believe you could have done what is alleged. I don't believe any civilised man could have. It's simply too fantastic.'

To confirm his belief in his son, Dore Senior offered his hand across the table, and Anthony made a show of accepting it. There, bond sealed, thought both. Man to man. Dore Senior replenished their glasses.

'I've previously thought that Priest was talented,' he said, 'mercurial. Now I think that he must be unhinged. Mercurial men can fly too close to the sun. Priest had some sort of breakdown in court. He accused you out loud of murder.'

'In court?' gasped Anthony.

'Yes.'

'In *your* court?'

'Yes.'

'Whilst it was *sitting*?' Anthony asked, imagining all the men who must have heard it.

'Yes. I declared it sub judice,' Perceval assured his son. 'If anyone puts it about I'll put them away.'

'There will still be gossip,' said Anthony, his guilt suddenly there, like a third guest at the table. So clear his father couldn't fail to see.

'Don't worry, Anthony. The law is with you. And a girl was in the gallery – I'm presuming she was the fiancée. Have you met her?'

'Yes, I have,' said Anthony. His ridiculous father couldn't see his obvious guilt. He suddenly despised him for being so gullible. 'Another young woman approached me and it was from her that I learned about Philomena Bligh's activities,' he said, being clever with the truth.

'Who is the other young woman?' asked Perceval.

'She said she was called Felicity.'

'Could she be called as a witness?'

Suddenly Anthony didn't feel so clever.

'Do you think it will come to that?'

'I wish you'd told me earlier, as soon as it all happened. We could have quashed it once and for all.'

'As I said, I was concerned for Priest, rightly, as it turns out. He'll be in trouble now, won't he?' Anthony tried not to look pleased.

'Major James is coming to the house tonight,' said Perceval. 'Can you join us? We can draw up a battle plan. He couldn't possibly tell me everything during recess. I need to question him properly. If we're going to deal with Priest I need to hear the whole story.'

'If he'll shut up, I'll still let him alone,' said Anthony, really not wanting the 'whole story' to be given the chance to emerge.

'Priest's thrown down a gauntlet and you must pick it up in some way.'

'I'm prepared to be magnanimous,' Anthony said, trying to make that the final word.

'That's all very well,' replied his father, 'but you must teach chaps like him a lesson.'

'I'd prefer not to have to *sue* him.'

'God, no. Everyone would hear of it. "Son of famous judge sues father's ex protégé over accusation of murder in war." I don't think so, do you? And by the way, you must never repeat that idea that you may have amnesia over a card game.'

'I didn't mean it seriously!'

'Seriously or in jest, never mention it again, especially to a third party. Never,' warned Dore Senior, poking his finger at Anthony's chin.

In those last utterances and gesture Anthony heard the old tone. His father was utterly dissatisfied with him. Anthony tipped his wine and whilst he drank he looked at the older man through the glass. This was one of those moments he hated his father with such intensity he felt he was liable to initiate a frenzied attack upon him. In this instance he could envisage leaning across the table, grasping his head, biting his face – he'd seize it between his teeth and tear chunks off it. He imagined his father blindly stumbling about the room, crashing into furniture, bleeding profusely from his wounds.

'You must never embellish or embroider in any way. You must stick to the briefest facts,' ordered his father.

'There are only brief facts,' said Anthony, making his voice sound normal. 'I took part in no such card game. I only wish Major Chiltern had survived to corroborate that Priest is making it all up.'

'If Chiltern were alive Priest wouldn't have made his allegation, would he? That would be stupid. His fabrication would be immediately obvious; we'd never have arrived where we are now. But he's got so much to lose; that's what I don't understand.'

'Do the actions of a lunatic demand to be understood or should he just be detained for his own safety?' said Anthony, trying to make it sound as if he was thinking only of what was best for Jonathan Priest.

Perceval Dore shrugged. 'There are men who would bend over backwards to try and understand him.'

'Do you count yourself amongst them?'

Anthony launched that slur on his father's loyalty so slyly it took a moment for Perceval to catch on.

'I'm shocked that you even ask that. You are my son, my heir; of course I believe you. You are a gentleman. There's no doubt who is telling the truth. Priest must be insane. That can be his only defence.'

'But there is a problem, isn't there?' said Anthony, seizing the moment. 'He's popular. He can behave as badly as he likes and men will try to understand him. He must be a favourite or he would never have been elevated to being a barrister in the first place. He has a way of making people like him – I think it's an outrage that Major James even asked me about Priest's allegation! He shouldn't have given him the time of day! Why couldn't he accept that Fritz killed his friend? It was a war, for Christ's sake!'

'It was just after the war, wasn't it? In the following minute.'

'Are you still doubting me, father?' demanded Anthony.

'No, but those are the facts, aren't they? Forgive me, I just mean to establish the facts, not because I doubt you, but because they are our bedrock.'

'Yes, it was in the first minute of the Armistice, and I got the Kraut who did it.'

Anthony tried not to shrink as his father studied him. After a few moments Dore Senior jerked forward and grasped Anthony's forearm, clamping it to the table before he could snatch it away.

'That was well done, Anthony, well done,' enthused the elder Dore.

Philomena passed another line of shabby soldiers waiting patiently at a soup kitchen. Months after the Armistice the war wasn't over. The newspapers carried stories every day of 'mopping up' exercises in Europe and outbreaks of hostilities, whilst here in England all these neglected men who went off to fight for their country now begged on the streets – and Jonathan, and Anthony; they were still playing out some aspect of their war. Dan was killed after the Armistice – an armistice is only a truce, it isn't the end. Is the Armistice technically ended? What will come after the Armistice – the peace? That would be nice.

She remembered the soldiers and the middle-aged woman

making the clay battlefield. When she reached the gallery the American owner greeted her like a lost friend.

'Our most frequent visitor!' she declared, smiling, and, acknowledging Philomena's large paisley bag: 'Thinking of moving in?'

'I'm going home, actually.'

'And where's home?'

'Do you know the rest of England?'

'Not really.'

'Up north. Hills and moors and rain,' mused Philomena.

'I see,' said the American woman. 'So you're a tourist here like me?'

'Are you a tourist?' Philomena felt that the woman lived there.

'I dunno,' admitted the American woman, laughing. 'I was in Paris before the war. Came here when life started getting too uncomfortable. I was with a German man, you see,' she went on, her laughter fading.

'Oh,' said Philomena, wondering what difficulties might have resulted from that pairing.

'Mmm,' said the American, and they both looked down at their feet for a moment. 'Actually, you know what? I just told you a lie. I wasn't with a German man, I was with a German woman.'

'Oh,' said Philomena again, thinking that that must have been double trouble.

'She went home.'

Philomena thought that that would have been one way of

solving the problems they might have been experiencing, but self-defeating because it meant they were parted.

'Where she died in an air raid.'

'I'm sorry,' said Philomena.

'Mmm,' said the American, looking down as she scratched the instep of her shoe on the concrete floor. '*C'est la vie, c'est la guerre,*' she said, quietly. 'How about you?'

'I came down here to introduce myself to my dead fiancé's friends,' replied Philomena.

'I can understand that,' said the American woman. 'I'm thinking of making that very same trip to Germany.'

Philomena smiled wanly. 'I hope that you don't find over there what I found here.'

It was the American woman's turn to say: 'Oh?'

Then what a relief, because Philomena told her the beginning of the story, the next bit, and the next. She wondered if she should swear her to secrecy, but that might seem rude given how open she had been with her. The American woman occasionally interrupted to ask questions for clarification as Philomena told her more of the story, but leaving some things out, as you have to, otherwise the telling of a story would take as long as the events it described, and gradually the American woman had less need to ask any questions, and Philomena arrived at the present.

'And what are you going to do now?' asked her attentive listener.

'I'm going to catch my train, and go home.'

'Mmm,' said the American woman, in that way of hers.

'You're worried about Jonathan, I can see. But there's nothing you can do about that, you know? If someone's set on doing something to themselves you can't stop them.'

'I stopped someone the other day,' said Philomena.

'Oh?' said the American woman.

But, Philomena thought, if you follow this woman's logic, William Rust might try again. And suddenly she felt that she couldn't go to the train without first reassuring herself that the shabby young soldier was alive, and at home.

'I've got to go,' she said, picking up her bag.

'Your train?'

'No. Something else.' Moving now towards the exit.

'You can leave that loud bag here if you want,' called the American woman after her.

'Thanks, but I'll manage,' Philomena called over her shoulder, tightening her grip on it.

Out of breath when she reached the tenement, she paced. How to get to see inside William Rust's room? She needed to be up as high as him, back in her recently vacated hotel room, in fact. She entered the foyer to be faced with the surly porter. He saw her and made a move to disappear into the office behind the counter, but Philomena didn't give him a chance to avoid her:

'I think I left something in my room and I'm late for my train – please, please, let me go up there. Nobody's moved in, have they? Please, please.'

The surly porter was about to decline, but he'd only just taken over from the pleasant day porter, who heard the breathless female and came out to see who it was. It was he who said: 'No, nobody's moved in yet and it hasn't been cleaned. You're welcome to go up.'

The surly porter seemed about to protest, but the pleasant porter held out the room key. Philomena grabbed it and sped up the stairs. Once in the room she dashed to the window. Across the way, there were no signs of life in William Rust's room. She felt the energy go out of her. Her shoulders became too heavy. Then her head. She leaned on the dusty windowsill and rested, standing up, enervated. Footsteps arrived in the doorway behind but she was too tired to look. Someone cleared their throat.

'Have you found whatever it is, miss?'

It was the surly porter, being less surly than usual.

'No,' she said, without turning.

'Was it valuable?'

The hairs on the back of her neck stood up. Why was he asking that?

'It isn't money or anything, no.'

Her attention was taken by the flicker of a flame in the recesses of William Rust's room. She could see tantalising glimpses of a figure as it lit a lamp. The figure came closer to the window, pulled up a chair, and sat. William Rust was returned to his room opposite. The only difference to him was that he had a brace around his neck. He saw her and, with a shy smile, raised a hand in greeting. She reciprocated and carried on looking towards him for a while but he made no further movement. Tears poured down her cheeks unchecked. William Rust was all right; therefore Jonathan could be all right. She could go home now.

She smeared her tears across her cheeks with her hands, brushed past the surly porter in the doorway, mumbling 'thank you'.

When she got to Euston she had just enough time to write a letter and post it before her train. *Dear Jonathan*, she began, but didn't know what else to say . . . Give up? Apologise to Anthony Dore? Don't kill yourself? Don't kill him? Her train appeared on the departures board. She couldn't find the words in the short time available. She'd compose the letter as and when.

She walked onto the platform and along the train, peering into each carriage, seeking one that contained another female. There. She stepped up, nodding to the older woman. Philomena hoisted her luggage bag up into the rack and made herself comfortable on the bench seat opposite. She opened her leather everyday bag and located her ticket, ready for the inspector's approval. She fussed at her hair and watched the engine's steam drift past the window. She handled the sheaf of envelopes. On top was the photo of her that Jonathan had had. Part of her wished he still had it. If she 'returned' it to him, that would be inviting further contact . . . Would she ever see him again? Her hands started fidgeting. They were back. A life of their own. Her fingers flicked through the sheaf of envelopes and stopped. Something was missing. Trying to damp down her panic, she began to sort through them — she always kept them in the same order — there! One was out of place. Outside, the guard's whistle sounded and doors slammed shut. She began to breathe more heavily as she searched through the sheaf for the out of place letter. No, no. It was definitely missing. She looked up to the older woman opposite, pleading.

'Whatever's the matter?' the woman gasped.

'I've lost one,' Philomena whispered hoarsely and stuffed the sheaf of papers into her open bag, yanked her hat on, opened the carriage door, dropped her bag, picked it up, screamed because someone slammed the carriage door shut again, yanked the window down, reached out to the handle and forced the door open once more.

'It's departing,' a guard shouted, 'you can't detrain!'

'Your bag in the rack!' her fellow passenger was shouting.

'Throw it after me!' yelled Philomena.

Ignoring the guard keeping pace with her carriage Philomena pushed the door wide open and leapt off the moving train, striking the guard a glancing blow. She fell to the stone platform, right onto her back. She lay dazed, full length for a moment, her belongings scattered around her, erupted from her everyday bag. In her prone position she watched, dazed, as her paisley bag landed further up the platform and skidded to a halt. Another guard ran alongside the train and succeeded in shutting the open door.

As other people began to arrive on the scene, Philomena hauled herself up, stuffed her belongings back into her bag, collected her paisley, apologised profusely to everyone without making eye contact, and hurried shakily away.

At the hotel she caught the surly porter skulking behind his desk.

'You're worried that somebody took something from my room, aren't you? You know somebody's been in there, don't you? Did you let somebody in there?'

The porter said nothing.

'Deny it,' she challenged, 'deny it.'

'I don't know what you're talking about,' said the porter, unable to maintain the veil over his shiftiness.

'Liar,' she retorted. 'He paid you, didn't he?'

And before he could respond she marched out of the hotel and hailed the first taxi.

The darkness thickened as they drove. Lights showed in the windows in the square when she burst out of the vehicle as it came to a stop outside Anthony's house. She marched up the stone steps and hammered on the front doors. A servant opened one of the pair, and, keeping his booted foot behind it, took her in with a contemptuous glance.

'Stop it and go to the side,' he hissed.

Philomena ignored him. Still possessed by the same demon energy that had propelled her off the train she hammered on the door that remained closed and shouted that she wanted to see Anthony. 'Get Anthony here, now. Get Anthony here! He's got my letter! Anthony Dore has one of my letters!'

Inside the house Anthony appeared at the top of the stairs and his father emerged from a ground-floor room. They listened for a few moments. Anthony felt his head go fuzzy. Perceval went to a window looking onto the porch and peered out.

It was the girl, wasn't it? What the hell was she up to? He shot a quizzical look at Anthony, who was transfixed. Outside, Philomena was still shouting that Anthony had her letter. Looking out of the window again, Dore Senior saw another taxi pull up. He caught sight of Major James squinting out from this one. At the same moment Philomena looked about herself for the first time since she'd begun hammering the doors. She saw Major James trying to hide in his taxi, swept down the steps towards him and began pounding on his window: 'What did you tell the judge? Anthony Dore's father; what did you tell him?'

Major James ordered his cabbie to drive and it sped away. Telling herself to stop ranting and raving, Philomena looked back up at the Dore house. The judge was bearing down on her; servants spread out on the steps behind him, a phalanx of flunkeys. Philomena opened her heart and beseeched, 'Please can I have my letter returned to me? Please.'

'Get back in your taxi and leave before the police arrive,' roared the judge.

Pressed back against the cold metal of the motor car, she fumbled behind her for the door handle and climbed in. The driver didn't need telling that he should drive on. Judge Dore was close enough to stare in at her through the flimsy glass, eyes burning, as they pulled away.

CHAPTER FIFTEEN

Following the episode with the girl Perceval Dore was extremely disappointed that Anthony had gone off without a word. He found his son in his apartment, which, in his annoyance, he entered without knocking. Anthony was sitting at his desk in his lounge, quite still.

'Have you any idea to what that girl was referring?'

'No,' replied Anthony, not looking at his father.

'You've no idea to what letter she referred?'

'No.'

'It's completely inexplicable to you?' spelled out Dore Senior, in a way that also communicated: 'For God's sake why don't you look at me when I'm talking to you?'

'It's plainly some plan she and Priest have cooked up to get him off the hook,' said Anthony, making fleeting eye contact. 'She throws more mud and they hope that some of it sticks.'

'It's strange mud to throw; to accuse you of being in possession of a letter,' replied his father.

'It's bizarre, I agree,' replied Anthony. 'Only they can account for the grotesque workings of their minds.'

Now his son looked at him directly, and Perceval could see the hurt in them. He silently swore to himself that Priest and the girl were going to pay for their cruel injustice. On the desk in front of Anthony he noticed his son's bible, the one he knew Anthony's mother had given him. His tone softened.

'Seeking solace?' he asked. 'Turning the other cheek is in Matthew, if I remember rightly.'

'I know,' said Anthony, again looking away. Hiding his upset emotions, his father speculated.

Perceval picked up the bible and it was all Anthony could do to stop himself snatching it from his hands. He tried not to stare at the hefty holy book as his father opened it at the index.

'Gossip spreads faster than a forest fire and is harder to extinguish. Has either Priest or the girl ever demanded money from you?'

'Money? No,' said Anthony, unable to stop his eyes widening as he glimpsed the stolen letter peeping out from between the pages of the Good Book.

'I don't understand what they're up to. If there was never any card game I don't understand what they're trying to achieve. I'm going to have to question them both, as well as Major James. Is there anyone else you can think of whom I should talk to?'

Anthony could only shake his head as he watched the stolen letter escape the pages of the bible and drop silently to the floor. He tried not to look at it as if, by not doing so, his father would fail to notice it. Indeed, Perceval had not seen it, so lost was he in his thoughts. The letter lay on the floor.

Anthony considered making an elaborate dive on top of it, but he couldn't imagine any explanation that could possibly account for such an action. His father paced, and turned sideways to look out of the window. Anthony seized the opportunity to rise from his seat and stand on the letter.

'The crowd's gone,' said Perceval. 'It's amazing how they materialise and disappear.'

Anthony didn't respond. He just wanted his father to leave.

'Shall we dine together this evening?' his father suggested.

Anthony suddenly took his father's arm and aimed him towards the door saying: 'Yes, let's have dinner together – my treat.'

Perceval smiled and tried to turn and replace the bible on the desk where it had lain. But Anthony didn't want him to turn back into the room, and tried to press him the other way.

'I still have your mother's bible,' said Perceval, handing it to his son.

'Do you want to borrow it?' said Anthony.

'Borrow your bible? No.'

'Are you sure?' said Anthony, still managing to keep his foot on the letter on the floor.

'Quite sure,' replied Perceval, thinking his son's behaviour rather odd. He offered it again to Anthony, this time successfully. Anthony tucked it under his arm and still tried to encourage his father out of the door.

'You're not taking a bible to dinner, are you? I think I'd find that rather inhibiting,' said Perceval, attempting levity.

At which point Anthony had to adjust his balance, which resulted in him having to put more weight on the foot that was standing on the letter, and he slipped on it. Perceval grabbed his son: 'Steady on!' and held him up. The letter had been sent skidding across the floor.

'Hold on. What's that?' said Perceval. 'You've dropped something.' He walked a few steps, bent down to pick up the letter, held it out to Anthony. As it passed between them Perceval glanced down and just caught sight of the addressee. It wasn't Anthony Dore. The intended recipient was Philomena Bligh. His son turned and unlocked a draw in a desk and slipped the letter inside. Whilst locking the drawer Anthony felt that in order to appear to be behaving naturally he must look at his father, but when he did so Perceval's back was to him. He was already gazing out of the window again.

At Jonathan's apartment block the concierge dialled him and passed Philomena the handset. 'Jonathan, it's me. I haven't gone home yet.'

Jonathan slumped against the wall. She'd come back! Despite his confessing to her that he'd fixed the fateful game of brag, she wanted to see him again!

'Jonathan?' he heard.

'Yes, I'm here,' he replied, huskily.

'I've something to tell you – something else has happened,' said Philomena.

'What's happened?' It sounded like more trouble.

'And I need more money to pay a taxi driver.'

'I'm coming down!'

Jonathan paid the taxi and it drove away in the evening darkness. Philomena hovered at the side of the doors, inside the vestibule, holding her luggage. When Jonathan came back into the building he tentatively faced her, didn't ask her what she was going to do now, didn't want to appear to assume that she wished to come up to his apartment.

'I've missed my train,' she said flatly, aware that the concierge would eavesdrop.

Jonathan nodded, awaited further information.

Wary of being overheard, Philomena leaned into Jonathan and whispered: 'Anthony has stolen one of my letters from Dan.'

'He's what?' exploded Jonathan.

Philomena silently shushed him.

'He's stolen one of—'

'Yes, I understood,' said Jonathan. 'I just can't believe it.' He remembered where they were, glanced around, saw the concierge not looking at them but almost definitely listening. He turned back to Philomena, whispered, over-enunciating: 'Look, I was determined not to ask this, but do you want to come up?'

'May I?' returned Philomena, relieved at his invitation, but not letting on how much.

He nodded and stood aside. Carrying her own bag she crossed the floor, passing close to Jonathan but not touching. They entered the lift and waited for the doors to close. The concierge studiously affected indifference. When the lift jerked into motion Philomena said in her normal voice, 'I think the night porter let him into my room when I wasn't there.'

'What did this letter say?' urged Jonathan.

'Nothing relevant. It was from weeks before the end.'

'It's not a letter that mentioned Anthony Dore?'

'No. Dan never mentioned him,' said Philomena.

'Why would Dore steal a letter from Dan to you?' Jonathan puzzled, still searching for a motive.

'I don't know. But I think he has,' said Philomena, sounding rational when in fact all she'd acted upon was a gut feeling and guesswork. 'I returned to the hotel and accused the surly porter and he didn't deny—'

Jonathan was incredulous again: 'You did what, the who?'

Philomena didn't reply because the lift had jerked to a halt at Jonathan's floor. He led the way to his apartment. The door was ajar the way he'd left it when responding to Philomena's request for help. In the kitchen she neither deposited her luggage nor sat down. He paced, picked up a bottle of brandy, paced.

She said, 'I went back and accused the surly porter of accepting money to let someone into my room and he didn't deny it. After that I went to Anthony's house and accused him.'

Jonathan stopped pacing and stared at her. 'You did what?'

'Please stop haranguing me,' said Philomena, 'I accused Anthony Dore—'

'I'm not haranguing—'

'Just let me explain. I accused Anthony—'

'To his face?' Jonathan interrupted, unable to contain himself.

'I didn't see him. I shouted it, at his house,' said Philomena, making it sound an everyday sort of thing to have done.

Jonathan's jaw dropped open.

'His father came out to warn me off – oh, and Major James was there, but he drove off.' Philomena transferred her paisley bag to her other hand. 'So that's how I missed my train,' she said.

'Tell me the beginning of the story,' insisted Jonathan, sitting down at the table.

'You know my sheaf of letters? Well I got onto the train and I noticed that one was missing, and for a moment I just felt desolate that I'd lost it. Then I had this sudden realisation that he'd stolen it from my—'

'Not like that. Put your bag down, take your coat off, sit down and tell me everything,' ordered Jonathan.

When she'd finished and he had asked all the questions he needed to, he poured himself a large drink. They sat in silence for a while. Jonathan couldn't help a wry smile.

'What?' she demanded.

'So now you too believe Anthony Dore is guilty of something that you are unable to prove.'

'Yes,' said Philomena, not smiling.

Jonathan blew out a stream of air.

'They're really going to come for us,' he said. 'I've been called to appear before my head of chambers first thing.'

'Is that bad? Of course it is. Stupid of me.'

'I'll be expected to resign,' said Jonathan. 'They won't be able to back me. What I can't predict is whether Dore'll sue me. If he does I'll have my day, or few days in the sun, picking away at him in the witness stand, but ultimately, no proof. They might not bother suing you as you haven't slandered him.' Philomena's eyes flickered. Jonathan's sixth sensed nudged him. 'You haven't told anyone about all this, have you?'

'Yes, I have actually,' admitted Philomena.

'Who?' demanded Jonathan.

'Someone who won't repeat it.'

'Who?'

'A friend,' she soothed.

'Who? Tell me their name.'

'I don't know their name.'

'What? How can they be a friend?'

'Because they are,' said Philomena, shrugging her shoulders.

Jonathan shook his head and looked askance at her.

'She won't tell anyone anything,' stated Philomena.

'So it's a woman?' pounced Jonathan.

'She − won't − tell,' repeated Philomena, separating the words for emphasis. 'I trust her. She confided in me and vice versa. She knows I'm not going to go around blabbing, and I know she's not.'

Jonathan appeared to finally accept this. He nodded several

times. But Philomena could see that there was still something eating at him.

'Did you tell her about me?' he asked, his voice catching.

'About you? Yes, you are a major part in the—'

'Did you tell her what I did?' he interrupted.

'Yes,' she said, meeting his gaze, 'yes I did tell her.'

Jonathan stood and moved away the few feet to a corner of the room. He stood side-on to a cabinet, running his fingers over the work surface atop it. Philomena rose and went the other way, to the window. Their conversation split into separate trains of thought for a few moments.

'Perhaps I should just announce what I did then I wouldn't have to worry about who knows and who doesn't,' said Jonathan.

'She's a good woman, American, my friend whose name I don't know.'

'In the old days Anthony and I could have had a duel,' Jonathan said.

'You must stay in the law,' said Philomena. 'There must be a way.'

'Not that I'm the type. Nor he.'

'Isn't there some kind of appeal you can make?' said Philomena.

Jonathan tossed his head back, emptied his drink. 'I'm not sure about this brandy,' he said.

'William Rust is back in his rooms,' murmured Philomena.

'He told me he was going there,' answered Jonathan, restoring their duologue.

'You've seen him again?' asked Philomena.

'Briefly. In hospital. I think he's going to be all right. The police officer in charge is a veteran. He doesn't want to charge him.'

'You *see*,' said Philomena, turning to him, 'you help people. People who really need it.'

Jonathan returned to the table, poured himself another drink. 'I should have told Dan I'd rigged the game. He would have scrapped the IOU.'

'I don't know if he would,' argued Philomena. 'He might have said that the Dores only got rich by cheating anyway. He said that anyone who was rich was crooked in some way, or their ancestor who'd become rich was crooked. He might have argued that it was all right to cheat a crook's descendant. Have you told anyone else?'

'That I rigged the cards? No.'

'It doesn't make it any less of a murder, does it?' said Philomena.

Jonathan looked sharply at her. Anthony Dore was guilty?

Yes, her eyes confirmed, she was saying that. She believed him. Those eyes!

She sat down. He mirrored her.

'That I rigged the game could be used to make Anthony seem like a victim,' Jonathan said, testing her commitment.

'But to use the fact that you dealt the cards he'd have to admit that there was a card game!' she countered, with twice his energy.

His eyes flared. 'I didn't deal them, I rigged them,' he

reminded her. 'That I confess to it doesn't absolve me. I told you because I was unable to hide the full extent of my involvement any longer – not just out of fear that you might learn it from Anthony Dore's version if it were to be published; I couldn't continue to conceal such a terrible secret from you. It was poison that would only spread.'

He was square on to Philomena as he said this, his soul bared again, as it had been in the public house following her first sighting of Anthony Dore. She was tempted to cross her arms, and he saw her impulse to do that, and he paused, in order that she could choose how to listen to him, open or closed. Fearing that if she gave in and closed she would be making the wrong decision at one of the key moments in her life, Philomena deliberately chose open, kept her arms unfolded, lifted her heart. He was offering himself – whoever he was, it was her human duty to meet him like for like, in the moment. Her behaviour should be such that whenever she looked back it was without regret.

'I don't expect,' he went on, 'that you will absolve, forgive, or pardon me for my complicity; you may not wish to, but also it's simply not in your gift. Living with the terrible consequences of my actions is going to be a life sentence, in a kinder gaol now that I've confessed, but the tariff remains full-term with no parole.'

Philomena pursed her lips and nodded. Jonathan shifted his weight in his seat, struggled for the right words.

'Philomena, you are being merciful, sympathetic, understanding – yes!' he raised his arms in a victory salute. 'At least now you understand me. That's quite something, no? To feel that someone understands you?'

'We mustn't be self-pitying,' she said, coming in lower, 'not that I'm saying that you are. You are being absolutely honest about yourself and the situation. Rigorously so. When someone else has said that they don't expect this or that from me I've felt manipulated, known that they do want exactly those things. But not you.'

Jonathan dipped his head to indicate his agreement and thanks.

She went on: 'There are thousands like us, millions, trying to pick their way through the aftermath. My friend, she's lost someone, a German, a civilian, who went back, and was bombed to death by us. She could hate the aviators who killed her lover, or hate all our airmen, but I don't think she does.' More thoughts sprang up, jostled to be rendered into speech. She began to speed up: 'Everyone must find a way of living without forgetting, or even forgiving, but you're right about poison spreading; it mustn't be allowed to – yours or mine or anyone else's – and I don't think that yours or mine is very strong poison, and we don't know for certain what's going to happen tomorrow. They might not ask you to resign, you might be surprised—'

Jonathan solemnly shook his head. Philomena reined in her unrealistic optimism.

'No,' said Philomena, reminded that she was a Saddleworth girl who sewed for her living. 'Well, then we're in trouble, tomorrow, but we won't always be. We have to hope – we just have to.'

She looked down, unable to trust her voice to go on if she kept looking at Jonathan. They both had their hands on the table. She glanced up. They caught each other's eye then looked away, then down at their hands, almost touching. The slightest movement from either of them, and they would be touching. Philomena's hands behaved themselves, but she wouldn't have minded if they hadn't.

CHAPTER SIXTEEN

Following dinner and formal goodnights, Perceval Dore went to his son's apartment a little after midnight and knocked on the door.

All through three courses, white wine, red wine, port, he'd avoided referring to the dropped letter addressed to Philomena. He'd been silent for much of the time, as had Anthony, but that was normal when they were together. What was unusual was that Perceval had been running the story of Anthony's life in his head, looking for clues.

He knew that his middle child – unlike his brothers – had never found his metier, but that wasn't an explanation in itself. Plenty of men at all levels in society plodded dutifully through life without becoming criminals. He'd thought about the effects of being a middle child. It was axiomatic that they felt overlooked, or they disappeared, or hid; but again, none of these could possibly explain what Perceval feared to be true about his surviving son. Yes, Anthony had always been the least clearly drawn of the boys. His mother had even gone so far as to describe him once as 'a stranger'. But strangerliness was also an unsatisfactory explanation for what Perceval had previously dismissed as impossible, become incredulous about, and was now bewildered by.

Next Perceval had dwelt on Anthony's failure to attract fondness. Edward and Albert, the brothers who bracketed him, were awarded nicknames from an early age, but Anthony had remained known only by his given name. A soubriquet that told of affection bestowed on him or the esteem he was held in would have reassured but there had always been something about Anthony that stubbornly resisted love.

During port Perceval had looked very closely at Anthony whenever his son's face was turned away, which was often, and had felt a deep anguish in himself. If his wife had been there he might have been able to begin to share all this with her, but as it was he was completely alone, agonising over what to do. After the meal he'd needed to get away from the boy in order to be able to think about it all properly. To try and see clearly what must be done, given what seemed to be the case.

Anthony answered his door. His father brushed past him, into the room.

'I've turned a blind eye too often,' said Perceval. 'About you failing to find a purpose, frittering your time away. So all that has got to stop. You are going to have to find some useful function in life and apply yourself wholeheartedly to it. But before all that, you have in your possession a letter that doesn't belong to you. If you're caught lying over that you're susceptible to be disbelieved about everything else, so it has to be disposed of. Now. Burn it. Now.'

Anthony couldn't help himself. He lied. 'What letter?'

Perceval stared at him. Under his father's intense scrutiny Anthony lied again, a new lie.

'I've already burned it.'

Perceval continued to stare.

Anthony's eyes hurt with the effort he was having to make to stop them sliding to look at the chest of drawers that covered the point on the floor under which the letter had only just been hidden, in the box with his special things. He felt a disintegration of himself. His brain frantically twisted in its attempts to devise a way out.

'Get the letter, Anthony,' said Perceval.

Anthony lost control of his eyes for a moment. They slid to the spot. His father followed them and went there, to the set of drawers.

'Is it in here?'

Anthony began to shake uncontrollably.

'Is it in here?' repeated Perceval.

When Anthony still didn't reply, his father pulled the top drawer right out of the chest and flipped it over in mid-air so the contents violently spilled out. Papers and pencils and odds and ends flew to the corners of the room.

'Is it amongst these? Is it? Answer me,' Perceval demanded, 'before I tear your rooms apart. I've all night and all tomorrow to achieve this. My case has been postponed thanks to you and Priest.'

Perceval took a strong grip on the second drawer and tugged. It slid open then stuck. He tugged harder, his anger taking him over. The whole set of drawers shifted, caught on something. Perceval redoubled his efforts and with a shout, 'YAAH!' yanked the chest of drawers with all his considerable might. The whole moved with a great *crack*! It shifted half a yard, leaving one of its feet behind, trapped by a slightly raised floorboard. Anthony gagged as if he was going to vomit. Perceval peered down at the raised floorboard, got down on his knees and grasped it.

'What's this?' he asked, more to himself than Anthony.

The board wasn't secured. Perceval looked at Anthony, his aghast offspring, and he decided that he had to know. He pulled at the floorboard until it was loose in his hands. Casting it aside he crouched and peered down into the exposed cavity. There was a tin box. He lifted it out and tried to open it. He stood up and placed it on the desk in front of Anthony.

'The key, please.'

Anthony nodded and rummaged in a pocket, held the key out in a trembling hand. Perceval took it, inserted it in the lock. With the lid open he could see oilcloth. He took it out and carefully unrolled it. He encountered a layer of tissue paper. When this was unfolded he found the photograph of his deceased wife, the letters between Anthony and his mother, the pressed flower, the French pornographic post cards, and lastly the letter to Philomena. Perceval took out a handkerchief, using it to prevent leaving any fingerprints on the envelope and letter, which he slid out to read.

'So then,' he said, eventually. 'What a terrible mess.' He fell silent again, and the feeling was that the terrible mess could refer to the present situation or the whole world. He replaced the crucial letter in its envelope. 'Australia or Canada, you decide.'

For a few moments Anthony thought his father had taken leave of his senses. What on earth was this abrupt invitation to judge between colonies supposed to mean?

'Your choice: Canada or Australia. Both big enough to lose yourself in. You're going today. Canada or Australia.'

Anthony began to protest: 'That item doesn't in itself prove that I—'

'Shut up, you coward,' snapped Perceval, stunning his son into silence. 'You lose yourself in either of those vast places or I hand you over to the police. That's the best I can do. I'm not doing the right thing in giving you the chance to escape, but I'm prepared to try and live with my decision.'

'Nobody else knows!' pleaded Anthony.

'They shall do if you don't leave.'

There was a pause whilst Anthony caught on to the fact that his father was threatening that if he did not go into exile he would be given up. In desperation Anthony made a grab for the letter. He laid fingertips on it. Perceval snatched it away with one hand, whilst with the other he swatted Anthony hard to the head.

'You leave today,' panted Perceval Dore. 'It's a chance. Take it.'

'I did it for you!' screamed Anthony, clutching his temple.

'You did what for me?' screamed back Perceval.

'I bet everything, I lost everything – I had to get it back!'

Anthony fell to his knees, begging, but all this served to do was further inflame his father, who bent down and pushed his distorted features close to Anthony's own.

'You had to?! Hmm?'

Anthony flinched as his father's spittle struck his face.

'I did one thing wrong!' he protested.

'*Which* is the one thing? You shot a German soldier *after* the Armistice and pretended it was he who'd shot your comrade? Was the German armed? Was he alert? Was he fighting? Did he think that the war was over? Mm? Or is the *one thing* the murder of the comrade, the shooting of a fellow warrior? Or is the one wrong thing your casting of a *third* comrade, the one who'd accused you, as a madman? That is three things, at least. You did one thing wrong? You can't even count!'

Perceval turned away and took himself to the furthest portion of the room where he paced, snarling to himself, scared that he might give in to his rage and exterminate his son.

'You wouldn't really give me up, would you? You wouldn't, would you?' whined Anthony.

'Stop that sound, stop that wheedling! Stand up!'

Anthony swiftly obeyed. Perceval walked around his son, looking at him from every angle, like a sergeant-major inspecting a particularly repugnant specimen of a soldier. When he got to Anthony's front he addressed him, gravely.

'Have you ever done anything like this before?'

'No!' squealed Anthony.

'Are you sure?'

'Yes!'

'How do I know that you're telling the truth?'

Perceval subjected Anthony to the longest, deepest scrutiny, using all his years of experience defending, prosecuting and presiding over countless instances of human depravity and mendacity. The judge stared deep into his son's eyes, searching through them, behind them.

Anthony felt that he was falling, shrinking and spinning; plummeting through nothingness, terrified it would never stop; the dark abyss was infinite. His father's voice brought him back to the room but the terrifying place he had just been continued inside him.

'I believe,' said Perceval, 'as far as I am able to discern that you're telling the truth about that. However, you've committed an act abhorrent and unforgivable, Anthony; try and be a man about it. You've a choice: a new life far away or stay and face the music. Either way, I wish that I'd never spawned you, I wish that you had died whilst either of your brothers lived – if I could make some retrospective pact with the Devil to that effect, I would.'

Anthony rocked back on his heels and had to take a step to avoid falling.

'There. I've said it.' Perceval turned away and leaned on the desk, panting in distress.

Still Anthony had one last plea: 'Mother wouldn't want you to—'

'Don't you dare bring your mother's name into this!'

exploded Perceval, turning on Anthony. 'Don't you dare! I'm giving you a chance to get away because you're my son and I must be in some part to blame for you. Why did you steal this girl's letter?'

'She was trying to trick me!'

'Trick you into what?'

Anthony didn't want to say.

'She was trying to trick you into telling the truth, wasn't she?' Something snapped in Perceval. He grasped Anthony's head with both hands and pushed hard, squeezed ferociously, tried to compress his son's skull, force his amoral mind out through his eye sockets. He heard a terrifying noise, like the death-wail of a hedgehog being slain by a fox. That shrieking, pleading. It was Anthony screaming from the back of his throat. That hedgehog noise had never stopped a fox, but Perceval, even at the height of his turmoil could calculate the consequences if he killed his son. He'd have to go down to his study, take out his old revolver and end himself. He let his hands drop to his sides, stared down at his son writhing on the floor. How could it be that he was his? Get away from him! He must get away. He went to the door.

'Start packing,' he ordered. 'You take only what you can carry.'

'If I disappear, people are going to think the allegations are true!' Anthony called after his father.

He heard the door to his apartment slam shut.

In the night Philomena dreamed that Jonathan and she had cornered Judge Dore, Anthony Dore, and Major James in a busy restaurant, where they were eating. She looked on whilst Jonathan sat down uninvited at their table and started to shuffle the pack of cards. Judge Dore told everyone to remain calm. Priest had dug his own grave earlier that day and now he was about to bury himself. Jonathan invited Anthony to declare in public that there was no card game, no betting, no IOUs, and that he hadn't killed Dan. Anthony didn't respond.

With the room watching Jonathan said he'd crack Anthony's defence. First; the proposition that there was no card game. Jonathan dealt two hands of three-card brag blind, one to himself and the other to Anthony, telling the latter that if he won, his version was the truth. Anthony didn't move. Jonathan asked him if he'd forgotten how to play, and turned the cards. He won. He dealt another two hands, saying to Anthony, if you win this one there was no bet. Again Anthony didn't move, apart from his mouth when he said that he was sorry for Priest – his mind had been broken on the wheel of war. Jonathan ignored Anthony and won the hand, saying the cards never lie. Anthony said, loud enough for the room to hear, that he was prepared to help Jonathan by getting him the best medical help, reminding him that they were comrades once, however briefly. It was beginning to look like Jonathan was unable to shake Anthony.

Philomena stepped up to the table and greeted Anthony and presented him with a covered platter. When she had everyone's attention, like a conjuror she whisked off the lid to reveal the two IOUs; Dan's to Anthony and Anthony's to Dan. Anthony turned ghostly pale and there were gasps from all around and Jonathan said yes, very quietly, and Philomena felt exalted. Avenged! But whilst Jonathan looked into her eyes Anthony Dore snatched up a steak knife from the table and plunged it into Jonathan's body, not once but several times, punching it in, then embraced Jonathan, pulling his heart onto the serrated steel.

Jonathan was acutely aware that Philomena was sleeping in the spare bedroom, next door, just the other side of one thin wall. After he eventually dropped off he imagined that in the night she was hunched on the edge of his bed, rocking, sobbing: 'Don't die, please don't die, please don't die.'

Waking from her nightmare she'd stumbled into Jonathan's room and indeed begged him not to die. Having delivered this entreaty she'd returned to her own bed and fallen into an exhausted sleep. When she opened her eyes it was barely dawn. Jonathan was hissing her short name through her door.

'Phil! Phil!'

'Hang on!' she called. She got up off the bed and threw on the outer layers of her clothing and opened the door. Jonathan was white-faced.

'He's here, you must go!'

He turned. She watched him walk the landing, enter the kitchen.

Who was there? Who would Jonathan refer to only as 'he'? Anthony! Anthony was here? In the kitchen with Jonathan?! Jonathan was warning her, telling her to get out, save herself?

She craned to hear what was happening down there, fearing the sounds of an argument, or even violence. Had Anthony brought his lawyers or was he alone? Philomena slid along the wall of the corridor, stopping just short of the kitchen. The door was open. She edged closer, ready to peer around the jamb. Jonathan's wild face appeared, expecting to see her much further away. They both jumped.

'I said go!' he hissed.

'I'm not leaving you on your own with him – is he alone?'

'Yes.'

'What does he want?'

'To talk to me.'

'I dreamed he killed you!'

A figure emerged behind Jonathan, much larger than she was expecting. It wasn't Anthony Dore; it was his father. For a moment he looked startled but recovered quickly. 'Oh,' he said, glowering. 'The other one. Good.' Judge Dore stepped back into the kitchen.

'I thought it was Anthony,' mouthed Philomena.

'No,' mouthed Jonathan.

'Shall we talk?' called the judge.

Jonathan nodded fatalistically to Philomena. They entered the kitchen, a condemned pair. Philomena instinctively folded her arms protectively across her heart. Judge Dore was standing one side of the table, they the other.

'I wanted us to have a chance to sort this out, man to man – and man to woman,' nodding to include her. 'There have been some serious allegations, wild allegations some might say, made. One of you has accused my son of murder, the other of possessing a letter of hers.'

The judge looked at her and something detonated in Philomena's brain. Whilst the judge paused, as if giving them room to accept his invitation to withdraw their accusations, she searched for it.

'Needless to say my son denies both charges. Neither of you have any proof. Not a shred. Have you? My son, on his part, has accused you, Mr Priest, of being mentally unstable. Now I would rather not believe that, but your behaviour yesterday could be taken as an indication that you are that way, given that there is no evidence to back your allegation. So.'

Judge Dore paused. Philomena looked to Jonathan. She could see he was waiting, as she was, for the judge to reveal his precise purpose, or for it to become detectable. She became conscious of her rapid heartbeat. The image of Dore's huge house, a home for giants, returned to her, and the weight of the Old Bailey, where the judge was an insider and they were definitely not. She made herself look at the judge and try to see beyond his title, office, to see him as a man, a father, but his power inundated the room, threatening to suffocate her. But what had been that look in his eye when he'd mentioned her letter?

'Learning of the conflict between you and my son,' Judge Dore directed to Jonathan, 'has led me to understand, to reinterpret your abrupt departure from chambers and your subsequent behaviour toward me when I've offered you the hand of friendship.'

Jonathan nodded, affirming that the judge's interpretation of his behaviour was the correct one. The judge made a show of sitting down, inviting them to parley. Jonathan joined him. Philomena remained on her feet. The judge almost issued an order for her to sit, but decided it probably wasn't worth the effort. A tussle over that would distract.

'I'm prepared to negotiate a truce between you all,' he continued, 'with no admissions or further action on any side, without prejudice, and I am offering to take steps to ensure that no consequences flow from your actions in my court last afternoon. I know that your head of chambers has summoned you, but with your agreement that this affair is over – that you will never again make any threat or accusation or insinuation against my son, I will intervene on your behalf. And my actions here must not be construed as anything other than those of a man who desires an end to conflict, conflict between my son and a young man I hold in some esteem. And you, miss, you are also impressive, for your doggedness and determination, misguided though you be.'

Jonathan pursed his lips. Philomena looked away, reviewing Judge Dore's presentation. Disbelieving that he could be entirely genuine, she made herself look at him again – an act of will, requiring courage consciously summoned. She felt a sudden surge of confidence when, on meeting the judge's gaze she saw his eyes flicker, and his hands, flat and calm on Jonathan's kitchen table, twitched.

'We stop making accusations against your son and you

won't ruin us,' said Jonathan. 'Are you scared of him suing me, sir, because in that event I could cross examine him?'

'It would be far better for you if this was settled privately,' replied Judge Dore.

'I could cross examine him and the public would be able to decide for themselves what the truth of the allegations is,' said Jonathan, trying to sound game.

'You'd be financially ruined and forfeit your career and still not have proved your case. It might even be that you would find yourself facing a criminal action – slander, libel; gaol.'

'Or perhaps it would mean justice,' said Jonathan unconvincingly, his head dropping under the judge's searching gaze.

'Can you be sure that you haven't misplaced your letter?' Judge Dore suddenly asked Philomena, who saw that his fingers twitched again.

She shrugged, unable to claim that she was completely sure. Jonathan looked to her, hopelessness in his eyes. There was silence for a few moments then she had a moment of inspiration regarding what that earlier look of the judge's told her. She breathed in sharply and both men glanced at her. She caught Jonathan's eye and indicated with her head and walked out of the kitchen expecting him to follow. She heard Judge Dore exclaim: 'What?' and Jonathan apologise: 'Excuse me.' He was hot on her heels to the end of the hall, where in hushed tones he demanded:'What are you doing? He's offered to let us off and you walk out like that?'

Philomena searched his face. 'You want to give up?'

'Give up my folly, yes.'

'But he's scared,' she said.

'He's scared you say, but what can he be scared of beyond a scandal that we shall be ruined by? We should take whatever is on offer,' argued Jonathan.

'Perhaps we're more powerful than we know,' she said. 'Perhaps our position is stronger than we know.'

'If that's true,' he said, 'I wish you'd tell me how.'

'I think he thinks we're right,' she said.

Jonathan shook his head in disbelief. 'You mean he thinks my allegation is true? You're saying you believe it's possible that he thinks his son's the kind of murderer I've described? You think a father would believe that about a son?'

'We are more powerful than we know,' she repeated. 'We must be, or why make any offer at all?'

In the kitchen down the hall Judge Dore cleared his throat and she watched Jonathan glance over his shoulder as if the noise was a prompt, or command. She knew it was an immense effort for Jonathan to negotiate on equal terms with the judge. She, on the other hand, felt quite reckless, liberated by the heady events of the last few days.

'What was it,' demanded Jonathan, 'that made you leave the damned kitchen like that?'

'I can't tell you.'

'What?'

Jonathan pulled back his head and looked into her eyes. She nodded rapidly.

'When we go back in, I'm going to try something,' she said.

'Try what?'

'An idea.'

'What idea?'

'I can't tell you,' she said.

'Because?' demanded Jonathan. And then from the way she looked at him he knew why. She considered him a liability.

Philomena saw the thought hurt him and moved her head closer: 'Only I can word it,' she comforted. 'You weren't there when I was asking for my letter. It's about that. I know I've much less to lose than you, but at this moment going back in that kitchen and defeating Judge Dore is something within our grasp if only we take the risk. You've fought so hard, do you really want to give up now? We're on the cusp, Jonathan. I'm not sure what of, but we're desperately close to something.'

'Might it mean he'll withdraw his offer?'

'That's not important.'

Jonathan opened his mouth to argue but her passion, the way she looked at him, convinced him that he should defer to her; just. If she'd been arguing the opposite he could have followed her that way, too. He smiled but it was terribly forced.

'Go ahead. I'm bereft of ideas. Yes, yes. You, you, you can do it,' he stuttered. 'Let's not give up. Try it, whatever it is.'

There was only so much more he could endure. He bent close. She could feel the heat of his head, his breath. He whispered in her ear: 'Thank you.'

She pulled her head back just far enough so she could look into the depths of his eyes: 'Thank you for what?'

'For having an idea.'

Tears filled his eyes.

'Come on,' she said, and led him back to the kitchen. Judge Dore was still seated at the table where they'd left him. Philomena took a seat opposite him whilst Jonathan remained on his feet, leaned on a chair, fidgeted. The judge looked to Jonathan, then to Philomena because she seemed to be in charge.

'We're inclined to accept,' she said, making herself sound confident.

'I hear a but . . .' said Judge Dore.

'We're inclined to accept your offer, mostly on his behalf,' she nodded towards Jonathan, 'because I haven't anything much at stake, nothing material – you couldn't ruin me. You can imprison me, but not ruin me. But there's one thing I'd still really, really like, if it's at all possible, and that's the return of my letter, my letter from Dan.'

Judge Dore remained looking at her and didn't say anything. This was crucial – the fact that he said nothing was evidence.

'I know you have to play your cards close to your chest,' she continued, 'but that's what I'd like: the return of my letter from Dan.'

She started a silence and let it run. It was up to Anthony Dore's father to end it with the right words.

She turned her head so that she was watching Judge Dore out of the corner of one eye whilst also letting Jonathan know she'd set the trap. The silence grew. The focus tightened on Judge Dore. Philomena had hoped he'd miss something, and it appeared that he had. Now she was scrutinising him for any signs that revealed he'd caught on. His fingers twitched. That was good. He scratched his top lip, also good. He was looking from one of them to the other to see why they were not speaking. He was waiting for one of them to speak but it was he who should have been speaking. Then his whole body tightened, his hands pressed flat on the table and his eyes widened a fraction – he'd spotted the trap? He'd recognised that he'd walked into Philomena's trap. And it was too late to back out!

'I have to go.' Suddenly he was on his feet, making his way out of the kitchen. In the doorway he stumbled slightly.

Jonathan looked to Philomena and silently mouthed, 'What?'

'We will pursue the truth,' she called stridently after Judge Dore. 'We promise not to spread gossip, but we will still try to establish the facts surrounding the death of Daniel Case.'

Judge Dore walked on.

'We're going to Germany to look for witnesses from their side.'

Jonathan stared at her, frowning. She urged him towards the judge, who was now fumbling with the lock on the apartment door. Jonathan went to help him, solicitously, as one might an invalid. Philomena felt a tilt in the world and put a hand up to the wall to steady herself. She had some pity for Judge Dore. His lips were parted, his forehead shone with sweat, and his energy – that in its intensity had threatened to conquer her and Jonathan – was now disordered, chaotic.

He was at bay – no; he had the air of a man who couldn't wait to be alone.

'I set a trap, twice, just now, didn't I, Judge? I said I wanted the return of my letter from Dan but I never mentioned Dan when I was at your house. I just asked for my letter back. So just now you should have said something like, "Is that what the missing letter is?" But you didn't, because I think you know what the letter is. Your son does possess it; you've seen it, even read it. And if your son's guilty over my letter, that very strange theft, what else could he be guilty of?'

Judge Dore didn't turn around. He waited, rigid, as if for more. Jonathan looked to Philomena and she nodded, and he opened the door for the judge. Without speaking again, he left. Jonathan shut the door behind him.

Philomena and he fell silent for a very long time, either end of the hallway of Jonathan's apartment.

'There it is,' she said. 'I think we've got all we're going to get. For now. It's our own armistice.'

'Yes,' said Jonathan, 'that's exactly what it is.'

'And we'll get Anthony. One day,' she said.

A pause. They filed back into the kitchen, each in their own thoughts, both wondering what would happen next. There was still an atmosphere in the room. Jonathan opened a window.

'Did you mean that about travelling to Germany?'

'I don't know. But there is somewhere I would like to travel to. I'd like to visit Dan's grave.'

CHAPTER SEVENTEEN

Anthony's train was for Liverpool and the Atlantic passage. He'd looked out on the silhouetted London skyline, wondering if he'd ever see it again. He fretted about money. His father hadn't referred to the subject beyond begrudgingly shoving an envelope of cash into his hand. Would he ever be allowed to return? Would his father reply if he wrote? Would they ever speak again? Nothing could be counted upon anymore. His head throbbed from where his father had gripped it and he sported mottled purple marks. He had managed one case of clothes and meagre personal possessions. His father had made him carry the damned bible. Fuck the bible. He yanked the carriage windows apart, took aim and threw it out through the gap. The opening was narrow and his aim poor; the heavy bible bounced back and caught him on his tender bruises, further infuriating him. He snatched the book up and stuffed it through, ramming it out, tattering it.

Anthony felt aggrieved at his treatment, even though he was guilty. He still felt angry with Daniel Case, but he was mad with rage at Jonathan Priest, and with Philomena Bligh, too, and with his father. With some ease he pictured shooting

Jonathan Priest, and Philomena Bligh, in the presence of each other. Which one first? Ideally, both ways: kill him in front of her followed by her in front of him.

Canada, what was he going to do in Canada? It was a cold, uncivilised place, wasn't it? How was he going to survive? What were his talents? He had none. Everything that had come to him had been due to his birth. That was all he had, his family. Would he kill again? He'd done it that time to protect what was his but now he had nothing, relatively. He was damned if he was going to be poor, though, the poor penitent his father seemed to have in mind. Mentally he prepared himself to lie more, cheat, and if necessary kill someone who had something he wanted.

Also, he began to plot how to convince his father that he was redeemable. From across the ocean he'd work on his paternal affections. Yes, that could succeed! He would come across better on paper than he did in the flesh. He might even send a short message from England's edge: 'Dear Father' he began in his mind . . . but he quickly became lost for what to say next, as the enormity of it all struck him a hammer blow. He cursed the war. He would never have met Daniel Case if it weren't for the damned war. Fuck the war. Tears of self-pity threatened to well. He dug his nails into the palm of his hand, a habit from schooldays, to distract himself with pain.

He'd loathed the wet in his father's eyes as he'd said, in a voice thick with emotion, 'Goodbye, Anthony.' His father – would he change his will? Everything should have been coming to him! That was the good thing about his brothers' dying. The bad thing was that without them to hide behind he was exposed as himself. Was his father going to disinherit him? Was he even now at his solicitor's? Oh my God, should he return to London immediately and kill his father before he had a chance to change his will? Where was the train now? Nowhere. Fields. If he stopped the train by pulling the emergency handle how long would it take him to return to London by foot and taxi if any existed in this godforsaken place? Would that be quicker than waiting to get off at the next station, travelling back up the line?

And so on, and so on, thought Anthony Dore.

Philomena sent another apologetic telegram home to Jo, her business partner, before she and Jonathan took the boat train to Calais, where they hired a motor and its driver, purchased provisions – wine, water, pâté, cheese, baguette – and set off towards Dan's grave. Jonathan guided the driver along the straight, flat roads. They motored the late afternoon and some of the early evening before he was able to inform Philomena: 'We're in the area.'

A phosphorescent moon hung in the sky. In the metallic light the eerie, disturbed landscape was revealed; unnatural-looking shapes and undulations in the ground. The car's head-lights illuminated gashes and pits in the earth covered by a thin dressing of grass and early wild flowers. Hard evidence of the war emerged from the earth – the barrel of a gun, a tank track – Jonathan hadn't thought before just how much clearing up there would have to be. Ah, there; a low, broken wall off to the left. A turning came up, an unmetalled road heading south-east. Jonathan commanded the driver to stop the vehicle and got out. He sniffed the air. Philomena began to make moves to join him.

'Not quite there yet.'

He got back in, consulted the map.

'That's not our farmhouse. It's all looking quite different from what I remember. Of course. I hope I haven't led you on a wild goose chase.'

'We'll find it,' she reassured, trying to take the onus off him. 'Is there anything I can do to help?'

Jonathan told the driver to *allez*, at walking pace. The motor bobbled over the uneven terrain. Ghostly was a word for the place. How many men had perished here? Soldiers, airmen, tunnellers; all races, all nationalities; and the civilians, the animals, and birds – death had been plentiful, hounding life with varying degrees of insane ingenuity on, above and below this ground. What had thrived? The rat, possibly, the worm and insect and the carrion crow. They shall inherit the earth.

'I was wondering about Felicity,' he said, switching his mind to a more pleasant subject. 'What are you going to do with her?'

'I returned her to the shop,' said Philomena. 'But I could always get her out again. I might be her sometimes.'

Jonathan smiled, wondering if that meant Philomena was to spend more time in London.

'That's a hell-hole,' he said. 'Did I say hell? I meant shell.

I feel that we're in the vicinity.' Another low wall. 'That could be it. And over there; that could be the remains of the tank.'

He was out of the motor car whilst it still moved, more alive to the search now the scent was stronger. Like an alert dog he took a few paces one way, a few another. The driver stopped and idled the engine. Philomena alighted. Jonathan reconstructed the geography. He rotated a full circle, mentally filling in what was missing, straightened his arm.

'Over there.'

He set off, casting a long shadow as he crossed the motor car's headlights. Philomena followed, picking up her feet to avoid tripping. He waited for her at the edge of what appeared to be a ragged picket fence. Nearing, she realised it was wooden crosses, irregular rows of them. Her heart went in her mouth.

At the outset of their search she read each internee's name and took a few moments to think about the person buried beneath. But there were scores of them, so as time went on her eyes slid over names in her search for Dan's. She heard Jonathan call her name and hurried over to him. He silently indicated a cross, roughly engraved. Daniel Case. Second Lieutenant. Killed in action 11 November 1918. Scratched over the *killed*, weathered, faint even after this relatively short time, was the word *murdered*. Jonathan must be responsible for that. So here lay Dan.

She reached up to Jonathan at her side and kissed him on the cheek. Then she focused on Dan's grave. Jonathan felt he was intruding, so he retreated a little way and waited. In the moonlight he tried to more fully recreate where everything had been just a few months ago. A flickering light over by the ruined farmhouse caught his eye.

At the grave Philomena went through some preliminaries. She told Dan that she believed that he had been murdered by Anthony Dore in a most cowardly fashion. 'It's not over, yet,' she told him. 'Don't know what the outcome will be. We're not giving up. I'm going to fight as hard as ever I can, and let Jonathan fight, without it destroying either of us. That's fair, isn't it? That's all you can ask for.'

She shared her memories of their last day together. 'Bi-cycles. You laughed at me straining uphill. I thought you looked too thin. I could have raced you, I think, if I'd put my mind to it. How bony you were when we got in that pond – how cold was that!? When we made love I was trying to fill you up, inflate you with spirit. I thought if I achieved that you might become buoyant, able to float out of harm's way.'

After her last words had faded she began the funeral cere-mony, one she was making up on the spot. She took the photo of herself that Jonathan had returned to her, found a flat stone and scratched a hollow in the earth. Into this she placed the image.

'You can have one letter back,' she told Dan.

To choose which, she held each in turn and squeezed her eyes shut, trying to receive a telepathic instruction. That didn't work. She'd have to decide.

'I'll tell you what,' she said, 'I'll hang onto them.' She pushed earth over the photo. 'You came home with different eyes.

Death. We never spoke of it. There it was, always, though. On the table between us . . . I've seen other women deal with it. You look at them and you think: "She should do that; that'd be a good thing to do now he's gone." Or you think: "Poor girl, look what she's at, mad with grief; judgement's shot – should I intervene?" But you never do; you let them get on with it hoping they'll emerge without too much damage.'

Over near the ruined farm Jonathan was silently watching a woman, a man with one leg, and a little boy intently conduct a fingertip search for weeds in their patch of earth. The cultivated area was small. It looked as if it had been prepared to a fine tilth. The boundaries were marked by a makeshift fence; posts of salvaged weaponry stuck vertically into the ground, connected by recycled barbed wire. There were walkways that all three were fastidious in observing. The man had developed a method of leaning at a precipitous angle on his crutches, as if hanging off them, in order to reach and work the ground. The woman, then the man, noticed Jonathan and stopped working. He raised his hand. The man and woman spoke to each other, and the man hobbled nearer, taking in Jonathan's clothes, face.

'Hello,' the man tried, in a local accent.

'Hello,' replied Jonathan.

The man turned to the woman and nodded. Jonathan saw lines running front to back of his face, the side that had been away from him, that of the man's lost leg. He took them to be streaks of dirt. The man shifted. The moon lit that part of his face more clearly, showing a sheen of sweat. The man took out a rag and mopped his head. The streaks of dirt didn't leave his skin or smear. They were in the skin. Jonathan guessed they were tattoos, dark matter explosively driven into the man, etched into his epidermis, for ever recording the direction of travel of the blast that took his limb. It was a miracle he'd kept his eye. Jonathan and the man watched the woman and the boy continue working.

Jonathan tried some French. 'Ju swee eesee don la gare.'

The man nodded, as if he had thought that that might be the case. They both looked off into the distance for a few moments. A dog barked, setting off another, a second, a third, in a chain reaction. In a similar fashion, the dogs progressively fell silent. Jonathan could hear little clicks from the tools the woman and boy employed, and the rustle of their clothing. A horse or donkey snorted from behind the ruined farm.

'*Nous sommes fermiers*,' said the man, speaking a little too quickly for Jonathan to immediately comprehend.

He stared blankly, then understood: 'Ah – wee, wee. Ju com pron. Fermiay.'

The man called softly to the boy and he came running with a metal bottle of water. A reclaimed army flask. The man took it from him and offered it to Jonathan. He took a swig.

'Bon. Mersee,' he said, giving the flask back. He looked over to where Philomena now knelt by Dan's grave.

Philomena looked up. Jonathan was nearing one side of the motor. The driver stood impassively on the other, with one foot on the running board.

Jonathan angled slightly away from Philomena and the driver. He took out the elegant silver phial in which he kept his cocaine. There was some inside. More than enough for a buzz. He tipped it out, letting the light breeze catch it and carry it away. He rinsed the phial with brandy from his flask; took a swig.

At the grave Philomena pressed her fingertips into the damp earth and inhaled the odours of mouldering matter. 'You wild bastard,' she growled through gritted teeth. 'I'm furious with you!'

Oh. Oh. Oh, Dan. A place in my heart for ever yours. Journey safe. Goodbye.

Tears came, swelled, stung. She tipped her head forward and screwed her eyes tight shut; open, shut, open, squeezing the wet out of her, onto the earth. 'Grow,' she implored. 'Something grow. Something good grow here.'

Jonathan could see her bent over, facing the earth.

After a while she felt the cold seeping into her from air and earth so she rose, and without looking at the grave again made her way stiff-legged back towards the motor, to where Jonathan waited. He lifted his feet in turn and replanted them on the ground. The driver inhaled deeply on the dregs of a cigarette. Philomena caught her toe on the ground, stumbled, recovered, sensed rather than saw Jonathan step forward to aid her. Yards from him she said, 'Food. I need food. I'm ravenous.'

Jonathan opened the rear door of the vehicle and brought out their supplies. She accepted them from him with a wan smile. On a level section of the car's mudguard she set out the cheese and pâté, tore a chunk off the bread. Jonathan removed the stopper from the wine bottle and filled to halfway the two glasses he'd pilfered from the ferry. He caught the driver's thirsty eye. 'Monsieur?' he offered. As Philomena drank, the driver retrieved a tin mug from the interior, knocked the dregs of what smelled like coffee out on the raised edge of his boot. Philomena hungrily bit mouthfuls of bread. Caramel crust crackled, white inside melted. She prodded pâté and cheese into her mouth. The sense of dense fat just behind their pungent taste comforted her.

The driver coughed to get the English's attention. He became sombre, tipped his mug, dribbled some wine from waist height down onto the land. He didn't need to explain that this was for the dead. Philomena stopped chewing. She and Jonathan followed the driver's suit. There was a respectful silence for a while, before the driver ambled away, either because he wanted to be alone, or to leave a space for his passengers' privacy.

Philomena felt the wine hit. Warmth spread from her abdomen outwards, up to her brain, out to her limbs. Jonathan reached for some bread. His hand stopped when she spoke: 'It's my turn to say thank you,' her voice pitched so that her words carried only to him. Both completely still, she looked at him, he at the bread, for a few intense moments.

Then as if it had been agreed that the moment had run long enough Jonathan resumed his movement, took up bread, mutely offered it. She shook her head then nodded towards the cheese and pâté. Jonathan nodded, one-handedly broke off a modest piece of cheese, chewed it, took up the wine bottle and held it over her glass. She nodded, yes. After he'd poured for her he swallowed his cheese, washed it down with a swig of his own wine.

Philomena and Jonathan stood by each other, looking out in different directions, sipping. She inhaled deeply, held her breath . . . let it slide out.

'Okay,' she murmured.

'Okay,' he replied.